THE DEVIL OF TREHORRA

Chapter 1

The villagers had just about forgotten about the death of young Sammy Tremayne, whose body had been found in the sea only a month before, when whispers of a second tragedy spread like wildfire around the tiny Cornish village of Trehorra. Another suspicious death, another Tremayne.

The village is deep in a valley with whitewashed cottages dotted along each side of the small River Goran, which straggles its way into a small harbour which is made to look a bit claustrophobic with its black foreboding cliffs towering into the sky.

These very dangerous cliffs are the one single barrier which used to protect the only haven for the old sailing ships for miles and miles along this rugged coastline, particularly when they were on their way to the ports of Bristol, South Wales and Liverpool. For about half of every year since time began, fierce storms and gales from the Atlantic Ocean have been battering and pounding against the high, solid black rocks. In winter it is a rough and tough place to live but somewhat idyllic during the short summer season. All in all a peaceful place, but is it to be torn apart and shattered?

Life for most adults in the village was one long hardworking day after another, just work, eat and sleep. The monotony was broken by a couple of hours or more perhaps at one of the local inns. Gone were all the ale houses, some twenty-seven of them in years gone by. Three pubs remained, two of them in the harbour district of Trehorra, the other being at the opposite end of the village which was inland and completely separate, not only geographically but socially too.

There were four places of worship, two were Anglican, one Wesleyan and one Methodist. Generally these were well attended, particularly on Sundays during the long summer days. Sudden deaths of villagers were few and far between so the death of a young man a few weeks previously caused more than a few raised eyebrows to say the least.

It was now April, spring was here, the primroses, daffodils and carpets of lovely bluebells transformed the village. Gone was the black and earthy brown grass along the cliffs. The windblown heather looked beautiful now, and sea daisies were dotted everywhere. It miraculously seemed as if the village was transformed overnight.

Everyone was looking forward to the summer. There would be plenty of visitors from 'up country,' especially from London and the Midlands. They would bring much-needed cash to the villagers whose cottages were adequate enough to provide bed and breakfast accommodation. Even the always complaining farmers would benefit from selling the Cornish new potatoes and the famous Cornish clotted cream. Proprietors of the few small fishing boats left in the harbour would supplement their inadequate earnings by taking tourists for trips along the deadly coastline now, in the spring time, mercifully smooth and calm, relating terrible tales of the old time smugglers' dastardly deeds in and around the huge caves.

This, of course, was all in the dim and distant past, they couldn't possibly have dreamed of what was to come during the next few months. The village, peaceful and uneventful for hundreds of years, was in for a shock.

Sammy Tremayne's body had been found floating face down on the surface of the deep blue-black Atlantic beneath an area known locally as the Black Cliffs. It had been assumed that he had lost his footing whilst walking along the cliff top and had fallen over the unfenced cliffs to his death. It was a four-hundred foot sheer drop to the sea at the bottom of these treacherous cliffs. The official report had recorded 'Accidental Death.'

Chapter 2

Four weeks later almost to the day, Mrs Vanstock was awakened by a loud, somewhat frantic knocking at her front door. It was 8 o'clock on a Saturday morning and husband Eric had been up late the night before. Not that Friday nights were particularly rowdy or troublesome but the local pubs were generally full and there weren't too many the worse for drink, just a few choruses of "Show me the way to go home," as a mixture of Friday night regulars and a few early visitors were turned out of the pubs. The Trehorra policeman rarely had too many problems and last night had been no exception, although the coming summer months would tell a different story. The village population would be extended a lot and pubs' customers would be quadrupled with an invasion of tourists, or 'emmets', as they were generally referred to by the Cornish.

This early in the tourist season, Vanstock was hoping to take advantage of sleeping in so he was quite irritated to hear the loud knocking on the police house door. "Go down and see who the dickens that is," he grumbled to his wife. He needn't have given her such terse instructions as she was already in the process of putting on her dressing gown. She replied, "All right, all right, don't lose your hair, I'm going as fast as I can." Neither of them saw the funny side of her remark, for Eric Vanstock was completely bald.

Opening the front door, Mrs Vanstock was surprised to see a young boy. His freckled face was blood red and he was obviously excited. In a breathless voice he gabbled out, "Is the policeman in 'cause I've found a body." The policeman's wife was taken aback. "And it be a dead one," the boy repeated.

"I'll get him at once," she replied before shouting upstairs "Eric, did you hear that?"

"No I bloody didn't," came the answer as the half-asleep policeman was about to turn over for a few extra winks.

"Well you'd better put your skates on and get down here pretty damned quick."

He thumped his way noisily down the stairs. "You'd better come in, John, Mr Vanstock will be down in a minute."

"Now what's this all about, young man?"

Taking off his boy scout's hat, John Stephens managed to stutter out, "Er, well, I've seen a man's body in the horse trough by Minerva church."

"Who is it? Do you know who it is?" Vanstock could hardly believe what the boy had managed to blurt out. "I don't know who it is exactly but his head is in the water and his legs are hanging over the side of the trough, but I think it's one of those Tremaynes." The boy scout shifted uneasily a pace back from the domineering policeman.

That was the last thing Vanstock wanted to hear. "Well I suppose I'll have to go and have a look at him, won't I?" Vanstock threw on the rest of his uniform and grabbed his police helmet, all conveniently on the hall stand, took hold of his bicycle and squeezed passed the boy and out through the door. "Well, come on, boy, come with me." By this time, young John was wishing he hadn't discovered the body.

It took them about fifteen minutes to reach the horse trough situated about fifty yards higher than Minerva church. It had been built in a valley and was surrounded by trees, an eerie sort of place, particularly at night, not to mention in daylight as well.

Arriving practically breathless, Vanstock threw his bike into the hedge and muttered under his breath, "What a bloody nuisance this is." He approached the trough, put both his hands into the freezing water to gently turn the body over until the face was visible. "It be Colin Tremayne all right," gasped the young John Stephens, staring at the now partially bloated body.

"My God, I can't believe this," exclaimed Vanstock. There was only one thing for him to do, he must get back to the house and telephone his headquarters in Waterbridge.

Chapter 3

Rumours were rife in the village by ten o'clock that morning. The village smithy was busy as usual on this sunny but chilly Saturday. Quite a few of the local characters were there, as they always seemed to be on most Saturday mornings. Some were just biding their time away before the pubs opened at eleven o'clock, or just waiting around in the warmth of the smithy forge before going out to the football match at Plymouth. Soon the bus would arrive to pick up these rural supporters of Argyle.

The English league team's ground was at Home Park in Plymouth and was the nearest professional team to Trehorra. Apparently, the Cornish always called the team Argyle while Devonians always referred to them as Plymouth.

Never a brilliantly successful team, they nevertheless had had their moments since they had been accepted into the English league in 1920. A lot of their support came from Cornwall. The county had only had amateur football teams. Today's game was to be the best home fixture of the season and the supporters' bus would be full. It would start the thirty-five mile trip to Plymouth at the Riverside Inn. This was situated at the end of Trehorra's old steep road.

Wending its way up the hill around two hairpin bends, the bus would stop at the Castle crossroads. Here would be waiting the small group of all males. There was Clicky Beasley, a young local fellow of seventeen years of age. He was still apprenticed to Bill Sharrocks, the village carpenter, another Argyle supporter. Dan Gent, Bill's partner, was an ex-sailor who had no interest in sport but was quite willing to work whilst his partner enjoyed his Saturday afternoon of football. Always first to get on the bus would be several schoolboys sporting the green and black colours of Argyle.

The bus driver arrived on top of the hill at the blacksmith's forge. He was nicknamed 'Bumper', but no one knew why. Today he surprisingly had to get out of his seat and actually go into the Old Smithy to gather the rest of his customers. Usually they couldn't wait to jump on the bus but today they were all huddled around the blacksmith's fire engrossed in a very animated discussion, and it was not Argyle they were discussing.

They all supported the Argyle, and like all football fans of their time – only a couple of hours before the kick-off – they were all confident that the enemy from 'up country' would be soundly beaten. So Bumper broke up the party by hollering he would leave without them if they didn't get a move on.

"What can be so damned important?" he asked, "Get on the bloody bus or else we'll be late."

It didn't take long for Billy Old, Dick Bradley, Arthur Laycock and the others in the front to tell Bumper about the dead body that had been found that very morning.

"I can't believe that," the old bus driver said, as he moved into first gear to negotiate the rest of the steep climb to get out of the village.

"Well you better believe it," shouted Dick Sanders. Dick lived next door to PC Vanstock. He had, of course, been listening when young John Stephens had knocked the local copper up and told him of the body he had found in the horse trough near St Minerva Church.

"Might have been an accident," a young lad piped up from the back of the bus, "he could have drowned like his brother."

"Funny sort of accident," retorted the policeman's neighbour, "upside down in twelve inches of water, he was drowned all right."

These types of remarks were being thrown all over the noisy old bus. "Well it be a bit different from Sam Tremayne who they found in the sea a few weeks ago," offered Arthur Laycock, "he was drownded proper, all right, in the sea. How can you be drownded in twelve inches of water?"

Little did they know that by this time PC Vanstock was convinced that not only the boy had been drowned, but that it was indeed a Tremayne, Colin, the younger brother of Sam Tremayne, and it did not look like an accident.

Nearly everyone had been convinced that Sam's death had been accidental. The idea of murder or suicide was out of the question. After all, this was a quiet little village, this was Trehorra. The population was only just over five hundred. The visitor season did not start in earnest until June, or sometimes even July. There were no strangers to speak of.

PC Vanstock's face was already red and went even redder when he realised the problems he had got on his hands. A twelve-year-old lad who had found a local farmer's youth around eighteen years of age dead in a horse trough only fifty yards from a fifteenth century church which local historians had once said had been a monastery. Of course, being in Cornwall, it was said to be haunted. It was common knowledge to the locals that once upon a time the monks had wanted to move their granite-built monastery to the top of the hill. They would strive all day to move three or four of the huge granite blocks only to find them back in place the next morning.

Until PC Vanstock's present dilemma, the only recorded murder had been of some drunken sailor. He had been found with his throat slashed by a horseshoe nail. His body was buried in the St Lynn churchyard. The gravestone simply recorded 'William Thomas, sailor, died 1791.' There had been no big murder hunt. By the time that William Thomas's body had been found, the perpetrator was probably way out on the high seas. No one was ever caught or even accused. For Vanstock there was not such an easy way out. Drunken sailors, cheap booze, even loose women and the grand old sailing ships had long since disappeared.

Vanstock must get in touch with his superior. He had got to cycle back to his house to use the telephone. He did not look forward to this situation.

"You'll have to stay here, young John," he instructed the boy who had found the body.

John was beginning to wish he hadn't. "I can't," he protested, "I've got to be at the meeting room. I'm going to Penporth with the scouts. We're taking our life saving and swimming badge today and the scouts' van leaves in half an hour."

"Of course," Vanstock thought, "the way my luck is going today this problem had to be expected."

On second thoughts no one else was likely to turn up in this lonely out-of-the-way lane. Being Saturday no one will be going to St Minerva Church. Most people work five and a half days a week. Saturday afternoon was the only time for relaxation for the men and shopping in the nearby market towns of Lanson or Polpennan for the women of Trehorra.

"I suppose I could make you stay, but if you've gotta go you better be off with you then and I'll be speaking to you later."

John Stephens did not need telling twice, he was on his bike and off up the lane before the policeman could even begin to change his mind.

Vanstock, however, did have time to shout, "Now don't' tell anyone about this, young John."

There was no alternative but to leave the body of Colin Tremayne there by the horse trough. It would take him fifteen minutes or so to get back to the telephone. He'd speak to Inspector Bugannon, get back to the body and wait for the Inspector to arrive.

Mrs Vanstock opened the door. "Can't you go in the back way with those filthy boots on?" "No, I can't, I've got no time to lose, I've got a murder on my hands," her husband answered as he brushed past her up the hallway.

"You've what?"

"God damn it, woman, can't you hear, I've got a murder on my hands. Get me Inspector Bugannon, will you, while I pour myself a drink."

He poured himself a large whisky. He grabbed the phone off Mrs Vanstock as she offered it to him. "Inspector Bugannon, sir, Vanstock here. I've got a body, I've got a murder here, I need you to come here at once."

"Steady on, Vanstock, am I hearing you correctly, you have a body and you have a murderer?"

"You're hearing me say I've got a body but I haven't got a murderer, but it is a murder all right."

Inspector Bugannon knew that Vanstock liked his cups of the strong stuff but couldn't believe he'd be tanked up so early on a Saturday morning. "Now steady on, old chap, you're saying you've got a body and it's been murdered? I can't remember there ever being a murder in Trehorra."

"I don't know if there has or not but there is one now. It's young Colin Tremayne, a farmer's son, and I found him drowned in a horse trough."

"Ah, he was drowned, that's different. I'm getting you now, Vanstock. Where is the body?"

"I've left it at the horse trough. It's right by Minerva Church.

"Okay, Vanstock, I'm on my way. Did I hear you say Tremayne?"

The village bobby had already hung up the phone. He now had some sympathy from his wife. "Oh, you poor chap," she said, "I'm so sorry I shouted at you."

"That's okay, my dear. I'd better get going, I've got to get back to the horse trough."

"Did I hear you say it's a Tremayne? You mean one of that lot at Trewarmett Farm? Didn't one of them fall over the Black Cliffs into the sea the other week?"

She opened the front door for him.

"Yes, that was Sam Tremayne. It's Colin Tremayne this time and he's been drowned as well."

"What, in a horse trough?" shrilled the unbelieving Mrs Vanstock.

"I've got to go back there now," muttered her husband, "and damn it, I wasn't supposed to be on duty until tonight."

Along the main street he could cycle for about half a mile before having to push his bicycle up a steep lane. By Trehane Farm he mounted his bicycle again and quite surprised himself at the speed he got up to for the last half a mile towards the church and the horse trough. Fortunately it was getting milder, one of those lovely fresh May days, a slight breeze but a bright blue sky. In this area that meant a good gardening day, but there would be no gardening for Vanstock today.

There was a slight incline down to the horse trough so he was glad to be able to stop pedalling, and going through his mind was that the only other person to have actually seen Colin Tremayne's dead body was John Stephens and he was off on his bloody scout trip.

He dumped his bike into the hedge, gazed at the drinking trough and could not believe his eyes! No body! He stared at the empty

drinking trough. The water was still clear. There was no sign that a body had been in it only an hour before. Vanstock peered over the back of the trough and slowly worked his way around the area . . . absolutely no evidence at all that a body had been anywhere near the trough.

Suddenly it dawned on Vanstock, "I'm in big trouble now all right, this is not my day."

Inspector Bugannon got quietly out of the car. Vanstock slouched wearily up to him and managed to remember how to salute his superior; the longest way up, the shortest way down. Bugannon ignored the village policeman's courtesy salute.

"Where is he then?" he snapped.

"I don't know," blubbered the now nervous copper.

"You don't know? You told me he was in this horse trough. Aren't we at the right place?"

Poor Vanstock was almost lost for words. "Sir, he was here," pointing to the horse trough, "his head was in the water, his legs dangling over the side. Young John Stephens from Trehane Farm along the road was here with me, sir."

"Well where is the boy now?"

"He's gone off to Penporth with the scouts."

"You mean you let him go off with the scouts and left the body here whilst you phoned me?"

"Er, well, yes, I did. You see, sir, I didn't think the body would be moved. No one uses this lane on a Saturday morning, what else could I do?"

"If it wasn't so early when you telephoned me, Vanstock, I would have thought you'd been drinking."

Vanstock's face could not go redder as he thought of the rather strong whisky he had drunk before returning to the scene of the young man in the horse trough.

"Whether the lane is used or not, Vanstock, someone's moved the body. I suppose this Tremayne, did you say, I suppose he was really dead?"

Vanstock immediately thought of the monks and the moving of the granite stones but quickly dismissed that story. "Oh, yes, sir, he was dead all right. Blue in the face, he was, when I saw him, and his body swollen and full of water."

"Well somebody must have wanted him out of the way. How far have you looked?"

"Oh, all over, sir. I've even been down to that old tree and looked over the hedge," replied PC Vanstock, pointing to a large oak one hundred yards down the lane. Bugannon wondered if a vehicle had been used to take away the body.

"Not much chance of that, sir. The lane narrows so much going that way," said Vanstock, "they can only get through to St Martin's woods either by walking or on horseback. If they had a vehicle they would have come towards the village, and I would know about that."

"Well, I'm glad you know about something," said Bugannon, with sarcasm in his voice. "What a bloody to-do, Vanstock, something has got to be done and bloody quick too. What about a search party?"

"Yes, sir, but by the time most of the village men get home from work or watching or playing football it'll be dark. I suppose I could organise a search party for tomorrow, sir, get some locals out and look over the area. The body's got to be here somewhere."

"Okay, Vanstock, you do that, and you'd better notify the Tremayne family of what you've found. Perhaps they'll be able to throw some light on the problem. And get me a written report about it by Monday morning. I don't want the chief to be calling in the Yard already."

"Yes, sir, I'll do that," replied Vanstock, selfishly thinking at the same time his weekend had been totally ruined, if not this, his last year too.

Now he'd got to get hold of some local volunteers to look for Colin Tremayne's corpse. Then there would have to be a written report to be done. Just as he was thinking there could be no more problems, it suddenly dawned on him that on Monday there was to be a funeral at Minerva church. No ordinary funeral either, it was to be the most important funeral in years. The lord of the manor, Sir John Bolitho, was to be laid to rest.

"Whoever removed the body couldn't have carried it far unless they had a vehicle, could they?" asked Bugannon.

Chapter 4

Meanwhile, John Stephens was busy concentrating on gaining his life-saving and swimming badges a few miles away at Penporth. Success in this test would mean John would become a King's scout, one of the highest awards in the boy scout movement. He had been practising for the past six weeks, ever since he had gained his pathfinder badge so he simply had to be successful today. Nothing else was on his mind.

The pathfinder badge was important and certainly more difficult than he and his scouting pals had ever imagined. They had had to learn about all the roads, the lanes and footpaths within a ten-mile radius from their headquarters in Trehorra.

Other scout troops further inland thought the Trehorra scouts were fortunate because half their territory was in the Atlantic Ocean off the rugged coast of their small Cornish harbour. But the Trehorra scouts knew differently; they had to have knowledge of the coastline, the caves and rocks too.

Standing in line were Derek Allen, his brother Toby, and John Stephens.

"Right, boys," shouted the scoutmaster, "who's next?" John, who was patrol leader, wasn't too keen to follow Derek Allen in diving down twelve feet to find a brick weighing seven pounds and then bring it to the surface. Not too difficult a feat for most of these boy scouts but this was one of John's weaknesses. Although good at most things, he could not open his eyes under water and knew he would be simply groping for the brick, and more likely than not, by the time he located the object his lungs would be bursting.

Derek had come up to the surface holding his head aloft the brick. "Okay, Allen, that's very good," the scoutmaster encouraged the boy, "Now throw it back."

It was John's turn. There were others taking the badge this afternoon. All of them spent a great deal of their time in the sea during the summer months. Most were strong, excellent swimmers. This, though, was early summer, the pool, full of sea water, was very, very cold, no more than sixty degrees.

The scoutmaster, Reverend Bowering, had worked hard with the boys and he had no doubt in his ability to pass on all of his knowledge and skills to the young scouts.

The rule stated that ordinary clothes had to be worn during the entire next test, which was swimming six lengths of this large pool. No mean feat for these eleven to fourteen-year-olds. The pool, hewn partly out of the cliff, was built up so that when the tide went out the pool remained full of the chilling sea water.

Also included in these rigorous tests was not only jumping in and saving a drowning person but also pulling them to safety. Each scout would take their turn to be the drowning person. John, who had failed to bring that brick to the surface in the time allowed, was still in the water so he was to be the first 'drowning person.'

He was treading water and so leaned on his back and floated out to the centre of the pool. In fact John was more confident on his back than any of the orthodox strokes, probably because he preferred to muck about just sitting in a pumped-up inner tube.

"Don't forget, in a real emergency if the drowning man proves too difficult and struggles violently, you have to gain control, you have to knock him out, you have to be cruel to be kind." Bowering shouted this reminder at the fair-haired Stuart Abbyn, who was getting ready to save the 'drowning man.' "But don't hit John, will you, Stuart, he's only pretending, you know."

This scoutmaster, who doubled as the village vicar, was an extremely good instructor. He tutored boys in the majority of their pursuits. Only for ball games and activities such as roller-skating did the scoutmaster Eric Bowering bring in outside help. At 5pm he blew his whistle. "That's enough," he shouted, "you can all get changed now."

The boys had been standing around, and although wrapped in towels they were shivering and their teeth were chattering. The test had to end prematurely as a strong north wind was beginning to sweep around the pool and the tide was coming in.

As soon as they were back in the scout van, the scoutmaster eventually managed to make himself heard over the excited din the boys were making. He had to blow his whistle. "That's enough," he ordered, "You've all done well and we'll be back here again to allow those of you who were unable to finish another chance to get the badge. Just one reminder of that last life-saving test, if the drowning person is panicking, think nothing of knocking them out. You have to be in control. You don't want to be involved in a struggle."

He continued to drive back to Trehorra and was extremely patient in answering the myriad of questions which were being flung at him.

"How did I do, sir?"

"When's out next troop meeting?"

"What's our next test, sir?"

"Will we have time to practise?"

"Will the chief scout present the King's badges?"

At last they were all back at the headquarters. "I'll see you next Wednesday evening at six o'clock."

John was inwardly relieved that there would be a second opportunity for him. He knew he had at least to become more proficient at swimming even if it was only the breast stroke.

Surprise, surprise, then when piling out of the scouts' van with all the other eager, noisy boys, the scoutmaster took John to one side. "You will get your badge the next time, Stephens." The other boys were too excited to notice him encouraging John.

Chapter 5

John was fast asleep when he was awakened by a loud knocking at the front door of the quaint little ivy-covered cottage his mother rented from the lord of the manor whose family had owned the parish of Minerva for three generations.

"Is John in?" the youngster heard the policeman ask.

"He is, but he's in bed. What has he been up to now, Mr Vanstock?" his mother asked.

"Oh, nothing, but I have to speak to him now."

John certainly knew why he was wanted and he was halfway down the stairs before his mother could shout up. "John, come down here at once, my boy."

All three went into the front room. "I'll put the kettle on," said Mrs Stephens.

"Thank you, Mrs Stephens, I just want to ask John a few questions. It's nothing for you to worry about, Colin Tremayne from the farm at Trewarmitt is dead and young John found his body, that's all."

"Nothing to worry about and there's a young man dead? But surely you mean Sammy Tremayne. I can tell you, Mr. Vanstock, my John's had no trouble with those Tremaynes."

"I know he didn't. Just let us be, Mrs Stephens, and I'll be out of your way in a minute."

As soon as Vanstock was left alone with John, out came his notebook and very painstakingly he took down the youngster's story. He had been taking a shortcut back to his cottage after taking Mr Jack Metteral's cows back to their field after the early morning milking. He was hurrying past the horse trough when his dog barked and ran to the trough. He followed the dog and came upon the body dangling over the side.

"You know the rest, Mr Vanstock, I got on my bike and went straight to your house and went back with you to the horse trough.

"Yes, I know that and you know that, but after I let you go off to your scouts' thingummy . . . "

John interrupted, "You mean my swimming tests at Penporth?"

Vanstock wasn't used to being interrupted and was getting slightly impatient. He did not want to be sidetracked and was intent on getting his story right.

"Now, John, be you sure you saw Colin Tremayne in the horse trough when you came back there with me, and was he still there when you left? Are you sure you didn't tell anyone about it? Did you meet anyone on your way to the scouts' meeting place?"

The boy hesitated, "Er," and blushing slightly he muttered, "Er, of course I'm sure. You turned him over, didn't you?" Then he added, "Oh, I did tell some of the scouts when they asked me why I was late catching the van, but I didn't meet anyone else. Why do you ask me that?"

"I'm asking you, my boy, because when you left to do your swimming thing, I had to go back to my house and phone headquarters. I gets back to the horse trough and he's gone." Vanstock snapped his notebook shut.

"Who's gone?" Young John wasn't following the policeman's drift very well.

Vanstock got up to leave. "The bloomin' body, of course, and I'll want you to get some of your mates to help look for it tomorrow morning and you'll have to sign a statement too." He walked to the front door of the cottage. "Now you get back to bed, my boy."

Chapter 6

St Minerva church was being prepared by the female villagers. Extra chairs were to be put in the aisles alongside the family pews. The dulling brasses were to receive an extra bit of polishing. Flowers were to be placed around the granite pillars and on the shelves by the stained glass windows.

Vicar Bowering was adamant, there was to be no interference with his preparations for the most important funeral in Trehorra for many a year.

Vanstock informed Bugannon that a search of the church grounds would be halted until after the funeral of the lord of the manor.

"And this we will do, and we'll do it thoroughly, Vanstock." Bugannon was convinced the answer to the missing body would not be far from the church, if not in it.

It was a small church and there were several small rooms which were used by the choir to change into their surplices and cassocks for Sunday services. As it was once a monastery there were several underground vaults where the monks would store their wine. Plenty of nooks and crannies where, according to Bugannon's thinking, it would be comparatively easy to hide a body. But whoever did it, why abandon a dead body only to return to remove it? Which led to the question of was the drowning an act of passion and the murderer panicked only to realise afterwards they had better get rid of the body. Bugannon knew that the longer it took to recover the body, the less chance they had of getting a lead. These views had been put to Vicar Bowering but the answer to all requests to search in and around the church was a very definite "No way." And that was his final decision.

The grave for the lord of the manor was ready. It was the regulation six-feet deep with the dug-up earth heaped along one side, a neatly folded green tarpaulin to cover the hole in case it rained. And there were planks of wood along the sides of the grave to prevent it crumbling inwards.

Sam Teath, the local gravedigger, as always, had done his job to perfection and he understood why Vicar Bowering did not want any search party roaming over the carefully prepared burial site.

Chapter 7

All the locals who had been notified, and some who had not, were grouped together by the Celtic cross at the Castle crossroads with PC Vanstock trying to assemble them into some sort of order. A very motley collection of individuals, he thought to himself, before going through his introduction.

"Just in case of the unlikelihood of anyone not knowing anything about what this early morning gathering is for," Vanstock made it simple, "what we're looking for is the body of a young man of about eighteen years of age. He was fully clothed when I saw him last and he was wet through, his body very swollen. He is about five feet seven inches, not very heavy and his name is Colin Tremayne. He was living at Trewarmett Farm with his father John, mother Ann, sister Madeleine, and his brother Duncan and twin brothers Gerald and Joe. His grandfather also lives with them, and until last month, his eldest brother Sam. You may know that poor Samuel was found drowned in the sea."

Lots of murmurs from the gathering were prompted by this grim reminder by Vanstock. There must have been seventy or eighty men and boys.

It was only 8 o'clock on this greyish Sunday morning, but news travels fast in a small village. And practically the sole conversation in the pubs and the men's snooker club was not the Argyle's great win, it had been the story of the missing body of Colin Tremayne. Some even doubted if there was a body to find. PC Vanstock was no Sherlock Holmes, thought most of the volunteers, but here he was trying to look at his most important.

Standing on an old orange box, he continued, "Now this is what we have to do. Get yourself into groups of three or four. Once we get to the Minerva horse trough we'll spread out. I want you to cover all that farmland from there up to Tredennis. We'll look all over St Martin's Woods inch by inch. Look in all those old, disused barns and tin mine ruins. Keep in touch with each other. And if you do find anything suspicious, stay by it and get a message to me. Oh, and one more thing, most important this, do not go into the Minerva church or churchyard." He took a swift look at his watch, got down from the orange box and led the way to the horse trough.

It was a somewhat seedy, sombre procession that was making their way to Minerva church. Nearly all of them were smoking cigarettes but a few of them puffed at their pipes.

Some of them, unable to get out of their Sunday habit, were wearing collars and ties, most of them wearing big leather boots, others relying on their 'wellies'. Nearly all were wearing cloth caps. None of them had become the least bit friendly with any of the Tremaynes, not even the young men of the same age as the missing boys. Practically all of them had pretty arduous jobs as fishermen, farm labourers, builders' labourers or quarry men.

Certainly their hearts were in the right place, they were willing to give up their only full day of a long working week to spend their day off searching for a missing dead body.

They had not been given one single clue, not a hint of where the body of Colin Tremayne could be. "It's going to be a long day," remarked Gerry Halford, a budding part-time local reporter, who had teamed up with Petherick Carnack and Tom Queen, his assistant at the blacksmith's forge.

After Reverend Bowering had watched Vanstock's search party go off to their various allotted areas, he hurried over to St Minerva church to meet up with Sam Teath, the gravedigger. Not a well educated man, but he was nevertheless a formidable villager and did take pride in his job. He was putting the finishing touches to the empty grave for the lord of the manor.

Could he have been the one to have convinced Reverend Bowering to postpone the search of the churchyard until Monday? "I don't want them lot tramping all over the grave site and walking all over the place," he had told the Reverend, "There's bound to be a lot of people who will be bound to come to the funeral and will be around the grave site. I suppose we can't stop them, but that'll be after the funeral service.

"They will want to go in the church as well, you know, Mr Teath." The Reverend has always addressed Sam in that way. It was if he was in awe of Sam. "I don't like the idea of the police swarming all over our church and churchyard. I can't think of any way or any place they're going to find poor Colin Tremayne's body, do you, Mr Teath?"

Sam was completing the cover over part of the open grave. "Well, as you know, sir, I've been digging graves here for thirty years or more and my father before me, and I've never heard of anything like it. But if it's true what I 'ear, the poor ol' boy can't be too far away from that blessed old horse trough."

The Reverend was sidestepping Sam Teath as he continued to tighten the cover of the open grave with the tarpaulin. "That's certainly true, Mr Teath. I agree with you, and I can assure you they will have to wait until after the funeral before they search the churchyard and the church. In any event, what can happen to a dead body in the space of twenty-four hours? Wherever it is hidden it will remain there for certain."

"You be right there, sir. It's true what they say, dead men can't walk, can they?" chuckled Sam with a somewhat cynical tone in his gruff Cornish accent.

"Er, something like that, I believe, Mr. Teath," smiled the Reverend. "Make sure no one comes into the church or churchyard." With that, the Reverend adjusted his black trilby hat, turned, and re-entered the church. Mrs Bowering looked up at him, smiled, and continued to supervise the ladies from the village who were quietly preparing the church for the funeral service.

Chapter 8

None of the search party had shown any sign of discovering anything. There were not even any false alarms.

At 6pm Vanstock had had enough, it would soon be too dark. He would be up half the night writing out his report for Inspector Bugannon so he blew three large blasts on his whistle.

The call to halt the search was passed on from group to group. Gradually they all trudged wearily back to the village. Darkness was descending, nothing more could be done. Vanstock thanked the ones that he saw, but most of the searchers went straight back to their homes.

Apart from searching the church and churchyard, he could not think of what to do next. He had told the father of Colin Tremayne. Still shocked after hearing the news of his son, and nervous as he was, he had valiantly joined the search party with his other three sons, young Duncan and twins Gerald and Joe.

It was in the early hours before Vanstock at last completed his report. He pushed it aside, had his usual tot of whisky and went straight upstairs to the bedroom.

"Bugannon's right," he whispered loudly to his wife, "Colin Tremayne's body has got to be in the church or churchyard."

She just sighed, groaned, and turned over once again, and returned to sleep immediately.

33

Chapter 9

THE FUNERAL

The church was full to overflowing when the coffin containing the body of the lord of the manor, Stanley Bolitho, was being carried by the employees of the estate of Trehorra.

Along the cold stone floors of the aisles between the huge granite pillars, the cortege slowly proceeded led by the Reverend Bowering of Trehorra. The organ was being softly played by Evelyn Menhennick in a long black dress with a hat to match.

The congregation, which completely filled every pew in this tiny church, was made up of a fascinating mixture of people. There were the hardworking tenants of Stanley Bolitho. There were the farmers who also rented their farms from the lord of the manor. And sitting in reserved front pews were quite a few of the notable country gentry, which included a smattering of the hunting crowd.

Tucked away in the very last pew next to the vestry, where most of the sacred vessels belonging to the church were kept during the week, were four tall men all in police uniforms. The Chief Constable of Devon and Cornwall with his assistant, Major John Sharp. They were flanked on each side by the indomitable-looking Inspector Bugannon and the plumpish figure of the local policeman Eric Vanstock.

The chief and his assistant had travelled from Exeter that very morning. They were keen to have a look at the locals after being alerted to the strange deaths of the Tremayne brothers by Inspector Bugannon.

Much against the will of Bugannon but with no apparent progress, the chief constable was thinking that he would have to call in Scotland Yard, so he was taking this opportunity to have a look at the Trehorra community.

Inspector Bugannon was convinced that a local person was involved in the strange deaths of the Tremayne boys, and he too wanted a close-up view of the locals.

The service over, the coffin was carried out through the heavy oaken doors to the special plot which had been reserved for the lord of the manor. The bearers were the men who had been employed by Stanley Bolitho for most of their working lives. There was Bob Appleby, an experienced carpenter who acted as foreman of the estate's manual staff.

On his left was Joe Sleet, a mason. Joe spent all his time working on the slate roofs and thick walls of the old village cottages. Billy Dawe was a Jack of all trades, giving a hand, when needed, to Joe and Bob. These, and the three remaining bearers, were all being closely scrutinised by the policemen.

There was Mark Colton-Taylor, who was probably the most important man of the lord of the manor's relatively small staff. He not only collected all the rent money, but it was he who decided when and where any repairs or improvements should take place. So naturally he was not all that popular with a lot of the manor's tenants. It was impossible to please everyone, and he certainly did not.

He lived by himself in one of the better houses. Apart from his estate duties, he was a bit of a recluse. He was never seen at any of the village functions. This was a man to speak to as soon as possible, noted the chief constable.

The other two bearers were Arthur Alley and Douglas Higgins, two teenage apprentices. No danger there, thought the watching policeman.

Following the flower-laden coffin was the Reverend Bowering with men of the choir following him in pairs. Bringing up the rear of this sad procession was a dozen rosy-faced choirboys in their whiter than white surpluses over their long black cassocks.

They all filed around the grave prepared by village gravedigger, Sam Teath, which, when pronounced by the locals, rhymes with 'death', rather grim to strangers. Some even doubted it was his real name. In fact it was his true name and he had been digging the graves at Minerva church for so long that very few could remember anyone else doing the job. He sported a long, bushy black beard which covered his face to the cheekbones. He really was a somewhat frightening character, especially to the youngsters of Trehorra.

Young Gerry Halford, who was attending the funeral for the business of reporting it to the local weekly newspaper, remembered very well how nervous he had been at a previous meeting with the gravedigger when he was checking some gravestones to back up a story he was working on. He had been so glad it was during the day. As it was, he was certainly nervous but he had never forgotten that meeting but was keeping that in mind.

Most of the congregation had now filed out through the main church door and had also gathered in as close as they could around the grave. Reverend Bowering finally uttered the last prayers as the coffin was lowered into the six-foot deep hole which had been dug with such precision by Sam Teath. The sides were smooth and perpendicular. To the grave digger it was a work of art, and long after the mourners had left he would be filling up the grave with the black Cornish earth.

The chief constable and his assistant were noticing some of the strange characters and wondering how to discover the motive for the deaths of the two Tremayne boys.

At a post-funeral discussion at Vanstock's police house in the village were the chief constable, his assistant, Major Sharp, Inspector Bugannon and PC Vanstock. They sat around the Vanstock dining table in the police house dining room. Having had enough to eat at the wake, the chief wanted to get down to some serious discussion immediately.

He addressed the group. "Gentlemen, let's be quick about this. First of all, have we got any suspects? I've seen some of the locals but, Vanstock, you know them all, have you any idea?"

"It beats me, sir. These Tremaynes were not real villagers. Their farm is three miles away from Trehorra so they haven't mixed much with my locals."

"We have dismissed the possibility that these deaths could have been accidents, haven't we?" the chief asked, more in hope than anything else.

Bugannon placed his coffee cup down with more force than was necessary. "Well, I thought the first boy to be found did accidentally fall off the cliff and the official report does say 'accidental death', but when Vanstock discovered the second boy in the horse trough only to lose the body later . . . "

Vanstock stared at Bugannon as the inspector seemed to make a deliberate pause. The inspector continued. "I have now changed my mind and I think the deaths are linked. The fact we can't find the body of Colin Tremayne makes me all the more suspicious it certainly was no accident."

He drummed his fingers on the old oak table and took a good look at Vanstock again. The chief constable was quick to observe there was no love lost between Bugannon and the village policeman – and he did not like it.

"Your search around the area was pretty thorough, was it, Vanstock?" The chief could see that progress was going to be slow at this rate.

"Well, yes, sir. I had over fifty men out all day yesterday and they be pretty smart, some of them anyway, and none of them found any sort of a clue."

Bugannon cut in, "I didn't like the fact that Reverend Bowering was so adamant against us searching the churchyard and the church. Any clues that may have been there are no doubt destroyed, the body could even be moved again." It was all getting a bit much for Vanstock, who could not forget that he was in the final year of what had been a very undistinguished career.

It was also getting too much for his superiors, but the chief smoothed things by saying, "Well, it was quite understandable that the vicar wouldn't want a search party in the churchyard the day before the funeral."

The chief already had it in the back of his mind that Scotland Yard detectives could be called in. It would certainly appear to be an admission of failure on the part of all the local police forces. The area's weekly paper had already published several articles doubting the ability of the local police force to solve these apparent murders.

As one door appeared to be closing for the ageing Vanstock, another could be opening for another village character, young Gerry Halford. This part-time journalist on the local paper had visions of escaping this dull, dreamy little village. He saw this catastrophe as a way of achieving his ambition, a job in London on a national newspaper. He would, no doubt, cynically attempt to increase the pressure on the police with his weekly contributions to the Echo.

The chief constable was getting worried. Inwardly he was certain that the local police force headed by Bugannon and Vanstock were not capable of handling this abnormal situation. However, he wanted to keep it local.

He said, "I somehow think that these murders will turn out to be committed by a local person. There must be some people in the village who have a suspicion of who murdered these two young men."

Vanstock thought the chief was putting the onus back on him. "Yes, sir, I think you're right there. I had no problem in getting people to search for Colin Tremayne's body and most of them thought that, even if they didn't say it openly."

Bugannon felt that he ought to put his 'oar' in. Looking at Vanstock, he asked, "There's got to be someone hiding the killer and that's got to be foolish. No doubt you'll be keeping your eye on that."

Vanstock had been sipping at his whisky and ginger ale. "You're right there, sir, I think there's one or two of the locals sleeping very uneasy in their beds lately."

Bugannon continued his hostility. "Well, you'll have to find out who they are, won't you, Vanstock?"

The chief constable could see they were getting nowhere at this rate. There was too much supposition, not enough facts. No one could suggest any names, let alone the motive, the opportunity or the means.

"First thing, gentlemen, we must do, now the lord of the manor's funeral is over, is look for that body.

"There's no objection to that now, is there? I take it as definite that the only reason you were prevented from searching the church area was the funeral?"

The chief's assistant, who had quietly been taking notes, looked up. "I can't see what harm your search would have done or how it would have affected church or churchyard."

Vanstock was now on his third whisky. He suddenly seemed to become more confident. "Well, I did ask him several times, sir, and he always was sort of agitated.

"In fact, I was surprised at his blasphemous remarks."

"What did he say exactly, constable?" asked the assistant chief.

Vanstock realised he had all their attention now. He turned a page in his notebook reading slowly and distinctly, and with just a hint of pleasure and triumph, he said, "Ah, this is it, sir. 'Bugannon can go to hell as far as I'm concerned. You'll go into the churchyard tomorrow over my dead body!'"

The chief constable forced a smile at all the double entendres which he had just heard. Bugannon touched his nose, a sign of nervousness all right, but he refrained from making any further comment.

It was getting late and the chief's assistant, Major John Sharp, reminded his superior that they still had a good two-hour drive to get back to Exeter.

The chief replied, "You're right there, officer. Well, gentlemen, thank you for your contribution. I want you to understand that it is no reflection on you all, but I think I may have to call in the Yard unless you find the missing body. I'll give you forty-eight hours."

Bugannon and Vanstock were not surprised, probably relieved. "Chief, shall we see how the churchyard search goes?" Inspector Bugannon was simply trying to buy some time and put the call for Scotland Yard on hold. As they all rose from the table, "I'll arrange that myself, Chief, and you can be assured we'll turn the church and the churchyard upside down and inside out if necessary. I'll make damned certain of it, sir." "Yes, I'm sure you will. Keep me up to date, Bugannon, maybe if you can find the body it will give us some leads," the chief concluded.

The chief and his number two had left it pretty late before deciding to return to Exeter. After discussing the situation during their two-hour journey the chief constable decided they were none the wiser after their look at the locals and their discussions with the men on the spot, Bugannon and Vanstock. No suspects, no motives. Not even the slightest clue. It was a bitter pill to swallow.

"I think we'll have to get Scotland Yard involved, sir," suggested Major Sharp, "Bugannon and the PC can't handle it."

"I'll have to sleep on that one," replied the weary chief. He had never been involved with the Yard before and he knew that the calling in of the London detectives was a last resort. It would cause a bad reflection on the county police forces and, of course, on the chief constable himself. He said, "We'll wait to see if and what the body might turn up. We'll give Bugannon one more chance."

Chapter 10

PC VANSTOCK'S TURMOIL

The Trehorra policeman had not been sleeping well. His thoughts kept turning over and over. Every night lately they would twist and turn this way and that way and they would be turning as often as his body. He was convinced Scotland Yard would be called in. And if they were would his present position, even his pension, be put in doubt?

Mrs Vanstock had gone into the spare room several nights previously. He knew he was not the most popular man in the village. He had been policing in Trehorra for the past three years and that certainly wasn't long enough to become accepted as Cornish, let alone a Trehorran.

He had come from Plymstock in south Devon and thought he was going to fill in his final years in the force before retiring to the peace and tranquility of this idyllic little village. That dream was truly shattered on the day young John Stephens had knocked on his door early on that fateful Saturday morning to tell him of the body he had discovered in the horse trough.

Maybe Vanstock had caught the odd cyclist riding at night without lights. He had suspected two or three of the villagers of poaching. Some of them had even gone badger baiting. All in all, however, this Cornish posting should have been a sinecure, but now one murder for sure, maybe even two. And to add to his problems, no body from the second discovery.

His thoughts scrambled on. If Sam Tremayne had not fallen over the cliff accidentally, then he was pushed, but what would anyone be doing on the cliffs at that time of night?

He had discovered that this eldest son of the Tremaynes had had it as good as many youngsters of that age, born in similar circumstances. On the threshold of manhood, happy to work on his father's farm, he had been noticed going out with a local teenage Trehorran girl, Ethel Weare. She had apparently been distraught at learning of the death of her very first boyfriend.

Still tossing and turning, Vanstock was delving further into his thoughts wondering if there was any link between Sam Tremayne's death and young 'pimpers'. PIMPERS?

In this part of the country these were young boys who played what to them was a fairly innocent game. It consisted of following courting couples who would stroll along the cliffs looking for a secluded spot where they could (and would in some instances) indulge in some advanced stages of love-making. The boys' game, of course, would be to want to get as close as possible. Vanstock recalled that on occasion Sam Tremayne had complained about the 'pimpers'.

The couple, Sam and Ethel Weare, actually named a 'ringleader' as a certain Steve Treleaven. There had been a meeting with the young boy's father when the PC had given him a very severe warning. Steve's father was not a popular villager. He never seemed to have had a regular job, but his family seemed to be adequately provided for.

Vanstock's thoughts were now rambling too much. Perhaps Steve Treleaven's father had taken some sort of revenge for Sam Tremayne going to Vanstock, followed him one night with the intent of giving him a warning and in a struggle the Tremayne lad had fallen over the cliff. This, thought Vanstock, was a bit far fetched, but his troubled mind took him even farther. Perhaps Sam Tremayne had taken the law into his own hands, given the Treleaven boy a beating and the father was simply retaliating. Family feuds in small villages like Trehorra were not unknown.

Vanstock's problem was finding a motive for Sam Tremayne's death. He could not make up his mind whether it was a revenge of father Treleaven or son Steve, or perhaps Sam had sought to sort matters out for himself.

Now there was an added problem – the death of Colin Tremayne. If only Vanstock could discover a motive for either murder it would go down well with his superiors and perhaps it would delay the Yard from being brought in.

His thoughts continued to wander and he recalled a tiny bit of conversation he had not written in his notebook. Sam had once threatened, "Wait till I get my hands on that bugger Steve Treleaven, I'll kill the little sod." Of course there was no evidence that the Tremaynes and the Treleavens had been at loggerheads since it had been necessary to warn them.

His mind would jump ahead. How long would it be before the young reporter Gerry Halford would be replaced by someone more experienced or, an even worse scenario, the national newspapers would get involved? Finally he would drift off into a fitful sleep.

This would happen to Vanstock night after night. He would neither keep awake, nor could he sleep soundly.

Suddenly his thoughts would be interrupted. "Cup of tea, dear?" His wife would be by the bedside. "Already?" the weary Vanstock would reply, "I haven't slept a bloody wink all night." Trying to soothe him, she began, "Never mind . . . "

". . . perhaps the chief constable will call Scotland Yard." But there was no consoling him. "That's all I bloody need," he decided.

Vanstock, who had previously been such an easygoing character, was now a constant worrier. With the likelihood of the Yard being called upon, where would this leave him?

Inspector Bugannon's position would also be queried. And with the chief constable not trusting Bugannon and the latter thinking Vanstock was a liability, calling in Scotland Yard was inevitable.

Chapter 11

One person who certainly did not think he would be replaced was Gerry Halford. He was hoping the nationals would hold off for a while because nineteen-year-old Gerry had ambitions to become a reporter on a London newspaper.

His grammar school headmaster had recommended that he was quite capable of becoming a successful journalist. But mother Halford had other ideas for her only son.

For quite some time she had been working as a part-time cleaner in the office of the local Corn and Coal Merchants, and on several occasions had hinted to her bosses that she hoped they would find a place for her son Gerald when he left grammar school. "After all," she had hinted to Gerry on more than one occasion, "where else will you get a nice office job?"

He had set his heart on becoming at least a journalist, if not a famous writer of the future. Many a time he had tried to persuade his mother to let him realise his own ambitions.

She was adamant. "Where else could you find a job and still live at home? And don't forget, Gerald, you could one day own the business. The present two partners of the business started off as office boys." She was constantly reminding him of this.

Eventually Gerry had given in to his mother's wishes. Perhaps the fact that his Merchant Navy father had been lost at sea many years ago influenced his decision. So here he was, for the time being, fairly happy to be a part-time reporter on the local paper and pleasing his mum by working in the Corn and Coal Merchant's office.

He did not know the Tremaynes so he saw their deaths as a heaven-sent opportunity to realise his main ambition in life to become a real journalist rather than looking upon the happenings as a sad time for the Tremaynes.

Maybe this would help him in his big ambition to get out of this place and go to London. He was constantly thinking, "I've got to get over that hill and out of Trehorra."

With the story of the second Tremayne's death and subsequent loss of the body, the Echo editor had increased his interest in the Trehorra events. "Forget your garden fetes and flower shows for the time-being," instructed the grey-haired editor, Percy Hunt, "send me all you can about the Tremaynes."

At this stage young Gerry did not know much more about the dead brothers than did the rest of the community, but he intended to. He was not going to miss what he thought was a great opportunity.

His office hours were the usual nine to five with an hour for his lunch. When he had the time, this budding young reporter would join the local lads who used to gather around the castle crossroads in the evenings. That was how he learned much about the Tremaynes, their preference to walk out with local girls instead of mixing with the local boys and that they all worked on the farm at Trewarmett for their father and grandfather.

He discovered that their education had been very limited. They never went to church or chapel, had never joined the scouts or the local boys brigade, and they had no interest in any sport.

Gerry thought that the ageing Vanstock was overcome by the whole business, was so busy with official details and reports that the discovery of the perpetrator or perpetrators was a long, long way off and he decided to write to that effect.

Gerry, who lived only a couple of doors away from the village police house, decided to do some keener investigations on his own. Whenever he joined a crowd of about nine or ten teenagers at the castle crossroads he would start a discussion about the Tremaynes, not that that was very difficult. The strange deaths were now the number one topic everywhere in the village, among men in the pubs, of course, and women in the shops too. In fact the Tremaynes' deaths had been more of a conversation piece than the weather and in these parts the weather always was number one, particularly during the summer months.

Much depended on the sunshine. There were the harvests to consider. There was the growing tourist industry and, of course, all the local fetes, shows, and sporting events.

At one such gathering at the crossroads, "I know who's done it," shouted Tom Ward, "I knows all about all of 'em."

Of course this brought howls of laughter and guffaws at the tinker son's sudden outburst. They all knew that Tom was subject to fantasizing, particularly when the moon was full, it seemed.

But Gerry Halford encouraged him to carry on with his ramblings. "What about Sam Tremayne? You said he was murdered. He just fell over the cliff, didn't he?"

"Oh, no," Tom Ward said, "I was there and I seen the one who did it. I saw him running away after he had pushed Sam over but I kept out of his way, he didn't see me."

More raucous laughter came from the group of village youths. "What were you doing, Tom?"

"I was out on my evening training run, you know, I'm going to enter the races next month."

"You entering the Trehorra sports? You've never entered it before, have you?" "We didn't know you even trained, you never told us."

"I haven't got to tell you lot everything. You'd only laugh and take the 'mick', I know."

"So who did you see running away then?"

"I wasn't that close to him and it was dark, but I saw him all right."

"How was he dressed?" Did he have a hat on? Had he got a flashlight? How did you know it was a him?"

Endless. Tom was now enjoying being the centre of attention but he did not expand on his first sensational outpouring that he "knew who dunnit."

"Have you told policeman Vanstock about all this?" asked Gerry.

"Oh, yes, I told 'im all right and he'll catch 'em. He told me so."

Whether or not Tom had spoken to Vanstock was anybody's guess. But Gerry noted it as interesting.

"Anyhow," Tom added, and by this time he was shuffling his feet from left to right, "now that Sammy is out of the way I'll be courting Ethel now. She always wanted me better than that farmer boy Tremayne."

"Perhaps you pushed him over the cliff then," shouted someone.

Well, of course, this last remark was greeted with huge yelps of laughter. To their knowledge, Tom Ward had never been out with any girl during the twenty-one years of his somewhat, to some, sad life.

Tom ignored that remark and he pushed his way through the group of teasing lads, turned his back on the jeering crowd of youngsters and jogged off down the road.

Gerry Halford, having started the tormenting of Tom, had kept himself on the fringe of this group while the taunting was taking place. He had always felt somewhat sorry for the village tinker's backward son.

He knew that Tom always had a trick of appearing suddenly in the most unlikely of places. There was one time when Gerry had been a member of the first Trehorra Boy Scouts. He had been to a late night campfire and singsong with some visiting scout troops from the Midlands. It was held on the cliffs over Pentarth Bay. Only twelve or thirteen years of age at the time, he had stayed rather late.

There was an extremely thick mist, which often came down quickly in these parts. It was just past nine thirty at night. On his way home Gerry got confused with his directions and was completely lost, when suddenly out of the dense fog who should be facing patrol leader Gerry Halford but Tom Ward!

"Have you lost your way then?" was all he had said.

In the pitch black darkness and a heavy thick mist, he proceeded to lead the young scout to the main road. From there it was easy for boy scout Halford to get home but he was more than a bit late.

Gerry had never forgotten that incident. He began to think that perhaps Tom's story of seeing a man running along the cliffs away from the spot where it was thought Sam Tremayne had gone over could just have a vestige of truth in it.

Gerry had dug deep into all the tales, tittle-tattle, rumours and riddles, which he had been busy gathering and listening to over the past few days. And although it would be mainly conjecture, he felt sure that his next weekly contribution to the Echo would be his best so far.

A couple of days later Gerry was summoned to Mr Hunt's office. "Gerry, you know I can't publish half of your story, you cannot criticise the police the way you've done."

Gerry was surprised. "I only mentioned facts. 'That despite such a lot of local knowledge and with only such a tiny population that police were nowhere near having a suspect, let alone an arrest for the deaths of the Tremayne brothers.' That's true, isn't it?"

The editor continued to peruse Gerry's report. "Now look here, Gerry, on page five you say you've spoken to people who know who murdered these young men. Shouldn't you have told the police?"

"I did, Mr Hunt, but Mr Vanstock brushed aside suggestions. I thought at least he could have asked some questions but he didn't seem interested in my notes."

"You also say you know what happened to Colin Tremayne's body. Now that is a monstrous mistake, young man. Didn't you join in the official search party yourself?

"But you write, 'Over fifty searchers and not a clue turned up.' Then you add you know where the body is."

The editor was not used to this sort of problem. He got out of his leather-lined swivel chair, took three or four paces and stared out of the window.

Gerry was a bit surprised at the editor's attitude. It only made him more determined to discover the answers himself. "Well, I was reading this book and the story was about a missing body. And it turned out that is was . . ."

At that precise moment the telephone on Mr Hunt's desk rang loudly. "What?" The editor yelled down the phone. "No, I can't see anyone right now." He slammed the phone back on the receiver, turned his attention to Gerry, who was beginning to lose a bit of the confidence he thought he had when entering the editor's office.

Mr Hunt quietened down, put his two hands on the young man's shoulders, looked him straight in the eye. "Now look here, Gerry, what on earth are you thinking about?

"This is the real world, not a Comic Cuts mystery cartoon. Forget all the myths, magic, ghouls and goblins, you can do better than this. My advice is for you to go back to Trehorra, find out the truth and get to the bottom of things. It's bound to be a local person who's behind it all. Get some serious stories that we can print. No more fairy tales, young man, stick to facts."

"Yes, sir." Gerry picked up his briefcase and quickly sidled out of the editor's office. He thought to himself, "Reminds me of the time a few years ago when I was reprimanded by my headmaster when all I did was complain about the sports master's selection of the cricket team!"

Chapter 12

GRANDAD AND THE TRACTOR

It was a nice sunny morning; Grandad Tremayne had just been served with his usual full breakfast – bacon, eggs, mushrooms, sausage, fried potatoes with of course the obligatory fried bread. Granddaughter Madeleine, who always did the family cooking, was disappointed as he pushed his plate to one side but she understood the old man's situation. He had always looked forward to his weekly trip into Trehorra on the farm's old tractor. "Can't believe Samuel won't be able to drive the tractor into the village today," he said. "Think we'll have to leave fetching the feed stuffs this week," John Tremayne answered, staring at his still untouched breakfast. Grandad suddenly perked up.

"You can't do that, John, we be out of most of it anyway."

"Yes, I know, but somehow I don't think it's right now Sam's gone and Colin too. Can't think what in the hell we're going to do."

Grandad stood up. "Look, John, we're farmers, we've got to carry on. It'll be no good givin' up or givin' in, I can drive that ol' tractor all right."

The young men's father, his mind obviously elsewhere, meekly replied, "I suppose you're right, Grandad, but I don't like the idea. I don't know what it is but I have this strange feeling about any of us going into Trehorra for a while yet."

Daughter Madeleine, clearing away the uneaten breakfast, said, "You don't think anyone's got it in for just us Tremaynes, do you?"

John was leaving the breakfast table and was resigned to letting Grandad drive the tractor. "Maybe not, but it certainly looks like it, don' it? Some of 'em in Trehorra be a bloody shady lot if you ask me."

Daughter Madeleine disagreed. "You shouldn't think like that, dad, some of 'em are all right." She was obviously thinking of her Trehorran fisherman boyfriend, Peter Williams.

Out in the yard the old man climbed on to the antiquated machine. It really was a monstrosity. He hesitated at the top of the two wooden steps to squeeze behind the wheel. He put his hand on the ignition key but never turned it. If he did he knew no one would be able to hear him because of the old engine's loud noise. He turned to John Tremayne, "Did you ever take it in to those two Brummies in the village and have 'em look at this engine?"

With all the recent family turmoil it was no wonder that Grandad had forgotten that the Pascoe brothers had been.

"No, I didn't. They came out here, don't you remember?" John was forcing himself to get on with his extra work now that his two sons were missing. "This tractor never did sound too clever, anyway."

"That's about all I need to hear and er . . ."

Whatever else Grandad said was drowned as he started the old tractor. The engine roared as Grandad put his heavy boot down on the accelerator. Smoke poured out of the exhaust.

"Nothing wrong with that, he shouted, as a flock of crows, blackbirds and magpies flew off in different directions. The old man stuck it into gear with the huge gear lever and off it stuttered with its usual 'kangaroo' start. A few old rotten turnips and discarded vegetables rolled around with a none too pleasant a smell in a four feet by four feet wooden contraption which stood perched above the tractor's huge wheels. These were so caked with mud and straw that all the debris flew all over the farmyard.

John Tremayne turned to daughter Madeleine, who had come out of the farmhouse to join her father. "I don't like the sound of that thing, I don't think he should be driving it at his age. There's something suspicious about it. I don't know what it is, but I still have a funny feeling about any of us going into Trehorra."

"Oh, don't be silly, dad. You keep saying it as if somebody's trying to do away with us Tremaynes, and especially Grandad?" She turned her back to avoid the smell of the fumes the tractor had left behind.

"Well it certainly looks like it," said John Tremayne, "our two boys have gone and I know it wasn't any accident. I have to say I mistrust the 'ole bloody lot of 'em in Trehorra."

Madeleine, still thinking about her fisherman boyfriend, "Oh, dad, you musn't think like that, they can't all be bad." She walked into the house to resume her housework chores but with a heavy heart.

John Tremayne shouted after her, "What I was thinking, the boys have done well taking those Pascoe tractors around to the other farms and you'd think those Pascoes at least would look after us and let us have a newer one." His daughter was out of earshot but John Tremayne continued. "They promised us one nearly two years ago now. I hear that the Browns over at Pennycrocker Farm have had a new one. I'm not going to stand it any more." No one was listening in any case.

The noise echoed all over the farmyard as the eldest living Tremayne, perched high up on this ridiculous machine, swallowed just a bit as his scarf slipped over his Adam's apple. Pigs squealed, the hens flew in all directions. John grimaced as he watched his seventy-five-year-old father and that machine simply corner into the lane adjoining the farmyard. "I hope he doesn't kill himself, heaven help him," he was thinking.

Daughter Madeleine, now upstairs, shouted down from the bedroom window, "Do you think Grandad will make it?"

"He'll be lucky," shouted back her father, finding it difficult to make himself heard over the still noisy but disappearing tractor machine.

Grandad Tremayne sank back into the homemade seat in what served as a cabin. It was perilously perched on the top of the tractor, a ludicrous homemade contraption.

Grandad had confidence that no harm was coming to him. He was thinking, "I know every bend, every bump, even the cracks in the road, and even the puddles when it's raining. Nothing can throw me off."

Son John, on the other hand, had not changed his mind from a few moments ago. Now he was not so sure. He had a feeling that his father's experience was not suitable to take what was virtually an unsafe vehicle through the Trehorra village.

What damage would be done to property if this thing took off and he lost his nerve? Suppose Bill Tate was taking his cows back to the meadows after their morning milking session? Suppose the last of the children were not inside the walled school play space? They usually had to be in by 9am and it was already only minutes before the hour.

"Well it won't be my fault anyway. I've warned him enough. And I'll be after the Pascoes for more than another one if any harm comes to my father."

As far as John was concerned that was the end of it. Que serra serra. Grandad had driven the tractor several times before, although it was mainly the boys who worked the other farms with the tractor. So John walked on to the farm's small vegetable garden neatly laid out behind the farmyard. "At least I'll get some peace here for a while," he thought.

Meanwhile the tractor was simply hurtling down the road. The oldest living Tremayne gasped under his breath, "Perhaps I shouldn't be bloody well doing this." He was losing a bit of his confidence. "It ain't fair. Oh, my God, what the hell is that stupid Mrs Bowering doing standing in the middle of the road?"

Actually, the vicar's wife was in the street, standing back admiring her handiwork on the church hall's notice board. She proved to be no slouch as she adroitly leaped to one side, the tractor missing her by inches. Posters, pins and paintbrushes were scattered everywhere.

Fred Mawgan was standing by his bicycle when he heard the roar of the Tremayne tractor's engine as the vehicle came sweeping around the next bend. Lucky for Fred he had not yet loaded up his basket with letters and packages yet to be delivered. He dropped the red painted post office issued cycle and leapt into a convenient empty porch. No time to look, "Who the hell be driving that?" he shouted. There was no one else around to answer.

The tractor went zooming on its seemingly uncontrollable journey down the steepest part of the street leaving columns of smoke behind it.

Gerry Halford was in a sort of a daydream, casually walking along, pushing his bike on the way to his office. A noisy engine roar, a huge clatter suddenly made him wake out of his dreams. He exclaimed, "What the devil's going on?" This was his first thought until he turned and saw the Tremayne tractor hurtling along the street looking as if it was out of control. He threw his cycle to one side and leaped behind a convenient tree. His quick reaction had obviously saved him from at least being knocked over and probably even killed.

The Pascoe twins were tinkering around with one of the few cars possessed by the villagers. This one happened to be owned by the Reverend Bowering. The Pascoes had commandeered the area around the village duck pond for a work space, which is better described as a waste tip.

These elderly twin brothers used it to carry out running repairs on a few motorbikes, some cars and tractors, which they were introducing to the area. They did these repairs for 'special' people who wanted a quick job doing on the cheap. The temporary but sturdy fence guarding the pond and the waste tip was severely tested as the tractor, with its now terror-stricken driver, crashed into it and came to a stuttering standstill.

Surprisingly, PC Vanstock for once in a long, long while was in the right spot this time. He immediately stepped over to help the trembling old Tremayne down from the steaming, smoking hot machine. Vicar Bowering, waiting for his car, also came to help thinking how fortunate it was that his car was on the other side of the duck pond and even more fortunate that the tractor had missed hitting him.

The Brummie twins simultaneously lifted their bald heads out of the Armstrong Siddeley's engine. They could not believe their eyes. Fred Mawgan had, by this time, barged breathlessly on to the scene holding the handle of his bicycle as if his very life depended on it and went straight at old man Tremayne.

He was in shock, standing still and absolutely bewildered. Fred was furious. Sensing trouble, Eric Bowering bravely stood between them in an attempt to calm things down before something more serious happened.

Vanstock stepped in also and took Grandad Tremayne to one side. The village bobby came straight to the point.

"Now what are you doing driving through this village like a madman?"

Grandad Tremayne, still trembling, stood up to the taller and much bigger policeman. "I've done this trip hundreds of times," which was probably an exaggeration, "and I've never before had a bit of trouble. I'm telling you, Mr Vanstock, there's something wrong with that tractor.

"When I put my foot on the brake nothin' happened, nothin' at all."

"Well when was the last time you drove the tractor?" Vanstock was getting slightly impatient again, thinking to himself that this was another Tremayne incident he was not wanting to deal with.

Gerry Halford arrived on to the scene and was confronted with a badly mangled fence, a smoking, steaming old tractor and PC Vanstock looking as if he was going to arrest someone. Fred Mawgan was leaning on his bike fuming, and on the other side of the duck pond were the Pascoe twins looking as cool as ever standing behind the vicar's car.

"Things could be getting out of hand," Gerry thought. He tried to look as if he had an official interest in the situation. He pulled out his notebook and began to take notes. Was this another Tremayne incident gone wrong this time?

Grandad Tremayne scratched his head, stroked his stubbled chin, "Well I usually just ride with one of the boys, but they over there," pointing to the Pascoes, "yesterday they came up to the farm and were supposed to have mended the tractor and seen that it was in good nick."

By this time the Pascoes had strolled over and joined this small group of irate villagers. Vicar Bowering, as one would expect, was attempting to quieten the atmosphere. He gradually succeeded. After a lot of toing and froing, it was agreed to have the tractor inspected there and then by John Taylor, the taxi man, whose garage was nearby.

Fifteen minutes went by before taxi man Taylor arrived. Under Vanstock's instructions, he got to work examining the brakes on this demon machine.

Grandad Tremayne seemed quite composed now and patiently waited until Taylor emerged from underneath the tractor.

Moving his dirty, oily cap to the back of his head, he announced quietly to Vanstock, "Somebody didn't want this tractor to stop."

"What do you mean?" Vanstock looking very concerned now.

"Well there's a deliberate cut in the brake tube."

Taylor invited the policeman to get under the tractor and have a look. "Look 'ere, Mr Vanstock, there's another deliberate cut in the brake lining."

Vanstock did not need to get under the tractor. "I'll take your word for it, John, but what does that mean?" He was writing his notes as quickly as he could.

"It means that whenever you touch the foot brake pedal, fluid is released and there's pressure to put the brakes on. The cut pipe would prevent this, so really there's no pressure on the brake to stop the tractor."

Even Petherick Carnack had joined the small crowd. He had, as far as Gerry could see, not been anywhere near the tractor's perilous journey. So the fact that Petherick was complaining bitterly about the old Tremayne and his tractor puzzled Gerry.

Stepping close to the village smith, Gerry tried to be as nonchalant as possible. "What's up, Mr Carnack?"

"What's up?" Petherick kept his voice as low as possible. "You must know, Gerry, what's happened, old man Tremayne has damn near killed six or seven people driving that tractor through the village."

"Did he?" Gerry replied. Thinking of his own narrow escape, "I know he just missed me. I suppose he's not used to driving it."

"Course he is, silly old bugger." Gerry was really winding smith Carnack up now.

The blacksmith went on, "These bloody Tremaynes have been driving that tractor around all the farms for ages now. Them and those Pascoes are trying their damndest to get the other farmers round 'ere to use tractors."

Gerry could see there was no love lost between Petherick and the Tremaynes or the Pascoes. "Are they allowed to drive them on the roads as well as on the farms then?"

Petherick didn't reply, but he moved closer to the old Tremayne and Gerry didn't know what to expect, but he wasn't going to miss anything.

Quite a small crowd had gathered by this time, but apart from a lot of mumbling, they were all very quiet indeed.

After John Taylor had completed his verbal report to Vanstock they all began to realise what close calls there had been on the tractor's wild journey through the narrow bending streets of Trehorra. The place reeked of burning oil, burnt tyres and stinking exhaust fumes.

Grandad Tremayne suddenly thought to himself, "I wasn't supposed to have driven that tractor today, so if they are after Tremaynes, it's not me they're after, whoever 'they' are."

Vanstock addressed directly the Pascoe twins who had crossed over to join the crowd. "Now which one of you went to the farm to see to that tractor last night?" They just looked blankly at each other and then to Vanstock. "I don't want that 'it was him,' 'it was him' answer either."

He had suspected those crafty identical Brummie twins of playing this, 'it was him,' 'it was him' trick before, but this was serious business.

To give Vanstock his due, he decided not to scrutinize the identical twins in front of this small band of locals. "I'll be calling on you two later to make a statement so make sure you're in." With that the crowd gradually returned to their various jobs and homes.

Gerry had been writing vigorously. "Another scoop," he thought to himself, "was this yet another attempt to kill a Tremayne or was it a Tremayne attempt to gain revenge for the death of the younger Tremaynes?"

Chapter 13

Gerry still felt a little bit deflated after being called into the office of editor Percy Hunt when he returned to his home after the Tremayne tractor episode. His mother was standing at the door holding a small, yellow envelope.

This was a telegram. It was for Gerry. It had been delivered by postman Fred Mawgan before he started his post round.

Excited, Gerry ripped the flimsy yellow envelope open. He couldn't believe his eyes. It was headed "London Express, Fleet Street, London," and read "Request you telephone, stop. Crime desk, Daily Express, stop. Malcolm P. Boucher, Chief Crime Reporter, stop."

Mrs Halford excitedly asked, "What's in it then, Gerald? Fred Mawgan said it was from London."

He never answered his mother. "This is it," he thought, "I'm on my way. Even if Mr Percy Hunt didn't like my article on the Tremaynes, then obviously this well-known newspaper is interested."

Almost trembling with excitement, Gerry dialed the London number. "I'll put you through to Mr Boucher," the operator replied immediately.

Gerry was a bit nervous now. He was actually going to speak to a Fleet Street journalist. A voice with a strong London accent came straight to the point, "What's happening down there? Have these two farmer's boys met their death accidentally or not? How far have the police investigations gone? Are there any suspects? Where do you think the missing body has gone? Think about these answers, young man, and phone me back as soon as you can get a reasonable story together. You can always reverse the charges, you know." With that brief message the call was ended. "Yes, sir!"

Gerry swiftly thought back on his previous articles about the Tremaynes' mysterious deaths which Percy Hunt had turned down. He quickly turned up his files on the Tremayne deaths, looked over them, and considered that he had not missed a thing in his reports. He had not accepted the official report or the opinion of PC Vanstock that Sammy Tremayne had accidentally fallen over the Black Cliffs. Of course, everyone else had but Gerry was inclined to believe Tom Ward's story.

He had reported when Colin Tremayne's body had been discovered by young John Stephens in the horse trough near the St Minerva Church. He also believed that the body had been seen by the local policeman only to later disappear. Gerry simply reported those facts. He had joined in the vain search for the missing body.

He was rather proud of the fact that the Echo had given him twelve column inches to accompany a picture of the search party. The local paper only wanted facts, but this is the London Express, this is different, they would like opinions.

Gerry got busy immediately. He looked up the stories he'd written which Percy Hunt had not accepted as relevant. In one the young reporter had posed a question as to why Sam Tremayne was out above Black Cliffs at about 10pm. This was the time it was presumed he had gone over the cliff on that fateful night. Mr Percy Hunt didn't like it.

Gerry had spoken to the other brothers and they had told him that Sam was not a collector of birds' eggs so that was not a reason to climb these dangerous cliffs. He had also extracted the 'pimpers' story from Vanstock only for the Echo editor to turn it down, but Gerry assumed that the 'pimpers' story would be accepted by the London paper. Editor Hunt had put paid to the story that Sam had simply been looking for a better secluded spot to take girlfriend Ethel.

"That's tittle-tattle," Percy Hunt had told him, "get some facts."

Gerry thought he had, and his story of Sam and Ethel visiting Vicar Bowering at the vicarage on that fateful night was also ignored by the editor when Gerry suggested that there may be a link there somewhere. He remembered that Vanstock got really annoyed when Gerry implied that Sam had been pushed over the cliffs.

The policeman had answered irritably, "Sam wasn't the first man to fall over, was he? There was a London chappie who fell over in the same place several years back, wasn't there? I've told Carlton-Taylor, the lord of the manor's agent, to put a fence up there ever since. I can't do no more than that, my boy, can I?"

Editor Percy Hunt didn't want to pursue that line either. "It was an accident and the official report said so." The editor repeated, "Until they say different we're sticking to that report."

"Another full stop," thought Gerry, "perhaps I should get this to the London Express too and see what their crime editor makes of it." Mr Hunt probably wouldn't suspect Gerry if it ever did get published.

He was a very happy young man when he turned up at the coal and corn merchant's office the next morning.

Chapter 14

The bedroom window of Harbour Cottage opened with a bang. A rather slight, silver-haired old lady thrust her head out of the window yelling at the top of her voice,

"I'll get you, Petherick Carnack. I'll get Policeman Vanstock on to you. You be always an interferin' old bugger, but you won't catch me next time." Poor demented widow Myrtle Smith was just experiencing another of her 'upsets'.

For years and years she had been a respectable member of the village of Trehorra. Quiet, industrious and meticulously clean, she had taken care of her pretty white cottage and her husband for the whole of their fifty years of marriage. She was now seventy-one years of age and lived with her spinster daughter who was getting on for fifty years of age.

During the past couple of years dear old Myrtle had had several of these 'upsets'. From being confined to her dainty little cottage and almost constantly confined to her rocking chair, she would suddenly get up and run right out the door. For an hour, sometimes two, she would stride around the village going practically berserk. She would run to the fields or out on to the cliffs. She was somehow able to summon up abnormal strength from somewhere. Her usual day would find her sitting and napping most of the time in her rocking chair, but these upsets were always imminent.

Her daughter Serina waited on her hand and foot, cooked her meals, bathed her and even put her to bed and tucked her in at night. So when this dear, frail old lady would get these upsets, the neighbours would all rally round and help Serina to chase and catch her.

On these occasions Myrtle would seem to have the strength of two or three men. And, indeed, it sometimes did take a couple of strong villagers to control the little old woman, who was always dressed in black.

Best friends to old widow, Myrtle Smith, and her daughter Serina, were neighbours, Petherick Carnack and his wife Sybil. They looked after Serina's dear old mother when on the few occasions she wanted to go out, which would only be to a whist drive or to a service at the local Methodist church. So it was strange that Myrtle Smith should be so hateful against them both as she often demonstrated during her 'turns'.

It was Tuesday afternoon and half-day closing for village shops. When she ran out of the house so suddenly, Serina missed her, so Petherick Carnack's old smithy was near and it was to there, yet again, that she hurried. Would Petherick please help her to find her runaway mother?

Immediately Petherick dropped the work he was doing, gave some swift instructions to his assistant, Tom Queen, and set off out towards Minerva Church, for this was where Mrs Smith was heading when she was last seen.

Gerry Halford, on his half day off from the office, could not help but overhear the disturbance at Mrs Smith's end of the street and, as always, was drawn to a commotion. He was soon joined by other youngsters. John Stephens always hung closer to Gerry than his shadow. Peter Rogers and Stuart Abbyn always seemed to be around on these occasions. Being young, they quite enjoyed the old lady's antics, which was a part of the village life.

It was quite astonishing from where the little old lady got her strength. Until recently, for years she had not been outside the house but she seemed to know where she was going every time she escaped the watchful eye of her faithful daughter.

It was fully half an hour before one of the boys, Stuart Abbyn, shouted that he had seen Mrs Smith dodging into Trewarmett Farm. Petherick Carnack was soon on the spot, and knowing Trewarmett Farm very well he called into the farmhouse to explain what had happened.

"I bet she's in one of those barns," said Grandad Tremayne, "I've seen her up here before and she's a bloody nuisance."

By this time Serina and the other lad, Peter Rogers, had joined the group at the farmhouse door. Poor Serina was in tears and Madeleine Tremayne suggested she go inside and have a cup of tea.

Grandad Tremayne instructed the party that the men could search the barns, he firmly added, "Don't go anywhere else, I'm warning you. We've just put in some new plants and seeds."

He was joined by his son John and they entered the barn by the huge doors. They were half blocked by the farmer's huge binder, a machine used to cut the corn and tie it into sheaves during the harvesting period. Upon reaching the barn, Stuart Abbyn remarked, "I love the smell of this hay."

"You never mind stoppin' and smellin' the hay," snapped the smith. "Be careful, I'm thinking she will fight a bit if she's cornered," was the advice given by Petherick Carnack. He had been on these particular jaunts several times before. He knew that at times like this Mrs Smith possessed phenomenal strength. Old as she was she would fight like a tiger.

After spending about ten minutes in the dark, dusty old barn, Petherick, hearing a slight rustle, looked up towards the rafters and there she was, sitting down on a bale of hay and looking down on the searchers with a huge, toothless grin all over her thin, wizened face.

"Come on down, Mrs Smith," said Petherick quietly, "we've got a nice cup of tea in Mr Tremayne's kitchen for you."

"I don't want no tea, you get on with you, Petherick Carnack. I don't know why you keep chasing me out of my house. Why aren't you working?"

"Come on, missus, let's have a cup of tea. Serina's 'ere waiting to take you home."

Dixie Dixon had joined in the blacksmith's pleas for Mrs Smith to get down. "It's pretty high up there, Petherick, I don't think she can get down."

"Well we'll have to get up there and fetch her down then." Carnack started to climb up the bales of hay. He was always inclined to get things done quickly. As soon as he was within an arm's reach of Mrs Smith, the old lady leaped away from him, lost her balance and went slithering downwards on some shiny straw with a considerable thump on the floor of the barn. There was a lot of spare loose hay and straw which thankfully softened her fall, and she was certainly shook up but quickly recovered.

Gerry Halford and Dixie Dixon were quick to get to the old lady. After she had dusted off her long black dress, they held her arms until Petherick climbed down from the top of the stacked hay. Surprisingly she quietly let them take her into the farmhouse kitchen where she sat down next to Serina as if nothing had happened. "Nice big kitchen you 'ave 'ere," she remarked.

It was a fairly long walk back to the village past the Minerva Church. As they passed the horse trough near the church, Stuart Abbyn asked Petherick Carnack if that was the one where Colin Tremayne had been found dead and then disappeared. The blacksmith took a long hard look at the trough with the clear stream water trickling in at one end and trailing away across the lane at the other end. "Yes, it certainly is, boy, there ain't another one that I know of. T'was a funny ol' do, that was, my boy. I was born and bred here and I can't for the life of me think that those things could happen in such a short time. It was all done in about half an hour if you believe Vanstock's story. Did you join the party who searched for him on Sunday?"

"Yes, I did, Mr. Carnack, I was out all day with my dad and we didn't see a sign of anything."

"Course you didn't." Mrs Smith had not lost her hearing. "I heard all about that and the other Tremayne boys as well," she chipped in surprisingly. "I knows who done that to those boys and I knows where he's gone. I know it all right. But those Tremaynes baint no good anyway. They be having no business coming into Trehorra. You haven't seen the last of 'em, I can tell 'e."

She attempted to shrug free from Petherick, who nearly let her go. He was so surprised at her forcefulness. Fortunately, Dixie was holding her other arm.

"I just can't believe what I'm hearing," Petherick said. Here she was talking so rationally about a situation he never dreamt that she had even heard of. Normally she never joined in a conversation, never read any newspapers. She was generally quiet, frail and like many old ladies of her age, very uncommunicative until she got into one of her upsets, then she would rant and rave and scream expletives at the top of her voice.

Serina raised her eyebrows in surprise at Petherick when she heard her mother. "Be quiet, mother, you don't know what you be saying, you don't know anything about those Tremaynes."

"Oh, yes, I do." She seemed to be in full control of her faculties but appeared tired and she was now leaning heavily on the two boys who had taken over her support.

Gerry Halford is still there in the group and was at Petherick' shoulder and he's thinking, "I'll have to see if I can jog the old lady's memory, maybe she does know something. I'll try to see her before Vanstock calls on her."

Myrtle Smith's search party were dispersing quickly, the boys laughing as they went their different ways to their homes. Petherick took out a packet of Woodbines, offered Dixie one, but retrieved it immediately. "Didn't notice you'd still got your pipe goin', Dixie."

"Oh, I like me pipe, boy, I thought you liked yours, too." Dixie drew hard on the black stem of his pipe, while Petherick was without his usual pipe. "Thought I'd try a cigarette." "Strange," thought Dixie, but it went quickly out of his mind. "Got time for draughts tonight? Feel I've got the beating of you after last night," Dixie asked.

Petherick had cupped his hands to light his cigarette with a match. "You have, have you? Well come round about seven and we'll see. The missus is going to the Mothers' Union meeting tonight."

Dixie walked away quietly but turned around, "Mine too. See you at seven then."

"Hey, Dixie, before I forget, was you there when Grandad Tremayne warned us not to go wandering round? 'Just stick to the barns' he said."

"Yes, I heard him say that. Thought it was funny at the time, I did, seeding and new plants at this time of year. But now you mention it, it makes me wonder. But don't suppose there's anything in it." Dixie obviously thought it was of no consequence and confirmed, "See you at seven then."

Chapter 15

THE LONDON TO LAND'S END RALLY BEGINS

A month or two, which included some nice sunny days, was enough to allow the villagers to forget the morbid stories of the late winter and early spring. The deaths of Sam and Colin Tremayne, plus the loss of the lord of the manor, Stanley Bolitho, was in the past. There was plenty to look forward to. It certainly was not as boring as some outsiders think.

Two weeks for Londoners and Midlanders is quite enough for them to relax and to get away from the hustle and bustle and stress of the city life. They mostly came for the sea, the sand and the surfing. They would wind down and leave the country folk to carry on what they all thought were contented peaceful lives.

The locals were more keen on the annual church fete, always held on the magnificently manicured lawns of the vicarage, or the annual garden show which also held tremendous interest for most of the village men folk. They would have the opportunity to show their best potatoes, cucumbers, onions or the longest kidney bean, in addition to their finest flowers.

The 'emmets' were not as interested in these activities as they were in the London to Land's End motor rally, as well as the circus and funfairs which toured all the local villages and towns during this time of year.

Nevertheless, to one and all, the London/Land's End Rally was a highlight of the early summer season. There were three starting points for this world famous event. Commencing in London, the three routes converged in Somerset and then continued into north Devon and down the north coast of Cornwall. Among such historic venues were Beggar's Roost, Crackington Haven, Strawberry Mills and Trehorra. Part of the rally was held in the area because of the exceedingly difficult terrain; narrow lanes, steep inclines, fords and hairpin bends.

The drivers of 1930 cars usually found it almost all they could do to get around the hairpins without stalling, positioned as they were on steep inclines. The three-wheeler Morgans fared no better than some of the bigger cars like the Bentleys. Some would have to take two and sometimes three attempts to negotiate these blind, often dangerous, curves. Most of the crowds would congregate on the hillside overlooking the hairpin bends, which constituted a natural grandstand view, hoping to enjoy the spills and thrills as the cars came through. They were not often disappointed. A few smaller knots of people would be straggled around the course. Volunteers would act as stewards and would take up their positions practically the same year after year.

Vanstock on his cycle would cover most of the points, so it was going to be a busy day for him. Stewards would help the cars when breakdowns occurred and when spectators might stray into dangerous areas. The first obstacle on the Trehorra stretch of the rally is the Strawberry Mills ford. The duties for this 'station' where the ford was shallow, were not considered to be very arduous.

Duncan Tremayne was succeeding his brother Sam at this point in the rally and arrived well before time, a good thirty minutes before the first car was expected. He found a bend in the lane, which would be his best vantage point, to see the cars approaching and negotiating the ford which would be their first obstacle of the day. This was twenty-feet wide. Caution was to be the drivers' watch word. Too much speed and the water could get on their brake drums. The plugs could also get wet. The riverbed was full of smooth stones and sharp rocks and could also present problems for drivers.

The day went well for Vanstock. No accidents, no spectator problems and no complaints, so he was able to go straight home as soon as the crowds dispersed. He enjoyed his whisky nightcap and thought to himself, "I'm glad that's over."

It had been a tough day for all the competitors in this part of the London to Land's End Rally. The weather had been kind. Plenty of dust in the country lanes, no mud, which usually caused the trouble, particularly on the hairpin bends, and, although watered, these were negotiated safely. The sun had been shining all day, a very pleasant day for watching this annual event, which by 4pm was all over for the competitors. Over, that is, until eight a.m. the following day when the final lap to Land's End would complete the three hundred and eighty mile rally which had started from Tower Bridge in London on the Saturday previous to the holiday Monday.

Most of the drivers and their navigators stayed the night in the many small hotels and boarding houses around the area. After a shower or a bath and then dinner, most of them would pay a visit to the nearest tavern to relax and relate their thoughts on the thrills and the spills, if any, of the day.

There was quite a mixed crowd at the popular Riverside Inn. Landlord Cecil Batten had hired extra part-time staff to deal with all the additional custom he was expecting. Evelyn Menhennick was playing the piano. This would encourage a good old singsong and a great way to bring the bank holiday to a close.

Evelyn was not only very popular but a very clever girl. She had progressed from the junior school of Trehorra to the grammar school in the neighbouring market town of Dundagel, but her exceptional talent was to be in music. Brought up by her widowed mother, Evelyn had received lessons from Mrs Lobby, the local village piano tutor. Starting when she was only eight years old, Evelyn had made such swift progress that by the time she attended the grammar school she had won every piano competition in the county. It was obvious that with her talent she could eventually progress to the Royal College of Music in London.

Widow Rosina Menhennick supported her daughter and herself by cleaning some of the various big houses. They included the vicarage, a rambling old building with large lawns and grounds situated just along the lane from where the talented Evelyn and her hardworking mother lived in an ivy covered, two-bedroom cottage aptly named Ivy Cottage.

It was rumoured that the vicar paid for the music lessons. Evelyn also played the church organ at most of the services taken by the village parson. The young teenager, with her long blond hair, enjoyed the life she had in the tiny village of Trehorra. Although so talented, she had no desire to go to Plymouth or London to further her career in music. You could say she lacked ambition, but she was only sixteen and a half years of age and was quite content. She would sometimes take time off from her education and earn some useful pocket money from her church duties and other functions in and around the local villages, such as this rally drivers' evening in the inn by the river.

It was at a similar function, a Saturday night hop at the village hall in nearby St Beth, that she had met Duncan Tremayne. What an unlikely couple they were, even for teenagers. He was just a simple country farm boy with very little education. He could milk a cow, drive a tractor and was excellent with horses. He was only slightly built and, considering he spent a lot of time working outside in the open air, he had a strange, very pasty, pale face with a haircut which could only be described as unkempt. Like his brothers, his hair was cut, or rather, chopped off, by his father. Unlike his brothers and even his sister, who all had dark brown hair, Duncan was fair. He always stood at the back of the old Trehorra village hall when the music was being played there for dances. Gradually, the group of youths who were standing with him would filter off to dance with the local girls. They would be sitting on chairs placed around the oblong-shaped floor. Of course, the village hall had many uses, from flower shows to mothers' union meetings.

Duncan Tremayne, from his very first visit to the village hop, could not take his eyes off the long-haired blonde girl who played the piano. So, overcoming a great shyness, one night he plucked up courage to walk over to the piano, picked up the tin of resin which was kept on top of the piano, and proceeded to sprinkle it over the floor. This was his way of getting close to Evelyn. Although she played the piano, she did not dance, and this obviously suited Duncan. He was soon fetching her a glass of lemonade or a cup of tea during the interval. So started a most unlikely courtship. No one could understand what she had in common with this apparently dull, uneducated farm boy.

Nevertheless, it was said that it was because of him that she was reluctant to pursue her musical advancement. A great part of her life included music. She would play the church organ for the Sunday services and for weddings and funerals. Two or three times a week she would be needed to play piano in the local village halls and pubs. Whatever spare time she did get, she and Duncan could be seen walking hand in hand around Trehorra. It appeared that once a Tremayne boy had met a girl, they seemed to want a long relationship. There was no flirting like most of the village boys, who passed their girlfriends from one to another quite frequently.

Duncan and Evelyn were noticeable everywhere; in the county lanes or watching the small boats steer into the calm of the harbour. They would throw bread crusts to the screaming seagulls. Duncan seemed to get more spare time than his brothers and spent most of it with Evelyn.

Evelyn's mother was very disappointed with this liaison. After all, she had to work damned hard to get her pretty daughter through her grammar school years and also to help provide those private piano lessons. Her daughter was on the verge of a very promising musical career, but this talented girl seemed destined to become a farm labourer's wife. Would all this talent be wasted?

In her mother's eyes, if Evelyn got serious with Duncan Tremayne she would be living in a one-up, one-down cottage with no electricity or running water way out in the 'wilds' of the country; that is, if she was not living with all the other Tremaynes at their farm. Not a particular pleasing prospect, she thought. One thing was for certain, Rosina Menhennick was adamant that if the couple married they would not be living with her. It was more than disappointing for Evelyn's mother. She always did her best to discourage this relationship. To her it was a tragedy of immense proportions.

The whole village was full of gossip such as "Whatever does Evelyn see in that Duncan Tremayne?" "What a come down for such a clever girl." "It won't last, they've got nothing in common." And so on. The remarks went on and on. Never to Mrs Menhennick of course, she kept her thoughts to herself, that her daughter was too young to get into a serious relationship. Evelyn would not have listened to any of the malicious talk anyway, she thought she was madly in love. Her mother hoped it was just a teenage crush or, at most, a mad infatuation.

The customers of the Riverside Inn that night were a great mixture of locals and 'emmets', plus, of course, a fair sprinkling of the London to Land's End car rally drivers, navigators and friends. Between the usual pub songs, the conversation would be totally around the rally; the cars, the accidents, the route, the good times had, the bad times had. These topics would naturally be discussed in some instances in great detail.

Bill Marlow, driving an MG for the third year running, had had a great day. No problems. He was full of praise for the route, the officials and the weather, he just could not fault it. And with a good performance on the last lap tomorrow, he could possibly win the trophy.

Martin Carruthers, who was driving an Austin Seven for the first time in the rally, was not so fortunate. He had stalled in the very first ford he had had to negotiate at Blue Mills. "There I was, stuck right in the middle of that first ford with only my navigator to help, and getting drenched as other cars came screaming through."

"Where was the steward?" Bill Marlow asked, "there's always one at the first ford."

Carruthers had hardly heard what Marlow said, it was getting so noisy in the pub. "Steward? I didn't see any steward. I guess I was unlucky. I've heard none of the other chaps got stuck in there." "Bloody good thing too, I'd say."

Marlow could not help smiling. "You were damned unlucky, old boy."

Cecil Batten, a local committee man for the rally, was behind the bar listening earnestly to this conversation. He said, "Well, there should have been somebody on duty, so where was he?" And turning to the unfortunate Carruthers, he said, "You were unlucky. A steward should have been there."

Marlow turned serious now, "If there was a steward there, he should have at least been able to warn the other competitors. That's his bloody job when there's a car stuck. All he has to do is wave his yellow flag and slow the other buggers down and Bob's your uncle."

Apparently there had not been another mishap. So the fact that there was no steward at that point was soon forgotten. The talk and the singing drowned conversation and continued way into the night.

The inn had got a special late licence but the music was to stop at eleven p.m. Evelyn at the piano was getting just a little bit anxious. Duncan had promised to take her home. He was never late for an appointment and it was five minutes to eleven and no Duncan. The pub was crowded but she knew he would come straight to the piano if he did arrive, so she continued to play a never ending number of requests. She loved doing it and the time always passed quickly, but not tonight. She found it difficult to concentrate. She was deeply concerned that Duncan had not appeared.

It was getting towards midnight. Cecil Batten had put the towels up which meant no more drinks, so the pub soon began to empty. Still no sign of Duncan. Cecil Batten scratched his head, wondering why Evelyn kept playing as the customers were streaming out the doors. Cecil was quite happy. Financially the night had been a good one, but he was concerned about the missing steward.

Evelyn, however, was far from happy. She played her last song on the piano and signed off with the good old standard pub song in these parts, 'Show Me the Way to go Home', to an almost empty bar. She collected her tips from the pint glass at the top of the piano, now nearly brimming over with silver and notes. She put her coat around her shoulders, looked in vain for her boyfriend, but there was no Duncan anywhere.

When it was noticed that he had not arrived to walk her home, she was not short of offers, so she left with three or four of the locals, the oldest of which was Archie Jasper. As the others wandered off to their homes, it was left to Archie to take her to her door. Archie was a local farmer now in his forties and shared his farmhouse, called Carnevas, with his sister Maggie. Neither of them had married, had never even travelled outside the village. Only on an occasion such as a bank holiday did they spare any time for leisure.

Although Archie did like his pint and most evenings called into the Pity Me at the other end of the village, he would sometimes go down to the weekly Saturday hop but would never dance. He was tall, dark, but not particularly handsome. Interested in sport, particularly football, but had never participated himself, his hobbies were chess and drafts, and not many people in Trehorra could play those games.

Carnevas was quite a large farm so he had very little spare time. He was obviously delighted to see Evelyn home. Despite the fact that he was nearly thirty years older, he was dying to tell her that he would like to take her out on a date, but she was constantly talking about Duncan and wondering why he had not kept his promise to take her home from the Riverside Inn.

She cherished Duncan as always attentive, meeting her almost every evening. She carried on almost non-stop. "He has never let me down before, even when it's harvest time, he'll dash the best part of three miles to see me just for a few minutes."

Archie knew all this, of course. Even if he thought he had a chance, he probably would never dare to suggest to her that he would like to take the Tremayne boy's place. Inwardly he was boiling with jealousy and wished she would shut up. Unfortunately for Archie, he was nearer to the mother's age than her pretty daughter. So he simply said, "Goodnight," and added somewhat grudgingly, "I expect he'll turn up, but if he don't and he may not, you know, you know where I live."

"Course he will," she snapped, but thought how strange of Archie to say that. She thanked him for seeing her home and tiptoed into her cottage as her mother would have been in bed for some time. It was now well past midnight.

At Trewarmett Farm, Grandad Tremayne was still discussing the non-arrival home of his grandson Duncan with the boy's father John. "If he went straight to the inn after the rally had finished and waited to take that girl home, he'll be home late," he said.

"Well, I would have thought he'd have come home and had a wash first," said John, "especially after spending all day looking after those cars passing through that river station at the rally."

"You'd be right there, son," agreed Grandad, "but if any of them cars got stuck in the ford and he had to help to push the car out, he'd be wet through and muddy as hell. He'd never go to see her in that state. I tell you, John, I'm not happy about it."

"Well, it was a nice day so perhaps he dried out," concluded John. "I'm going to bed now, Grandad. Duncan has been later than this before now."

"I think I will, too. I hope the boy remembers it's his turn to do the milking in the morning, however late he gets in."

No electricity in this old farm, they had oil lamps, which were duly turned down until the last little flicker of flame disappeared. John Tremayne blew them out to make sure. Both trudged up the bare wooden stairs to their bedrooms. It had been a long day, it was long past their bedtime. It would be back to some serious farm work in the morning.

Chapter 16

The annual motor rally between London and Land's End had passed through Trehorra and was practically history. Bill Allen is making his weekly coal deliveries to customers in the village. Most of them only had one cwt during the summer so he's able to take his time.

Some of the cottages were so small he had to stoop quite low to take the bag of coal inside. Some would have a coal container at the end of their neat little gardens, which would be usually full of vegetables and flowers at this time of year. Some even had a coal cupboard under their cottage stairs.

Carpenters Bill Sharrocks and Dan Gent start work in their cosy little carpenter shop sharp at 8am, as usual. Petherick Carnack, who would reluctantly light the fire of the old smithy shop, also started at around eight o'clock. When the fire would get red hot he would start making shoes for the horses which he hoped the farmers would be bringing in throughout the day.

Postman Fred Mawgan would push his bike up the street delivering letters on the way before cycling his way around the surrounding farms. In Trehorra it was the start of another working week. All the villagers had enjoyed the previous day, a bank holiday, free from their daily toils. It was now business as usual.

Fred, one of the three village postmen employed by the post office for delivering mail in Trehorra, was responsible for the eastern part of the village and the outlying areas. This meant walking up the steep lane before getting on to his heavy, government issue red post office bicycle. It was fitted with a basket attached to the handlebars usually packed full of letters, done up in neat little bundles. A few parcels would be carried in a bag behind the seat.

Fred loved the open air and would start whistling as soon as he jumped on his bicycle and headed out into the country to deliver the letters and parcels to the isolated farms and hamlets. He enjoyed going to the farms, which had such fascinating resounding Cornish names such as Marisyan, St Erth, Ruthern Farm, St Endellian Farm, Trejeune, Tregonwell, Tremorra and Harrow Barrow. Sometimes postman Fred would collect a few eggs from one farm, some fresh vegetables from another in return for doing favours for the farmers, usually the farmers' wives. The basket fixed to the handlebars of his red Royal Mail cycle was always full. It would get pretty heavy at times. And Fred, well into his fifties, would have to take a breather or two and generally stopped at least once for a snack and to quench his thirst. One of his favourite stops was by a stream in reality but grandly named the Goran River by the locals. Fred chose his usual spot near the Blue Mills ford, propped his bike up against a tree and walked a hundred yards to get under the shade. He unwrapped his snack. Today Mrs Mawgan had put in a small Cornish pasty, the best sirloin steak and Cornish new potatoes cooked beautifully inside the pastry. After that, he had two of her homemade biscuits and would wash them down with a couple of cups of tea taken from his thermos flask.

The stream did not flow very fast at this point as it twisted and turned on its way to the sea. There were lots of smooth pools and plenty of trout to be seen. They would dart among the smooth stones and white spar rocks which were dotted all along the length of the Goran, only about twenty feet wide at its broadest point.

Fred looked at his watch, saw that he was in good time, and took a short walk to see if there were any trout farther up the stream wishing he had long enough to catch some. Approaching the first bend where the stream narrowed, he noticed what he thought was a bundle of old clothes discarded by some vagrant, but as he got closer, however, he could see it was bulkier than just a mere bundle of rags. He noticed a pair of rubber boots. Closer still, and he was now extremely apprehensive as he realised he was looking at what looked like a human body. Although the legs were on the bank of the river, the top half of the body and head was almost underneath the water. He lifted his peak cap with his right hand and smoothed his very thick greying hair with his left. He came over in a cold sweat. The Cornish pasty was almost coming back up into his mouth. He was not sure if he knew who it was or not. He was hoping it was someone he did not know.

There were several vagrants in Cornwall during the summertime. "Perhaps it's one of them," he thought, edging nervously a little closer to the body. Could be a gypsy, he was hoping. They often made frequent appearances around this area. He was trying to remember if he had seen any gypsy encampments recently, but could not. His mind was racing.

He was now within a few feet and he could see some straggly hair on the back of the head. It was caked in blood. "God damn me," he muttered as he suddenly realised who it could be, and thought, "It surely can't be a Tremayne boy." He knew there was one with blond hair. He bent down taking a closer look. He had delivered mail to the Tremaynes for years and had seen the boys grow up. He exclaimed, "By God, it is a Tremayne, it be Duncan."

Fred, although doing some volunteer work for the St John Ambulance unit, had no idea how long the young man had been in the water. After just a cursory glance at the body, although he knew it would be a ridiculous exercise, he felt for a pulse. There was none. The face was badly bruised and the forehead and forearms had several abrasions. The legs looked decidedly wobbly to Fred. He thought they were broken. They were at such a twisted angle to the body. He knew there was no one around he could turn to. Even if he started shouting, no one would hear him. The immediate panic and dismay at discovering a dead body was slowly disappearing. He thought about the other Tremayne boys, especially the one who had been found in the horse trough and had then mysteriously disappeared.

Could the murderer still be around? He did not stop to look. He rushed back to his bicycle, decided he would go to the nearest farm on his round. Fortunately, it was the only one with a telephone for miles. It was St Stithian's and it belonged to a widow, Mrs Billings. In fifteen minutes he was there. The seventy-year-old lady, who was hard of hearing, shouted to him, "You're in a pretty old state, aren't you?" She was, as usual, waiting for him at the front door.

"I must use your phone, missus," shouted Fred Mawgan. "I've got to ring policeman Vanstock. Where's your phone?"

"It's on the wall in the kitchen, but you'll have to ring the post office first."

"I know all about that, I work for them." Fred brushed passed her, got the phone and yelled, "Get me policeman Vanstock, and quickly."

Annie Hambly, the Trehorra post mistress, recognised Fred's voice. "Whatever for?" she asked. "Are you all right?"

"Never mind what for. 'Course I'm all right. Put me through quick as you can."

"All right, hold on, I'll put you through." Fred knew she would be listening in so he never bothered to tell her anything.

The phone rang in Trehorra police house and Mrs Vanstock, as usual, answered the phone. Recognising his thick Cornish accent immediately as her regular postman, she said, "Mr Mawgan, whatever do you want?"

"Is PC Vanstock there, I've got to speak to him."

"Well, it is his day off, Mr Mawgan."

"He'll speak to me when you tell him it's something to do with that Tremayne lot."

"Oh, my God, I'll get him to the phone at once. Eric! Eric!" she screamed up the stairs. "Come down at once. Mr Mawgan the postman wants to speak to you urgently."

Vanstock heard her. "Okay, okay, tell him to hang on a minute." He was very irritated. "Whatever does he want me for? Don't say somebody's stolen his bike."

"It's about the Tremaynes." The local bobby needed to hear no more. He almost jumped the stairs from the top to the bottom and landed in the hall. Mrs Vanstock was holding the phone. She passed it quickly to him. She waited with bated breath as he said, "Vanstock here, what the hell's up?"

"This be Fred Mawgan, Mr Vanstock, and I've seen Duncan Tremayne."

The instant reaction from Vanstock was, "Thank goodness for that." Old Grandad Tremayne had sent a message only a couple of hours previously saying that the boy had not been home all night. Vanstock, not thinking, had replied, "Boys will be boys, Grandad. At that age they have a night on the tiles occasionally." Changing the phone close to his other ear, "Where did you see him then, Fred?"

"In the Goran near the Blue Mills ford and he be dead."

Vanstock was stunned. "Oh, no, not another Tremayne." He had quick flashes going through his mind as he thought of Colin Tremayne's body which went missing. "Get back there to the body, Fred, as quick as you can, and wait for me."

They both knew Annie Hambly would be listening so were not surprised when she cut in, "It'll be all right, Fred, I'll keep open till you gets back."

Vanstock quickly said, "Before you go, Annie, get me John Taylor, I'll need a lift to the Blue

Mills ford." He wasn't going to risk valuable time cycling all that way.

There were not many car owners in Trehorra, but Taylor, the local taxi man, owned two of them. He decided to take the small Austin Seven and not the six-seater Austin Saloon he used for taking visitors on day trips to beauty spots along the lovely coastline.

Fred Mawgan had ridden his cycle back to where he had left the body. He was relieved; firstly, to see that the motionless body of Duncan Tremayne was still in the same place, and later to hear the sound of John Taylor's car as it came up the narrow lane and stopped where the postman was standing at the riverside by his gruesome discovery.

The bank of the river at this point was very steep, it did not provide a very good foothold for the three men. It was all they could do to get the body up on to the bank where they laid it gently on the grass. The body had obviously been in the water for some time. Rigor mortis had nearly set in.

Vanstock got out his notebook to set down in writing his observations. He noticed the legs appeared to have been broken, the face and arms badly bruised with several cuts and abrasions. Closing his notebook he looked up. "Well, thank you, Fred. I've certainly had my fill of dead bodies, haven't I? Just one more thing. I shall need both of you to confirm what we found here." Vanstock glanced at his watch as he put away his notebook. "I'll have to tell his father, I suppose. You're not going that way, are you, Fred?" Vanstock did not relish the task of informing the Tremaynes that another of their sons was dead.

Fred quickly replied, "I'm afraid not. I've already called there today and I'm going t'other way and I be late already." He too did not envy the task of revealing another Tremayne's death to the boy's father.

The body of Duncan Tremayne was crammed rather than laid, along the back seat of the small Austin car. "We'll go straight to Bawdry mortuary," instructed Vanstock. This would be a thirty-mile journey. He was taking no chances this time. He would telephone Bugannon upon arrival at the county mortuary. He could see no alternative.

The three of them had a brief look around the area beside the river. It was thick with bushes, ferns and young silver birch trees. No sign of a struggle. The lane itself had dozens of tyre marks left from the rally cars that had roared out of the ford and up the lane the previous day.

Taylor made a suggestion. "We can go past Trewarmett Farm if you like." It was almost his first contribution to the conversation. "Oh, okay then." Vanstock was ready to admit the situation was getting way out of his depth. "If he was run over by one of them rally cars, how the hell did he get this far up from the ford."asked Fred.

As all three stared at the body in the rear of Taylor's car, Fred said, "There be certainly some dirty work round 'ere, if he wasn't hit by a car and he can't have fallen off a horse, altho' it looks like it. In any case, somebody must have dragged him 'ere" said the postman.

Vanstock was almost lost for words. "I can't believe that all this is happening to me, Fred. Cecil Batten down the pub told me when I came here first, he said, 'You'll be all right, 'ere, Mr Vanstock, nothing ever happens in Trehorra."

Taylor walked around to the driver's side, popped his head over the car. "Shows you how wrong you can be then, don' it. How many's that now, Vanstock? Three, 'ain it?"

Vanstock stared back at Taylor. He had never liked the taxi man. "There's no need to rub it in, John, all I know it's too bloody many. Looks like the Chief will have to bring in Scotland Yard now." Vanstock took off his helmet, wedged himself into the front bucket seat along the side of the stone faced John Taylor.

Meanwhile, Fred returned to where his cycle was still propped up against a tree. He watched the Austin go up the hill from the riverside. It struggled in first gear to negotiate the hairpin bend. Fred continued on his round. This had set him back at least two hours. He fully expected that by the time he got back to the post office rumours would already be flying around Trehorra.

The small car chugged along quite comfortably until it got to a steep incline leading to the entrance of the Tremayne farm. "I'm really fed up with all this lot. In a way I'll be bloody glad if they do send for the Yard." Vanstock was talking to himself, he knew. He instructed John, "Now, don't go right in, and keep the engine running."

Vanstock was glad to see that only Grandad Tremayne was sitting in the whitewashed porch of the farmhouse surrounded by potted chrysanthemums and he appeared to be enjoying his pipe, still in his mouth. Standing by the car from a few yards away, Vanstock cupped and shouted to the old man, "We found Duncan, Grandad, I'm off to Bawdry now. I'll call in tonight when the rest of the family will be in."

Grandad Tremayne simply nodded his head, his chin dropped on his chest with the pipe still in his mouth. Vanstock was already squeezing himself back into the car. "Don't think he heard me. Come on, John, let's get going." He certainly was relieved there were no other family members in sight.

Taylor lifted his foot off the clutch and took off quickly almost before Vanstock had closed the door. "Here, steady on, John, I'm not in that much of a hurry now, I've got the body with me. But I think we'll wind the windows down, don't you?"

The smell from the back seat was pungent to say the least, despite the dead body being covered with a couple of sacks. Vanstock was not looking forward to the journey over the moors. "Ah, well, it's to Bawdry mortuary now, and Bugannon. Full steam ahead, my boy."

The taxi man was quite startled at the apparent light-heartedness of the policeman, but he still remained poker-faced.

The caretaker at the mortuary instructed Taylor where to park the car and they trundled out the gurney to carry the body through the old solid doors down a bare drafty corridor into a cramped square room with just a steel top table in the centre. Their sturdy hobnail boots echoed as they transported the body into this room.

As there had been no prior notification, there were no officers there to examine the body straight away, so after telling Taylor to wait for him, Vanstock went to phone Inspector Bugannon who would be in Waterbridge. "How long are you going to be?" suddenly asked the taxi man.

"I don't know, but never mind how long," replied the Trehorra policeman impatiently.

"I don't want to hang around here if that Bugannon is coming," Taylor for once expressed his dislike of Bugannon to Vanstock.

"Just keep out of his way and don't worry, you'll get paid for as long as it takes."

It would be fully half an hour before Inspector Bugannon would arrive. It seemed like a lifetime to Vanstock. Plenty of time to think about this multi-murder situation. There were so many questions Vanstock wished he had answers for. Was there any significance that all the bodies had ended up in water? Samuel's death was no accident, how and why did he fall over the Black Cliffs? Colin had been found under only a few inches of water in the horse trough, but with bruises around his neck, it looked like he had been strangled before he was put into that horse trough. Why? Now there was no body, so where was it taken? And why? Now there is a third body with bruises, abrasions and both legs probably broken, and again it was found in water, a river this time. But how and why? Was there more than one murderer? Because the first dead body had been found in the sea, the second and third bodies could well have been copied. Finally Vanstock pondered who would want to murder three apparently innocent siblings, who lived on an almost isolated farm. Whatever could be the motive?

The PC continued his pondering. These Tremayne youths did seem to make close friendships quickly with some of the Trehorra girls. Could the local lads have taken an exception to this situation? Probably a little jealousy, yes, but surely this was not enough to commit murder.

John Taylor's eyes were now closed. The fact that he had been carrying a dead body around in his car didn't appear to faze him one little bit.

Vanstock on the other hand was exactly the opposite, pacing up and down the mortuary's forecourt. He was profusely sweating and his puffed up face was very red. He had avoided a great deal of stress during his career by avoiding publicity and 'turning a blind eye' to several misdemeanors on his country patch. He knew that there had been some poaching and that there was a bit of badger baiting, which he knew was illegal. There had been drunken incidents between locals and sometimes with visitors to the area during the summer season.

A bicycle would go missing, clothing would be stolen while hanging out to dry. Kids would often play football in the streets, there would inevitably be some broken windows. A small gang of young boys would go 'scrumping' apples in the local orchards, and of course there was the problem of those young 'pimpers'. He rarely apprehended the young culprits and when he did it would nearly always end with just a warning. That was probably why he was still a constable after practically twenty-five years of service in the police force. He continued to pace up and down past John Taylor. He must have passed him a dozen times or more. His thought processes seem to work better when he was moving, but now he was involved with murder. The word had never even appeared in his vocabulary until now.

"For God's sake," he muttered aloud, "this is my last year." Surely there was no one with a grudge bad enough to want to embarrass him to get him dismissed, even deprive him of his pension. Try as he could, Vanstock could not think of any reason serious enough to kill for. Plenty of traditional family grudges were sometimes carried down from generation to generation, but surely not big enough to commit murder.

He was suddenly jolted out of his mental wanderings by the voice of Bugannon booming out from his car. "Not again, Vanstock." The inspector had arrived and as he approached the constable his body language made no secret of the fact that he was distinctly displeased at the circumstances which were now becoming extremely critical, not only for Vanstock, but for all the police force under his command. He realised he had so far been a bit fortunate in gaining several promotions without too much trouble. And he was ambitious no doubt, but he certainly didn't relish these extraordinary situations with which now confronted him. "What in the hell is happening in Trehorra, Vanstock?"

Vanstock, as always uncomfortable in the presence of his superior, managed to blurt out "It beats me, sir," and admitted firmly, "and I certainly can't do any more on my own."

"Well, I am damned sure I can't spare any more personnel, surely you can think of at least some reasons why these murders are occurring. After all, you been in Trehorra long enough, you know everyone, don't you, just bloody well try to think of at least some idiot we can pin it on, or else the chief will be bound to call in the Yard."

"I was thinking that myself, sir," and he wearily took a seat by Taylor, who had remained seated and apparently completely uninterested in the conversation.

Bugannon, however, was not keen on having Scotland Yard on his 'patch' and tried quickly to rehash the Trehorra happening from the day when Vanstock had telephoned about the body he had found in the horse trough. Although he had accepted the verdict of accidental death of Samuel Tremayne, he now said he had suspected foul play from the very start. "Look at the time that was lost because we believed that official report," and he was gradually trying to put some blame on Vanstock for not perceiving that the first death was no accident. "There's no doubt, Vanstock, there is quite a collection of canny weird folk in the area and one or some of them are hiding something. So before I go to the Chief Constable I want you to give me some names.

"For a start, I can't forget that that Reverend Bowering refused point blank to have the church and churchyard searched when we first asked his permission."

At this point, Taylor sat straight up. "Surely you don't think the parson did these Tremaynes in?"

Bugannon snapped, "You keep out of this, Taylor," and turning to Vanstock he said, "You know, constable, I'm not going to wait for the coroner's report on this Tremayne. What did you say his name was?" I'm assuming it's now three murders; two bodies and no suspects."

"He was called Duncan," Vanstock replied, and, now getting to his feet, he added, "I'll hate doing it, Sir, but I'll have to request the chief constable bring in Scotland Yard."

He got really fired up. He jabbed his forefinger into Vanstock's chest. "You can't bloody well do that over my head, Constable." He emphasised the word 'constable' and carried on, "Haven't you got the slightest idea who could have murdered these Tremaynes? Surely you must have some idea. After all, you've been living practically next door to some of 'em for bloody years."

Vanstock was now convinced that Bugannon was going to shift most of the blame for having no suspects on to him. Bugannon had not finished, though. "If you can't come up with any names in the next twenty four hours I'm damned certain the Yard will be called in, but that's the Chief's job – and it's my job to advise him."

Vanstock, now surprisingly faced up to the truth, "We have to admit we're achieving nothing but a dead end."

Before Bugannon could criticise the village PC at what seemed an admittance of failure, the swing doors of the mortuary swung open. Two stern-faced police doctors appeared. The taller one looked over the rims of his spectacles but read from his notebook. "Duncan Tremayne was killed by a blow to his head. It appears that both his legs have been broken. He also has abrasions on his face, hands and arms which may mean he has been hit by a vehicle of some kind."

Vanstock immediately stood up. "That's it, sir." He looked at Bugannon. "It must have been a rally car accident." His feeling of relief was soon shattered. The inspector shook his head "You cannot be serious, Vanstock!"

Chapter 17

The third brother found dead had filtered through to Fleet Street and the London Express decided to make it the lead story on their front page. "THREE CORNISH BROTHERS MURDERED – POLICE BAFFLED – SCOTLAND YARD TO BE CALLED IN?"

Gerry Halford was excited and when seeing the Express poster outside the little newsagent's shop belonging to Landon Perry, he dashed in immediately.

"I'll take the Express, please, Mrs Perry."

"You don't usually take that one, Gerry. Shall we deliver the Mirror as usual for your mother?"

"Yes please, Mrs Perry, I want the Express for myself."

He scoured the story to see if any of the copy he had sent through to crime reporter Boucher had been used. He was not disappointed, for now he knew the Express were on to the story, he was determined to send them even more details. Plus perhaps they would be more interested in stories which Percy Hunt of the Echo had refused to print. Now, for sure, he would get more stories and perhaps a byline when and if the detectives from Scotland Yard arrived in Trehorra.

Gerry thought he had written some good stuff about the missing body of Charles Tremayne. "I'll phone Boucher up today," he promised himself, before the Express decided whether or not to send a reporter down to Cornwall.

Chapter 18

SCOTLAND YARD ARRIVE IN TREHORRA

Constable Vanstock had remembered that a young couple had spent quite a lot of time and money themselves in improving what was nothing more than huge disused old barn. They had received special permission from the now deceased Stanley Bolitho to convert the ancient "building" into a six-bedroom guest house. Gilbert and Valerie Vasey were delighted to oblige Vanstock when he suggested they take in the two London detectives.

They both realised that there would be a lot of people coming and going. No doubt, the more visitors they had, the more popular their Pentire House would become, especially as they ran a small bar. It was inevitable that Scotland Yard detectives would soon arrive at Trehorra.

Vanstock was allocated the job of arranging the visits for all the people to whom the detectives decided they would need to talk.

The first request of Detective Inspector Barnes surprised Vanstock. It was to see the right-hand man of the dead lord of the manor.

Mark Colton-Taylor was not too pleased to be told he must go to Pentire House. Vanstock thought it a strange choice.

The Scotland Yard men had arranged the lounge of Pentire House to appear very informal and friendly. Knowing the traditional dislike the Cornish had of strangers, particularly those from London, they sat in armchairs, and the rent collector also sat in one.

The chat lasted just over an hour, during which Valerie Vasey had popped in with coffee. Mark Colton-Taylor was ushered to the front door by Barnes's assistant, Detective Sgt Norman Tripp, who thanked him for his time.

"Well, I'm a very busy man, you know, particularly since Bolitho is no longer with us."

"I understand that, Mr Taylor."

"Colton-Taylor, if you please," corrected the Trehorra Estate agent. With that, he shrugged his shoulders and walked quickly down the street.

Detective Tripp looked up from the notes he had taken. "Didn't learn much from him, did we, sir? I think he knows more about his tenants than he let on."

"It's early days yet, Sarge. One interesting point was, the Tremaynes were way behind in their rent. It will take time before we open these villagers up. This is a very close-knit community. I spent a holiday down here a few years ago, and it takes three or four evenings in the pub before they'll let you near a dartboard. They're funny buggers, these Cornish. Funny peculiar, not funny ha-ha, if you know what I mean." He looked at the list of interviewees. "Who's coming next?"

"Vanstock said the vicar would be coming in. He only lives around the corner."

With that, who should walk in the door without knocking, but the Reverend himself. "Good morning, gentlemen, I'm Eric Bowering." He immediately took the armchair facing the detectives.

"Ah, yes, sir, thank you for coming. I hope we're not inconveniencing you too much. This must be very sad time for you and your village."

"It certainly is," said the vicar. "Stanley Bolitho's passing will have deep repercussions on Trehorra."

"I was referring to the Tremayne boys," Inspector Barnes cut the parson short.

"Oh, yes, them too, very distressing indeed. It is very difficult for us village folk to accept the thought of three such young men murdered. All from one family, too."

"Have you any idea why?"

"None at all. You see, they did not live in either of my parishes." The vicar sounded just a little gloomy and the inspector could understand that by preaching in the church for such a long time, and bearing in mind the circumstances, the vicar had simply acquired this style of holding a conversation.

During the next question-and-answer routine, Detective Inspector Barnes learned that the Reverend Bowering was responsible for all the church services in both parishes, St Wenn and St Minerva. Also, the Sunday schools, confirmation classes, weddings, funerals and baptisms.

He also found time to visit people who were ill. His favorite hobby, he admitted to the two detectives, was being scout master of the 1st Trehorra troop, which he had founded several years ago.

"So as well as John Stephens, the boy who discovered the one Tremayne in the horse trough, you know the majority of villagers?" questioned Sergeant Tripp. "I wouldn't say I know the majority, quite a lot do not attend my churches, John Stephens. Yes. He's a very popular boy. A patrol leader, too."

When PC Vanstock asked him to stay and look after the body of Charles Tremayne by the horse trough near the church, he said he couldn't because he had to go to a scout meeting."

"Yes, that's right, there was no way he could have stayed, we had a very important swimming badge test that day at Penporth. There were several other boys taking the test as well."

"But if Vanstock hadn't been so lenient, then the body of that Tremayne could not have been taken away and hidden or disposed of."

"I suppose you're right, Inspector, but Vanstock could not really be blamed for letting John leave to go to the scouts. He could not have foreseen that someone would remove the body and have you thought that John may have been in danger had he remained by the horse trough?"

Barnes was surprised "Have you any idea, Rector, who would be around at the time of the morning?"

"No idea at all. I've racked my brains and I've quizzed the boys. Sometimes, you know, it's children who come up with solutions. It's nearly always kids who find lost keys, wallets or purses which adults have mislaid." He laughed softly at his own suggestion.

"Of the people you know in the village, Vicar, have you any thoughts why this family should be attacked like this?"

"It's a mystery. The Tremaynes are not that well known. Trewarmett Farm is three miles or more away from Trehorra, and, as I said, they do not live in either of my parishes. So I don't know any of the family."

"I understand Samuel Tremayne, the one who was found in the sea, was going out with a local girl."

"Yes, sir, he was. I believe he was engaged to be married to Ethel Weare. A nice girl from a very good family. In fact, she's one of my Sunday school teachers."

"There seems to be an even closer link to the village with the last boy we found dead. Wasn't he going out with the young lady who plays the organ in the church?"

"Yes, yes, Inspector. Evelyn is extremely unhappy and depressed of course. Her mother helps my wife in the vicarage too, and she has told me more than once she did not approve of her daughter's relationship with this young man, so yes, the death was that close to us, but I can see neither rhyme nor reason as to why these shocking events should happen in what has been such a peaceful little village."

The Reverend Bowering, so used to dealing with illness and death during his general duties, seemed to be getting very upset. He took out his handkerchief and dabbed the moisture from around his eyes. Inspector Barnes wisely brought the conversation to an end. "I do want to thank you, Reverend, for talking to us. Just one request I would like to ask you. If any of your scouts or Sunday school children come to you with any sort of finds or stories, please let me know. We'll be right here in Pentire House for quite a while yet. I would like another chat with you when you can spare the time."

Barnes stood up, as did the Reverend Bowering. "If I can be of any help, I will be only too pleased to assist you. Now, if you don't mind, I'd like to go back to the vicarage. Mrs Menhennick is looking after my wife. She's not too well, you know."

"I am sorry to hear that, Reverend, we'll try not to intrude too much into your very busy schedule. Thank you for your help."

The inspector looked at his watch, turned to Sergeant Tripp. "I think we'll have a break now, Sergeant, and go for a pint. You never know, we could pick up something useful in the Pity Me.

"Perhaps we'll get near the dartboard at this time of day, sir." replied Tripp, closing his notebook.

The inspector replied, "I wouldn't bet on that, Sergeant."

Chapter 19

Gerry Halford couldn't wait to interview the Scotland Yard duo. His nearest connection to that famous detective agency was simply reading about them, and that was mainly in novels.

Gerry was not the only one to realise that for Scotland Yard to have been called in meant that the Cornish and Devon police forces had come to a full stop.

His last piece for the Echo had led with some rather sensational remarks with a headline, "POLICE BAFFLED, THEY HAVEN'T A CLUE." "This murderer must be found before he strikes again and they have nothing to go on. Nothing at all. Even one body is missing. Every avenue Inspector Bugannon has pursued has hit a dead end. Even the vaguest of vague leads has gone nowhere. The murderer is either very clever or very lucky, and possibly both. Surely we must be looking for someone local."

Gerry went on to implore the Echo readers to write or telephone him with any information which could be connected to the murders of the three Tremayne brothers.

The editor had reluctantly given the young part-time reporter a little more scope in reporting the most sensational story to hit this part of Cornwall in living memory.

Gerry had his own theories of how and why these three brothers had been found dead, although details of the death of Duncan Tremayne had yet to be confirmed, but editor Percy Hunt still would not go so far as to allow Gerry's ideas to be published in full. He did draw a line and reminded Gerry that the Echo was merely a county newspaper, the only paper whose front page was full of advertisements.

"If you glean anything from your mates or other people who may phone you in the village, go straight to the Scotland Yard men." instructed the silver-haired editor. "Don't even tell me of anyone you think may have something to do with these murders. Oh, I hate that word, murder. It simply doesn't sound right for these parts, or my paper."

Young Gerry Halford was delighted to have been given a little more responsibility. His interest in the mundane work of the coal and corn merchants quickly took a backseat. He spent hours and hours poring over and writing his notes. He was tempted to give the Express a list of his suspects. Up to the arrival of the Scotland Yard men, he had at least half a dozen people who could well have been in the position to have something to do with these baffling murders.

He had, at one time, had dear old Myrtle Smith on top of the list. He thought she was quite capable of pushing a man over a cliff. Her sudden appearance out of the blue could well have surprised Sam Tremayne. Only the slightest of pushes, even if playful, could easily have taken him off balance, and the law of gravity would have seen to the rest. She was also capable of holding a person under water for quite a while too. Her strength was phenomenal, when she was having one of her "crazy" turns, but what could be her motive?

Both of the incidents involving Samuel and Colin Tremayne could have happened at night or early in the morning, the death of Duncan was presumably during the day of the motor rally, so Gerry decided not to pursue that very unlikely story.

It appeared as if the third brother met his death in a rally car accident, so this could throw a new slant on the whole torrid business. Gerry thought that Inspector Bugannon was convinced all three were murdered by the same person, but he would not be quoted.

Gerry was not so sure. To him it appeared that several people in the village might have borne grudges against the Tremaynes. If the first death by drowning had been an accident any one of the people holding these grudges could have seized the opportunity to kill the other two boys, and by placing them in water infer that the deaths had all been completed by one person. However, there was a snag. It had been confirmed that Duncan Tremayne's death had been caused by a blow to the head, and although he was in the Goran River his death was not caused by drowning. The fact that Duncan's legs were broken and that his body had shown some serious abrasions, led Gerry up another alley, and he was quite disappointed that he had not been asked to Pentire House, by the Scotland Yard men. He was not to know that Inspector Bugannon, had already presented Gerry's Echo reports to them, and supposed that the experienced detectives knew what they were doing.

Gerry knew that some of the locals considered that Tom Ward, the tinker's son, could possibly have something to do with the Tremayne deaths, if not actually committing them, but the difficulty with Tom was the same as with dear old Myrtle Smith. What possible motive would they have? It was generally thought among the villagers that neither was quite "all there". In some of his articles Gerry suggested that the murders could have been committed by three different people, in a sort of "copy-cat" scenario.

The more he thought of it the more Tom Ward entered his thoughts. During conversations he had listened to in Petherick Carnack's smithy, a lot of the older men thought that Tom was a "little barmy", especially when there was full moon. Gerry himself had on one occasion had a strange experience involving Tom Ward. Gerry had been enjoying a boy scouts' sing-song evening, with some visiting scout troops who were camping in the area. He remembered he had stayed later than the rest of his troop, and a very thick mist had gathered over the camp site, and setting out on his own he had become completely pixielated. Who should suddenly appear out of the thick Cornish mist but . . . TOM WARD!!

Gerry was so relieved to see Tom he never thought to ask him, why or how he was there. Yet, without a word, he had guided Gerry out to the main road and put him on the right road home.. Gerry had been so relieved to see Tom that night, that he had completely forgotten it until now. Perhaps it could be true that when Tom had bragged to the teenage group "I seen somebody running away from the Black Cliffs." And however much sympathy he had for the tinker's son, he decided, "YES he was quite capable of pushing Sam over." He also could have been on one of his "training runs" and met young Colin Tremayne in the lane by Minerva Church. The boy could have taunted Tom somehow, and on the spur of the moment, Tom could have led him to the horse-trough, intending to douse his head in the cold water, and not realising his own strength held the unlucky youth under too long. Tom could well have hung around until both

John Stephens and PC Vanstock had disappeared. He was nearly 6 ft tall and was quite capable of lifting the much lighter Colin Tremayne, and so with no-one around he hid the body. Possible – then again where was the motive?

For most of the time Tom Ward was a loner, so it was equally possible that he could have again been on one of his training runs, could have found the third Tremayne dead or alive and could have dumped him in the Goran river near the Blue Mills Ford.

His imagination was now running wild, and as Percy Hunt, his Editor at the Echo, had put down Gerry's theories, it was obvious that the Scotland Yard detectives would also dismiss his "stories". Nevertheless, he thought Boucher might be interested in his speculative ideas, so he decided his next piece would be headed MURDER IN THE COUNTRY – THE MEANS, MOTIVE AND THE OPPORTUNITY. Perhaps this would encourage some suggestions and may actually bring in some tips.

When Bugannon paid one of his infrequent visits to Trehorra, he went to Pentire House to find Detective Inspector Charles Barnes and Sergeant Tripp engrossed in notes taken from the long list of people they had interviewed.

"There doesn't seem to be anyone else who can give us any additional helpful information, does there, Sarge?"

He nodded to Bugannon to sit down. His Scotland Yard assistant, Norman Tripp, had just finished going through all the notes he had taken from the locals. He threw his notebook on the coffee table. "No, sir, you're right, I think the villagers know a lot more than they're telling us. They seem to get so far and clam up on us." He turned to Bugannon, "Do you know, Bugannon, not one of them has come forward voluntarily. I wonder why?"

Bugannon, now seated opposite the two Londoners, looked a little uncomfortable but agreed with the non-co-operation of the locals. They continued their discussion, which really was a interrogation of Bugannon, for a further few minutes.

Detective Inspector Barnes was on the point of closing the meeting and was not pleased with the stone-faced Inspector Bugannon. He had not added very much to any of their questions or conversations since the Yard men had arrived on the scene, so for a change Bugannon appeared delighted when Barnes invited him to contribute. "Look here, Bugannon, you know we are getting nowhere. I want you to make one last effort to help us" He emphasised the word last.

Looking thoughtful, "If you are looking for a motive" Bugannon came straight to his point. "There seems to be plenty of people who didn't like the Tremaynes. The older ones owe money all over the place. The younger Tremaynes have almost swept the field when it comes to getting the girls in the village. I think we can put Petherick Carnack and Dixie Dixon into the frame now, but forget the few "crazies" and "barmpots" we seem to have in Trehorra, like Tom Ward and the old girl, Myrtle Smith, that this upstart of a local reporter, Gerry Halford, keeps

referring to. They are definitely not responsible."

Bugannon was in full flow now. Inwardly he was thinking that these city slickers would soon find out what policing in a small Cornish village was really like.

Aloud he continued, "Vanstock, poor old chap, is way out of his depth and tells me he's been trying to nail those strange Pascoe twins for a long time. But whatever and whenever he suspects them of doing something, he says they always have alibis, and pretty good ones too. They cover each other so well, and that's difficult for Vanstock to deal with."

Tripp looked at his notebook. "Can't say we've seen them, sir. Do you think it's worth getting them in?"

Bugannon looked smug. "It would be a waste of time." He turned to the sergeant, "Of course let's face it, Tripp, weigh it up a minute. How many real suspects have we got? People don't murder for bills that aren't paid. People don't murder young men because they don't want them going out with their daughters and getting them pregnant, although both reasons are serious in these parts, but murder them? I don't think so. Neither of those reasons is, in my opinion, a motive for murder. So we still have to find a motive or rather you do, I cannot accept Tom Ward's hallucinations mean anything. And old Myrtle Smith, whilst capable of some unusual escapades sometimes, is surely not a serious suspect?"

"I guess, gentlemen, that leaves our cupboard bare. It certainly leaves the ball in our court, so to speak."

Both Barnes and Tripp looked surprised and puzzled at the local inspector's demeanour. It was certainly not a helpful one.

"I suppose there's some substance in what you say, Bugannon, but it's all negative stuff, isn't it?" Detective Inspector Barnes realised the area's highest ranked officer's little speech had not left them with any new information.

"Now, if we were in London, we would be able to call on our "grassers" and we would soon get a list of at least two or three suspects. These country folk seem to stick together well, whatever their motive may be."

"Haven't you any leads at all?" Bugannon looked blank. Sergeant Tripp slapped his notebook on the table. "if we don't get something soon we'll be called back to London. I reckon we'll have to get hold of that young reporter chappie. He seems to be putting himself about a bit according to his articles in the press."

Bugannon shrugged his shoulders. "He talks a lot of hot air. I don't think he knows any more than Vanstock, and that's next to nothing."

"Perhaps we'll bump into him at the fair, sir." Tripp attempted to be optimistic "Maybe, sir, the locals will be more relaxed this evening. Are you coming along, Bugannon?"

"I wish I could, but I've got to get back to headquarters."

"Of course you have," said Barnes with a hint of sarcasm, "Thank you Bugannon" and turning to his assistant, "Better put those girls and that Gerry Halford in the book, Tripp."

All three started to walk to where Bugannon's police car was parked at the end of the Pentire guesthouse. They watched several villagers walking past.

"Isn't one of them the village smith with a funny long name?" Detective Inspector Barnes was getting to know the locals now.

Bugannon nodded his head, "Yes, sir, Petherick Carnack. He's into most things in the village. Chairman of the men's snooker club, organises village whist drives, arranges darts competitions with visiting pubs in his local, which is the Pity Me. He is a member of the parish council and he's on the sports committee too. You name it – he's in it, or on it, but murder? No way."

"Can't remember having him up to Pentire. Seems like he could be useful to us, Tripp tell him we'd like to see him."

The Scotland Yard man turned to Bugannon and they shook hands. "Thanks for coming, Inspector, and we'll see you later I expect. Keep in touch, please."

Chapter 20

It wasn't that far to the entrance to the temporary fairground, and already they could hear barrel-organ music blasting out plus all the screams and screeches of excitement from the swings, the roundabouts and the rest of the fun of the fair. It was doing a roaring trade.

"Roll up, roll up, three balls for a tanner. Knock over just one coconut and you win a prize. Roll up, roll up."

This was the appealing message of the caller on the coconut stall, who was only one of the many colourful characters beseeching the locals to spend their hard-earned cash.

This was the scene which greeted Inspector Charlie Barnes and Norman Tripp as they entered the fairground, looking extremely relaxed in just cream shirts and grey flannels.

Some of the locals had been lucky. Lots of the children were holding on to their winnings – tiny goldfish in a glass jar full of water! Fewer kids were holding the star prize of huge cuddly teddy bears. All, however, were having fun. The terrifying happenings of recent weeks were momentarily forgotten.

The two Scotland Yard men were actually enjoying their casual stroll past all the sideshows. They even squeezed into a dodge 'em car, which had just been vacated by Gerry Halford and Tom Ward of all people.

That's Halford with his buddy," shouted Sergeant Tripp.

"Can't hear you, Sergeant, too much noise. Did you say that's the murderer?"

"No I bloody didn't," replied Tripp, anticipating an early crash as, with a huge jerk, the cars were set in motion.

If the two Scotland Yard men had not been such a tight fit, they would surely have been jolted out of their seats very early on. Their car was hit square on by the number 13 car with two young girls in it.

Charlie Barnes, good naturedly-shouted to them, "The name of the game is dodge 'em!"

Even Archie Jasper was in one of the cars. And who was with him, but Evelyn Menhennick! Gerry Halford, back in for another ride, was in another car, this time with the pretty young sister of Archie Jasper

This was all duly noted by the detectives. Although outwardly appearing to be enjoying all the "fun of the fair," they were still interested in who was with whom. In fact, the evening was turning into a valuable learning experience for them.

"Did you see that Archie Jasper with the girlfriend of Duncan Tremayne, Sergeant?" They had got out of their car without any further collisions.

"I certainly did, sir, and I saw that Peggy Dixon girl, you know, the pregnant one, she was in a car with that youth who helps Petherick Carnack in his blacksmith shop. Tom Queen's his name, I think."

"That's interesting, Sergeant, you have a lot of following up to do after tonight, won't you?"

It was nearly 9:30pm and the star attraction of the fair was just about to start Already a lot of people had gathered near the bright blue water tank at the end of the field. Rising up from the side of the tank, which was full of water, was 150 feet tower of tubular steel, built into a high construction which had a diving board at about 30 feet intervals. A team of Canadian divers would, for the third and final time today, attempt their dives from the various diving boards and would leap up to the exciting climax when the would-be world champion diver planned to dive for a world record from the highest diving board.

Before that, there was a lot of comedy diving and some more serious diving.

"Will anybody challenge our champion?" the compere asked. The usual "plant" in the crowd, a tall middle-aged man with a check shirt and a pair of white flannel trousers, shouted "I will." The compere accepted the challenge and the man was invited to climb up on to the diving boards. He pretended to be scared of course, and stumble up to the fourth diving board one by one and would pause for laughs. They would then proceed, of course, to finally tumble off and into the tank of water with a long, belly flop splash to the great delight of the assembled crowd, particularly to all the children who were squatted on the grass in a sort of semicircle around the bright blue painted tank.

There would be well over a hundred people watching when the champion diver was introduced and he made the most of his climb to the top of the diving tower.

The cheering and clapping was deafening as he treble somersaulted and swallow-dived his way down to what seemed a ridiculously tiny target of water. In fact, the tank was only 20 feet in diameter and just 15 feet deep, so there was no disputing that these artists were of the best quality.

The champion diver, after hurtling down from the top board, entered the water with hardly a splash. Even the two Scotland Yard men had to join in the applause and were pleased to chuck a few coins into the divers' collection tins as they were handed amongst the admiring crowd.

"I wish I had my kids here," remarked the sergeant, "They would have loved that lot."

"Unless we find out who's been seeing off those Tremayne boys, you'll not want to come back to Trehorra."

"We'll have to get 'em then," Tripp replied.

The music had ground to a halt. The lights were gradually being switched off one by one.

"I think we'll have a goodnight pint at the Pity Me before we turn in," Inspector Barnes suggested to Tripp.

"Okay, sir. That suits me. Never know who we'll meet in there."

He tapped his jacket pocket to make sure he had his notebook with him and going in through the side door of the Pity Me they never expected to meet Police Constable Vanstock, but he saw them first.

"Good evening, you two. How are things going? I was just going home after a day at the fair – on duty, of course, sir?"

"Well, you must be off duty now, Constable. You might just as well have a pint with us. You haven't got far to walk, have you?"

"No, sir, I'm only just up the road. I did want a word with you anyway."

At the bar, Inspector Barnes was 'in the chair'. "Three pints, please. What have you been up to lately, Vanstock? What's the word you've got?"

"Well sir, I've been having several chats with that young Gerry Halford. He's the Trehorra reporter for the local Echo, you know. I think you've been provided with some of his articles. Well, he's told me that Sam Tremayne and Ethel Weare had been to the vicarage the night before he was found dead in the sea."

"What! Together?" Sergeant Tripp took another sip from his pint of his Symonds Ale and out came the notebook. "How does he know that? We haven't spoken to the Ethel Weare girl but we have spoken to the vicar, and I can't remember him telling me that."

Vanstock was gaining confidence and he continued. "Well, that's what he told me, and he also told me that Peggy Dixon was pregnant and guess who the father is?"

"I suppose you're going to tell us that it's one of the Tremaynes?"

Vanstock looked totally surprised. "You be damned right there, Officer, how did you guess that?"

"It's not a guess, Constable. To tell you the truth, Vanstock, in a conversation we had with her father, we came to the conclusion, that it could be Colin Tremayne who wasn't very popular with her old man. 'Dixie' I think they call him. He told me that he had stopped her going out with him."

"I wonder how long ago that was then. Could be he was a bit late." Vanstock smiled at what he thought was a joke in there somewhere. Whatever the PC intended, Inspector Barnes chose to ignore it.

"Looks as if we'll have to find out a bit more about the girlfriends," He looked at Sergeant Tripp." We'll see Gerry Halford tomorrow. Looks as if he's got some knowledge that we've missed out on, after all he's around their age."

Vanstock continued. "He's certainly putting himself about, sir. I seen him at the fair with Tom Ward. He thinks Tom knows more than he's letting on, but Tom is harmless if you ask me".

The Scotland Yard man agreed with the local policeman's remarks. "I think he's a barking up the wrong tree there, Vanstock. The tinker's son is as daft as a brush, isn't he, Constable? Now tell me he is?"

"Course he is," Vanstock agreed. With that, the conversation petered out as some of the locals were cocking their ears and edging suspiciously nearer and nearer to the three policemen.

As soon as the barman called "Time, please, gentlemen," the bar emptied gradually. Barnes, Tripp and Vanstock drained their glasses and bade each other goodnight. Vanstock almost tottered into the gents toilet before taking the short walk to his house.

The two Londoners went striding off, in the opposite direction, to Pentire House. It was getting slightly chilly. Barnes, the older of the two, buttoned up his jacket. "I guess our time at the fair hasn't been entirely wasted, Norman."

"No, sir, or at the pub. Could be we're getting somewhere at last. I'll be chasing up young Halford for sure tomorrow. We certainly ought to have at least a friendly chat with him. Judging by his comments it looks as if he might throw some light on one of these murders at least. Being a local, he can perhaps get them to talk to him far easier than they'll speak to us."

His superior said, "Maybe you've got something there, Norman. We seem to get so far with these Cornish people and then a barrier seems to build up. I feel that they can't believe that one of them, as sure as hell, is responsible for these murders."

They were nearing their temporary headquarters at Pentire House now, and Sergeant Tripp suggested, "I'm thinking, sir, that sooner or later, they'll have to believe, it is one of them."

"I'm sure you're right there, Sergeant."

They briefly went through their programme for the next day. Interviews with Gerry Halford, Petherick Carnack, Ethel Weare, and Peggy Dixon were on the top of the list, but significantly they decided to invite Vicar Bowering for another "chat".

Chapter 21

The sign was crudely written and brief, 'HELP WANTED TO DISMANTLE FIXTURES AND LOAD ON TO LORRIES. APPLY CARAVAN NUMBER FIVE'

It was fixed on the entrance gate to the village sports field, which for the past few days had contained all the fun of the fair. A local gang of youths were grouped around the sign situated so that it would be seen on their way out. It was quite a while after the funfair had been closed for the night. To the surprise of all of them, the tinker's son, Tom Ward, with a sort of a swagger, was the first to come out of the makeshift office in caravan number five

"I've already signed on. Been doin' it for years, I 'ave. It's good money, you know," he advised the waiting group of young men.

Standing on the fringe of the group, Gerry Halford was invited to join them. "I've got to finish my weekly report on the Tremaynes," was Gerry's excuse, "And I've still got to get to work by 9am."

What he didn't want them to know was the other business he had to think of. It was his London Express arrangement.

Most of the others decided they could do with a little extra pocket money, so they all went along to caravan number five. Altogether, there were at least a dozen to twenty villagers already queuing up. The youngsters who had got in line were soon signed up for the dismantling.

"Be here at 6am sharp," ordered Barnie Bamford's number two, "We'll be waiting for you."

The crowd of prospective part-time fair workers dwindled away to get a few hours' sleep.

Chapter 22

Detective Inspector Barnes looked at his watch. Thought he was either seeing things or hearing things. It was only 6:30am but surely that was a somewhat loud knocking on his bedroom door. He automatically shouted, "Come in." Valerie Vasey opened the door immediately.

Balancing the tray, on which was the detective's tea and biscuits, the young landlady was not as composed as usual. "Sorry I'm so early, sir, but I just had a phone call, sir. You're wanted at the fairground at once."

"The fairground?" Barnes was now fully awake. "Who wants me there?"

"Policeman Vanstock rang up five minutes ago, sir. Said there was a problem with another Tremayne."

"Oh, no, are you sure? I can't believe that." He hesitated. "Thanks for the tea, Mrs Vasey, I must get over there immediately."

Fifteen minutes later, he and Sergeant Tripp were looking at the dripping wet bloated body of yet another Tremayne laid out on the grass. It looked rather bizarre. Standing over it looking even more flustered than usual was a very nervous Vanstock. Forgetting his usual salute he explained to the two detectives that this was Gerald Tremayne, and he was found in the diving pool by two of the men who had signed on to dismantle Barnie Bamford's famous Canadian diving platform. Vanstock had confirmed that Gerald Tremayne's twin brother, Joseph, was still at home. There was only a small group of people there. Even for the country folk of Trehorra, this was a bit early.

    The Scotland Yard detectives had to think quickly. They instructed Vanstock to get names of as many witnesses as possible. Tripp would take statements from all of them later.

    This could be the opportunity to solve all of the Tremayne mysterious murders. Perhaps the perpetrator has become too confident by committing another murder while Scotland Yard were in the area.

Chapter 23

Barnie Bamford had remained in his makeshift office at the end of his luxury caravan. Vanstock had already instructed him that his trucks, the fairground machinery and none of the live-in caravans or any of his employees would be allowed to leave the fairground until Scotland Yard had given their permission. He was also to provide a list of all the names of people who travelled with the fair. This was going to be a colossal, complicated task, not only for Vanstock but for Barnie Bamford.

The fairground boss would have details of only about fifty per cent of the males who travelled regularly with the fair. As for the other fifty percent, keeping tabs on them would be a mammoth task for him, also. A lot of them had families. Some of the children, some of whom were even under 14, worked on the various fun and gift stalls.

Gerry Halford was awakened early too. The phone in his mother's small cottage a few doors away from the policeman's house rang at 6:30am. His mother answered, "Yes, Mr Hunt, I'll get him down immediately – Gerald, get down here at once, Mr Hunt wants to speak to you."

Gerry had heard the phone and he literally jumped out of his bed and nearly down the whole of the tiny staircase. At the bottom, his mother was holding the phone with her hand clasped over the mouthpiece. "Mr Hunt doesn't sound too pleased." This stopped the young reporter in his tracks. He wondered what could have happened this early in the morning. He was soon to find out. Nervously he grasped the phone, "Er, hello?" he stuttered into the phone, and for the next few minutes, the only words he managed were, "Yes, sir. No, sir. Er, I didn't think, sir. Yes, I will, sir. No, I won't, sir. Thank you, Mr Hunt. Thank you." He placed the phone down quickly.

Mrs Halford was still standing by his side. "And what was that all about, Gerald?"

Gerry was half way out of the door. "Can't tell you now, Mother. I'll see you later."

And there he was, gone out of the door, grabbing his bike and off along the street.

Landon Perry and his wife were busy unpacking and checking the first batch of the London newspapers to arrive at their tiny newsagent shop, which was really only a converted sitting room-cum-lounge sometimes referred to as the front room in some small cottages.

Hearing the door bell Mrs Perry peered through the door window. "It's young Gerry Halford. Whatever does he want this early?" she asked.

At that moment, her husband, Landon, had just opened the top London Express out of a roughly bound bundle. He stared at the huge headlines, "ONE CORNISH MURDER MYSTERY SOLVED. SECRET OF MISSING BODY FOUND.

He couldn't wait to unfold the publicity poster the Express always included. Used as he was to eye-catching headlines, he could not help exclaiming, "Oh, my god, missus. This is sensational stuff all right. Look at this." He pointed to the large letters – FROM

OUR SOURCE IN TREHORRA. "Wonder if we can get another batch."

The door bell rang again, longer this time. "Come in, Gerry, my boy, look at this." Landon proudly pointed out the headlines. "This will put Trehorra on the map all right."

Gerry concealed his delight. "Oh, I think we're on the map already, Mr Perry." Nevertheless, he eagerly said, "I'll take six London Express, please." Mrs Parry noticed Gerry's excitement, "SIX!? Do you want your mother's Mirror as well?"

Gerry was engrossed in the paper. "No, no, no, thanks. You can deliver it as usual, please." He scanned the article. His name was nowhere to be seen. He didn't know whether to be pleased or not, but it was definitely his copy. He read on.

'The search by the police and their search party failed because the body had already been taken many miles away. No wonder the collection of farmers, poachers, rabbit catchers, even some huntsmen with their hounds, also in the search party, couldn't trace or find anything.

'The answer has been in these parts for years. Many sheep have been killed and eaten and only five miles away from Minerva Church. No humans, however, have ever been hurt or attacked. But this time it is a dead human which is missing.

'In the past, various papers and magazines have been covering the stories and rumours of missing farm animals. It has been said that even fully grown animals have been consumed. No one appeared to have

the answer – but a monster it definitely was. The stories had been so prolific that the story had almost been put into folklore category.'

Gerry was lapping this up. What a story the Express man Boucher had made of Gerry's suggestions. All Gerry's copy that Percy Hunt wouldn't print was included.

'It is a wolf-like animal. It has been described as similar to a panther or puma, which had probably escaped from a zoo.'

Gerry had to smile to himself as he read the final lines. *'Our source, direct from the centre of this mystery in Trehorra, has confirmed: 'The search party had no chance whatsoever. The body of Colin Tremayne had been picked up probably mistakenly by this mysterious beast, as it covered the ground so fast, the body of this poor Tremayne was very soon in the animal's lair miles and miles away. The culprit who stole the body of Charles Tremayne is obviously this superhuman animal aptly named The Beast of Bawdry Moor. SEE THE STOP PRESS.'*

He swiftly turned to the back page and to Gerry's amazement, it read, 'MORE REVELATIONS ON THE BEAST OF BAWDRY MOOR'.

The fact that Percy Hunt had earlier reprimanded him when he had recognised this Express story as one of Gerry's reports the Cornish Echo had decided not to print, worried the young reporter slightly. It made him more determined to find even more copy for the Express.

He thought "I'll send more copy tonight" as he folded the papers, tucked them inside his jacket and continued to the Corn and Coal office where he was anticipating another boring day.

Gerry was there so early he had to wait for the general foreman to arrive before he could get into his office. He was not to be bored for long! No sooner had he taken up a seat at his desk, than he heard someone pounding up the wooden stairs.

The early visitor did not bother to knock the door, he swept straight into the office and approached Gerry in a somewhat threatening manner. "Young man, I want you to come along with me," demanded PC Vanstock.

"I can't leave the office this morning, Mr Vanstock." Gerry was startled by this early visit from the village policeman and tried to protest. "I have a lot to do." he lied.

"Well, you'll have to leave it then. These Scotland Yard detectives want to see you up at Pentire House. I don't know what you've been up to, my man, but it's looking serious." PC Vanstock remained straight-faced. Although Gerry wanted to speak with the Yard Officers, this was going to be no friendly chat.

He was still on a high from reading his piece in the Express, so he jokingly asked, "Don't tell me you've found another body?"

"Now how did you know about that?" Vanstock was just amazed. "You are definitely coming with me, Halford." The use of Gerry's surname seemed to jolt the young reporter. He wasn't being arrested. Or was he?

"As soon as Mr Steward comes in, I'll ask him if I can go." Gerry was pleased that he was to see the London detectives, and couldn't foresee any problems.

"You'll go all right, Whatever your boss says." PC Vanstock had tucked his helmet underneath his arm. "Come on young man, I can't hang around here all day." It became obvious to Gerry that the policeman had not read the London Express. So as soon as his boss arrived, he asked permission to go with Vanstock.

"Certainly. But don't hang about, Halford, and come straight back. That's if Vanstock doesn't have to put you behind bars." He winked his eye at Gerry.

"In that case, sir, I would hope you will bail me out."

The fact that the policeman was ultra serious still did not seem to worry Gerry or his boss. Vanstock followed Gerry down the stairs, not looking too pleased with light-hearted responses he was getting from Gerry and his boss.

The two Scotland Yard men had returned to Pentire House from the diving pool site at the fair. They were seated in their familiar informal layout, Detective Inspector Barnes at the coffee table and Sergeant Norman Tripp leaning back in an armchair, notebook on his lap. Gerry sat on the opposite side of the coffee table. After introducing themselves, which really wasn't necessary, Tripp offered a friendly smile, thinking to himself that his own son was only a year younger than Gerry. The inspector nodded at Gerry.

"That's quite a story in the Express today, Gerry." And coming straight to the point, "Was there anything in it?" He was, of course, referring to the Beast of Bawdry Moor story.

Gerry looked thoughtful for a moment, for he knew that Mr Boucher at the London Express had certainly 'jazzed up' the facts of the 'Beast' report which Gerry had sent to him. "Well, sir, where else could the body be?"

The inspector stroked his chin, not sure whether Gerry was trying to be clever or not. To answer a question with a question was not what the detective wanted or expected. He had to agree though, that there was a slight possibility that the story could have some truth in it, in the absence of any other clues.

He now took some newspaper clippings from his file which had been provided by Vanstock. He next referred to another of Gerry's reports from the Echo.

Holding a cutting at arm's length, he read out, *"They must find this person before he strikes again. And strike he will. The police say they have nothing to go on. Nothing at all. One body is even missing. Every avenue Inspector Bugannon and his team have pursued has hit a dead end. Even vague leads have gone nowhere. The murderer is either clever or lucky and possibly both."*

He placed the cuttings down, looked straight into the eyes of young Gerry Halford. "Mr Halford, that's strong stuff maybe written very easily on this case. But what's more, you wrote this report when it was generally thought that the deaths were merely accidents. What made you think there was a murderer or murderers at the stage?"

"To tell you the truth, sir" – Gerry was surprisingly not a bit nervous – "I just knew that they couldn't be accidents. Sam Tremayne would never have gone to Black Cliffs on his own at that time of night, the time that he was supposed to have fallen over. So I naturally assumed that somebody must have coaxed him somehow and simply pushed him over. Tom Ward told me he saw somebody running away from the cliffs, round about the same time."

"I can see your reasoning there, but is Tom Ward reliable?" the inspector asked. Before Gerry could answer, he was asked quite pointedly, "But the second Tremayne who is missing, he was on familiar territory for him, wasn't he?"

"Yes, sir, he wasn't far from his home really. Either he hadn't been home all night or he had gone out exceptionally early in the morning, which is not unusual I was told. So it was obvious to me someone had met him by arrangement or by accident."

Gerry was quite pleased with the way the conversation was going. He was thinking the Express would be pleased that their "man in Trehorra" was assisting Scotland Yard.

The detective inspector now looked serious. "You're not the only one to criticise the police, but you must understand, Mr Halford, that critics of the police are in a different position from us, especially people like you. They can assume things – we have to prove them."

Gerry was sensible enough to acknowledge what the detective was saying. The inspector, too, decided that if he was to get into the locals' confidence, then this young ambitious reporter might prove very useful.

There followed a few more questions from Sergeant Tripp who took the opportunity of putting some of his own theories from the copious notes that he had gathered.

Gerry was completely honest and forthright and thought he had made a good impression on the two London detectives.

"Thanks for coming, Mr Halford, although we think that some of your witnesses and suspects don't fit the picture we have. You know the locals. We don't. But the names being bandied about like that Myrtle Smith and those Pascoe twins – we don't see these sort of people as murderers. As you have inferred, some things in your reports point to certain village characters. Could be any of those I've just mentioned. You may be correct in assuming that locals are involved, but not these sort of people. We have to find a motive. It's not easy."

"Yes, sir, I know that." Gerry felt the interview was coming to an end, and got up to leave but Sergeant Tripp hadn't finished with him yet.

"By the way, Mr Halford," said the detective as he half-rose from his chair, "what do you know of Gerald Tremayne's death? We understand that you mentioned another body when PC Vanstock spoke to you earlier."

Gerry was absolutely floored. What was he talking about?

He sank back into his chair. "Surely, sir, you mean Duncan Tremayne, don't you? He was the last one, at the time of the motor rally, I was only joking earlier."

"I don't have to tell you, this is no joking matter, Mr Halford. Gerald Tremayne has been found dead in the fairground only a few hours ago." The Scotland Yard man stood up, all six feet of him. "It seems your mate Tom Ward was one of the persons who found the body. What do you make of that? And may I remind you that this new situation is extremely serious, especially as in one of your earlier articles you all but named Mr Ward as a suspect, but I'm told you look upon him as a sort of mate."

"Well, sir, he's not really a mate. I latched on to him in the hope that he would provide me with some information. He does get around the village at some odd places and at odd times, but I honestly knew nothing about Gerald Tremayne's death until you just mentioned it, but could you please give me the details?" The inspector held out his hand to the young reporter.

"I'll see that you get our official statement" and with a firm hand shake reminded Gerry "Don't forget, Mr Halford, we'll be here for a while yet. I would like you to keep us posted if you discover anything that may be useful to us",

On his way out, Gerry met Valerie Vasey and, still shocked by the news of Gerald Tremayne, said "What about this latest news then Mrs Vasey?" She didn't answer him and brushed quickly past him into the lounge. He heard her breathless voice say to the inspector, "You're wanted on the telephone, Mr Barnes. It's a lady. I think she said it was your wife."

Chapter 24

Before the inspector could reach the phone, he could hear his wife's voice sounding very irritable. Before he could get a word in she was saying "How much longer are you going to be down there?"

"Calm down now calm down. I really can't say." The inspector was not unduly surprised at the tone of her voice.

"Well, you've been down there nearly two months now. The kids will have forgotten they have a father, if you stay there much longer, I'll have forgotten I've got a husband."

He tried to remain calm. "This is turning out to be a very difficult assignment. We've just had another problem only this morning."

These words seemed to go right over Mrs Barnes, "And you thought it was going to be easy – a piece of cake – you said."

The inspector was still trying to be cool, with Valerie Vasey hovering in the background. He said very abruptly, "Well, it's not."

She continued to be aggressive. "What? You're saying you can't beat what you said were "country bumpkins?" And I thought you and Tripp were supposed to be smart."

This last remark he did not like, so he snapped "I'm not here on holiday, exactly. Haven't you read the papers? Think we had three murders to deal with, and just today another dead body has been found only this morning. I have never known anything like it."

There was silence at the other end of the phone for a few moments. Mrs Tripp rang me last night and said you'd both been to a funfair."

The inspector maintained his patience. "All in the course of duty, my dear. We are not enjoying this one bit. It's a sort of hell down here. In fact I'm beginning to believe some of those old Cornish tales. I'm sure there's a devil here somewhere."

Mrs Barnes warmed up slightly. "Oh, come off it, Charlie, a devil in Trehorra? You forget I've been there."

Realising that everything he said was being overheard, the inspector was trying to keep calm. "Yes, I know you've been here. But this is different. I can tell you, people aren't so willing to say hello and welcome to us. They know that it's one of them. So no one, but no one, seems willing to offer us any assistance whatsoever."

His wife half believed him.

"So it's not the run-of-the-mill routine investigation you anticipated. 'Give me a couple of weeks or so,' you said. It's not going to be as easy as you thought then?"

She was softening a bit and the inspector went on, "I might have to ask for more help.

"It's too much for Tripp and me on our own. There's virtually only one policeman here."

"If it would mean you coming home sooner, then why not ask for it?" She realised that he was not on a sort of an easygoing break from his London duties. "Did you say there's been another murder? There's been nothing on the wireless about another murder." She was astounded!"

"We believe so – and it's another Tremayne!"

That convinced Mrs Barnes that her husband's job was no holiday. "Ah, well, that means you'll be even longer then."

"Not necessarily. But I keep hoping we'll get a break soon. Thanks for ringing. Love to the kids. Goodbye."

"Good luck, darling. Please come home as soon as you can." She gave a sigh and placed her phone down slowly.

Sergeant Tripp was patiently waiting for him. He glanced at his superior, raised his eyebrows and understandably exclaimed just one word, "Women!"

The inspector nodded in agreement, "That's for sure, and, let's see, we've got to interview a few of those youngsters. This bloody business at the fair won't help will it?"

Tripp thought for a moment. "Oh, I don't know, sir, we may get a break on this one and perhaps it'll help us solve the others."

Chapter 25

AUTUMN CARNIVAL

A few weeks had passed by with no further incidents. At this time of year the locals would usually be looking forward to their autumn carnival. However, the recent events, plus the presence of Scotland Yard, had made the villagers think of calling it off. It had taken a lot of persuasion from committee chairman, Petherick Carnack, to convince them that the "show should go on" as usual.

There were a few tourists still around spending a late holiday in the hope of getting an Indian summer, when they could enjoy the many changing hues of the countryside, combined with the beautiful sunsets at this time of year, as the summer gradually moved into autumn, plus of course some of them actually loved the old-fashioned carnival. There would be many decorated floats which would gather at end of the village in readiness to parade through the main thoroughfares. Most of the floats would be decorated wagons belonging to local farmers, and pulled along by magnificent Clydesdale horses. Only a few would be towed by tractors, John Taylor's two cars would also be used, with his Austin saloon being reserved for the carnival queen, who this year was to be Petherick Carnack's daughter Catherine. The parade would include individuals dressed up in all sorts of fancy costumes. There were also classes for doubles and trios. There was even a section for bicycles.

At the head of this colourful procession would be the famous St Endellion Silver Band. Illuminating the parade at intervals would be flaming torches carried by boy scouts, girls guides, and Boys' Brigade youngsters. The torches would be "home-made" from broom handles fixed into tins, with a paraffin-soaked cloth, which would be set alight. This long snake-like procession would slowly wend its way through the village streets.

About two hours later, they would take their turn to line up in the Riverside Inn car park pausing momentarily in front of the judges' stand. There would always be a magnificent fireworks display to follow the floral dance, led by young girls from the local schools.

Everyone was invited to join in. It was thought that these periods of relaxation would help the villagers forget the heavy black cloud of the Tremayne murders, which still hung over their heads but which they all preferred to forget.

The fireworks were fizzling out and the final one ended in a crescendo of multicoloured stars. The St Endellian Silver Band played the national anthem. The town crier would call for three cheers. This would signal the end of the Trehorra carnival parade for yet another year.

One more attraction remained – the carnival ball. A pall of smoke clouds from the fireworks was still hanging over the car park, which minutes before had been tightly packed with all kinds of people, villagers and visitors alike.

Those who did not proceed to the ball would make their way home gradually. Some of them were reluctant to leave the festivities, the music and the sort of togetherness which these occasions seemed to generate in a small village. There were plenty of reasons to stay. There were sideshows, coconut shies, roll-the-penny and much more. Several vendors were selling all kinds of hot and cold sandwiches plus brightly coloured candy floss, toffee apples, and special sticks of Trehorra rock with plenty of hot and cold drinks to wash them down with. Furthermore, the pubs had extended hours. All this was particularly attractive to the village adults and teenagers.

Inevitably, there would be a dozen or so youths hanging around. Some of them climbed up to the parapet where Petherick Carnack and his committee men had been setting off the fireworks display.

The boys were hoping they could find one or two of the 'dud' fireworks which had failed to go off and perhaps relight them along with the odd one or two which might have been dropped. This 'horseplay' was done to impress the groups of teenage girls who had lingered behind. Some of the crowd were already making for their homes or proceeding to the carnival ball.

PC Vanstock, hands held behind his back, was slowly pacing around keeping a watchful eye on things. He was hoping these late hangers-on would either leave to go home soon, or go to the village hall and the carnival ball.

Vicar Bowering was hovering around attempting to make sure his scouts who had been assisting in the parade were accounted for.

Several of the spectators, some of whom should not have indulged in that extra pint or two, were staggering unsteadily around and there was a buzz of conversation as people discussed the parade.

This scene was suddenly shattered by horrendous piercing screams. It came from one of the girls, Dorothy Case, who had sidled around to the wall surrounding the mill wheel pond. It was very dark in the area, where the water was silently lapping over the mill wheel blades and sliding gently and gradually into the pond.

Dorothy had thought she could get a better view if she stood on the wall. What that view was, no one could guess, but she did see something, and whatever it was, it caused her to scream so loudly that her friend, Mary Hoskin, who climbed on to the wall with her, lost her balance and fell in. More blood-curdling screams!

Every one of the late night stragglers stopped in their tracks. It could just be the ice-cold freezing water that had caused the screaming. The two girls who had screamed simultaneously were surrounded by the rest of the group. PC Vanstock heard them just as he was getting ready to leave for home. He turned and walked very determinedly towards the mill wheel. "I knew it, I damn well knew it," he muttered under his breath. "I guess one of those silly maids has fallen into the pond.

By the time he arrived at the mill wheel wall, the girls' friends had managed to pull both of them out of the ice-cold water. Wet through to the skin, shivering, trembling, teeth chattering 19 to the dozen, they were soon wrapped up, Vanstock volunteering his own waterproof coat. To the unlucky girls, he gave a stern warning "Now you two get off home, I'll be seeing you tomorrow." Some were still staring and pointing into the pond. The PC got out his police torch and the strong ray soon pinpointed what looked like a lump of flotsam.

Someone passed him a walking stick and with the hook of the stick, Vanstock was able to manoeuvre the lump' to the boundary wall. "Oh my God what have we got 'ere?" There was more screaming as he kept the "flotsam" close to the wall still half submerged, there were shouts of "What is it?" "It's a body! – "Is it dead? "Another loud voice "I bet it's a Tremayne!" followed by a cruel remark "Which one this time?" The situation was quite unbelievable. Vanstock was almost dumbstruck, but with some help he got the body over the wall and it was laid on the ground. As he knelt over the body he looked up and over the din shouted "Who said it was a Tremayne? Not you Halford was it?" as Gerry approached the policeman. He had promised Catherine he would take her to the ball after he had got a list of the prize-winners from the judges. However, as soon as he had heard the rumpus at the mill wheel, Gerry had assumed his "news-hound" role. "I'll just make sure what's happened"

"If it's a name you want, although I only got a quick glimpse, I am sure it is Joe Tremayne." Gerry was amazed at Catherine's prompt reaction.

Catherine held Gerry's hand more tightly. "It's the other twin, Joe." The tears began to flow. It was Gerry's turn to be shocked. She started to shake and shiver, although still wearing a thick coat over her long carnival queen's dress. Through the tears she sobbed "I really can't go the ball now and present all those prizes, after all this. I really can't."

Gerry was at a loss as to what he should do – make sure who the mill pond victim was or escort Catherine to the ball. He made a decision. He jerked his hand away from Catherine's. "I've got to see that body and I've got to see Vanstock. Look, Catherine, I'll only be a few minutes." He could see her father, Petherick, approaching so he dashed back towards the mill pond. "I'll take you to the ball and see you home afterwards, tell your father." He was still shocked that Catherine had recognised that lump of flotsam so quickly as Joe Tremayne. Vanstock and John Taylor were passing the body into the Austin saloon which a short time ago had been carrying the carnival queen and her two attendants. Gerry confirmed from Vanstock that it really was Joe Tremayne the twin of Gerald, and he quickly returned to where Catherine's father was pleading with her, "You can't back out now, Catherine, there's nothing you can do to help the situation here, and you must present the prizes." She was still protesting when Vanstock's booming voice from Taylor's car was heard. "Come here, Carnack, I want a word with you." The carnival queen's father turned to go. "Please go to the ball, Catherine, please don't let me down, I must see what Vanstock wants." Gerry got her arm "I'll see that she gets to the ball, Petherick, and I'll see her home afterwards. Don't worry." Then they heard Vanstock's loud voice again. "Come here, Carnack, what's keepin' you?" The village hall was only within walking distance, so reluctantly the carnival queen went along with Gerry.

She had stopped crying. Gerry could not get out of his mind how easily she had recognised Joe Tremayne. "I can't believe how quickly you said it was Joe Tremayne."

She had got a grip of herself now. "Well, I went with him for a while sometime ago. Didn't you know? I thought you reporters knew everything. In any case, Gerry Halford, why should you be concerned? It was quite a while ago, and when Dad found out, he stopped me seeing him, banned me from going out for a whole month, but when Joe started leaving me messages, he went berserk. He even went to Trewarmett Farm, threatened Joe not to go into Trehorra even! If he did, he would tell Vanstock."

"I can't believe all that," said Gerry, who was astounded, but inwardly wondering if this was a possible motive for Joe's "accident". The couple were now joined by a small knot of people and they were soon ushered into the village hall by some relieved committee members. Inside it was another world to the one they had just left. Dancers packed the dance floor, some of them still in their fancy dress costumes. Obviously the news of the mill pond death had not filtered through yet. In a way Gerry was relieved that the committee people had taken charge of Catherine, so, after promising to collect her after the presentations, he hurried back to the mill pond. It was now deserted, so he just stood there gazing at the mill wheel still going round and round, the water trickling off the blades into the pond. It was as if nothing had happened. So he had nothing to do but think and he certainly had a lot to think about. Catherine Carnack going out with a Tremayne, her father objecting, could Joe Tremayne have wandered up to where Petherick was setting off the fireworks? Could he have got in Petherick's way and could the smith have pushed him on to the mill wheel? He was suddenly aroused from all these wild thoughts by a huge slap on his back. Startled he turned around and relieved this time to see it was only Tom Ward!

Chapter 26

Bill Hawkin had been expecting his relief coastguard for the past two hours. He didn't particularly mind because he had spent most of his shift looking at the wonderful views on offer in which ever direction he chose to look. With his powerful coastguard binoculars the views were magnificent, especially today, as the previous night's storm had not yet cleared completely. The morning mist that followed had lifted quickly, but Bill Hawkin a voluntary coastguard was not there to admire the views, but to keep this part of the coastline safe for shipping, for to the south were the highest and most dangerous cliffs in Cornwall, and it wasn't many more miles to the Pentucket Lighthouse, whose flashing lights had warned the ships of the hazardous coastline in these parts for many, many a year. To the north were also fine views with several distinctive rocks dotted along the craggy coastline known locally as the Nine Sisters, whose only occupants were hundreds of screaming seagulls. To Bill it was even more sensational when one of those Atlantic storms hit the coastline. The coastguard "lookout" tower was over 400 feet above the seas level. In years gone by it was thought to have been used as a lighthouse, but the local youngsters imagined it to have been a castle.

In actual fact it had been built by Government revenue men whose job it had been to halt the eternal smuggling problem..

Bill Hawkin, being a bit of a romantic, would reminisce about those 'good' old times of which his grandfather had often told him. Suddenly, as he panned his binoculars around again to the north, he was amazed to see one of the local fishermen's boats heading out of the harbour below.

Putting his binoculars down, he walked over to the huge telescope and focused on to the small fishing boat. "My God," he exclaimed, "whatever be Pete Williams doin' goin' out now?"

The swell of the overnight storm had not yet abated. The waves were still quite huge, close to the rocks. As the swell hit the rock face, it hurled spray way up high. Apart from the large swell, the sea wasn't all that rough, but there would be undercurrents. That was the danger.

Bill, an experienced member of the Trehorra voluntary coastguards, didn't like the situation. He could see Pete was going to collect or lay some lobster pots, and thought it madness. Surprisingly he appeared to have a mate and even more surprising a female, thought Bill, although it was extremely difficult to tell until her hat blew off and out tumbled all the girl's dark long locks of jet black hair.

He followed the small boat and the couple on board through the telescope. The boat was rocking and Pete Williams was having difficulty dealing with the lobster pots from the side of the boat when suddenly the boat rocked a little too far for him. It was probably a freak wave and Pete, still grasping the lobster pot line, lost his balance, and fell overboard.

"I can't believe this," muttered Bill Hawkin." Reaching for the telephone without hesitation, he rang the Perian lifeboat headquarters just a few miles north from Trehorra.

Pete Williams was a strong swimmer, and he was able to keep near to his small boat for quite a while.

Bill Hawkin gave the Perian lifeboat captain a very accurate description of what was happening and where. There was nothing else he could do but watch, wait and hope that the lifeboat would get there in time to rescue the local fisherman, and his 'mate'.

While phoning the lifeboat station, he had momentarily taken his eye off the unfortunate Williams. Turning to the telescope again and swivelling towards the small boat and zooming in as much as possible, Bill was astonished to see Pete swimming towards the cliffs. He wanted to shout, "Hang on to the boat and wait for the lifeboat," but of course, there was no chance of sending a message or signal of any sort.

Pete Williams was bobbing about like a cork whilst attempting to get on to the rocky cliff. With a swell of some fifteen feet now, he would get no opportunity of getting out of the sea. The mate was hanging on for dear life. The boat's motor had stopped and the boat was just drifting.

To Bill's dismay, it was steadily drifting further and further away from Pete Williams and the shoreline. He gave up trying to get on dry land. Apparently changing his mind, he was now swimming back towards his boat, but with the unexpected undercurrents it was turning out to be almost an impossibility, and he was near to exhaustion.

The sea in this area was never very warm, and today it must have been less than 40°F. The ground sea currents made it even more difficult and dangerous.

Strong as he was, the young fisherman was now suffering from hypothermia. Despite all the drawbacks, he was actually getting nearer to his boat.

Bill Hawkin rotated the telescope around to the north. No sign of the lifeboat. He was helpless. Turning back towards where he had last spotted Pete Williams, he was staggered. The fisherman had completely disappeared.

Bill Hawkin thought that perhaps he had got back on the boat, although in his heart of hearts he knew that that was particularly an impossibility, but he dearly wanted to believe it. In fact, he became even more despairing now. Concentrating his vision on to the fishing boat, Bill could not see anyone. The boat was riding the swell of sea but was drifting away from the coast.

"Where, oh, where is that bloody lifeboat?" he grumbled to himself. There was one thing more he could do, although he did not have much confidence in it. "I'll telephone the police station."

PC Vanstock would probably be helpless but, to give him his due, he quickly replied. "I'll get over there – Tregarrick Cliffs, did you say? Okay, Bill, I'll be there as soon as I can." Vanstock put the phone down and didn't hear Bill's "You'd better get a move on."

A short time later, the lifeboat pulled alongside the small drifting fishing boat. The crew hitched a line to it and one of them jumped on to Pete Williams's boat. It had been a difficult manoeuvre but before long they were turning around, and headed for the safety of Trehorra harbour.

By the time the lifeboat reached the old-fashioned harbour and had moored both boats up, the usual band of locals had appeared. It is simply amazing how news travels so quickly in these parts, and bad news especially.

The captain of the lifeboat was in earnest conversation with Vanstock by the time Gerry Halford had arrived. Gerry had rushed down to the harbour as soon as he had heard the lifeboat had been called out. He pushed his way through the people who were crowding around Vanstock and the lifeboat captain. He was just in time to hear the captain say, "No, sir, there was no one on the boat and we've picked up one body only, a male, it's back there in the stern. We've covered him with a tarpaulin. You probably know who he is."

Gerry couldn't help interjecting, "It's Pete Williams, isn't it?"

Vanstock looked down at the youngster. "Now you steady on, Gerry, don't jump to conclusions so quick."

The budding newspaper reporter was not a bit taken aback. "Well, it's Pete Williams's boat, isn't it?"

"We know all about that, young man, but the captain here was told there were two people on the boat." Vanstock hesitated, "And we've only got one body." He suddenly stopped and he thought to himself, "Not another missing body!"

Gerry Halford understood why the policeman had suddenly stopped in his tracks and had scratched his forehead under his police helmet.

"It's a case of déjà vu, isn't it, sir?" he asked as politely as he could. But Vanstock didn't hear that remark and probably wouldn't have understood it, if he had.

Vanstock climbed on to the lifeboat, where he carefully stepped over ropes, buoys and other lifeboat tackle strewn all over the small deck.

One of the lifeboat crew was already standing over the body covered by the tarpaulin.

He lifted the end of it just a little. PC Vanstock took just one quick glance and solemnly announced, "It's Pete Williams all right." Inwardly he thought that it meant another trip to the mortuary with yet another body. He no doubt also thought that Pete Williams would be a great loss to the fishing community of Trehorra – at least it wasn't another Tremayne, but when was it all going to stop?

Aloud he said, "I better get the poor chap off this lifeboat, I suppose, and get John Taylor again." He didn't have to move away from the anchored lifeboat very far. John Taylor was standing among the group who had crowded along the moorings but were now beginning to dwindle away quietly muttering to themselves about how foolish Pete was to go out of the harbour in such a rough sea. Vanstock spotted him. "Another trip to Bawtry Mr Taylor. How are you fixed?"

"I'll be back in ten minutes, Mr Vanstock." Taxi man Taylor didn't need to be asked twice. He turned quickly and went to fetch his car.

"Bring your big saloon again, Mr Taylor," shouted Vanstock. He didn't fancy another rough ride in Taylor's little Austin Seven.

The lifeboat crew lifted the covered body of Pete Williams on to the wooden jetty and laid it down gently. After signing some paperwork and forms, the lifeboat captain turned to the policeman, "Well, I'll be off. I'll be back to Penrian now. There's nothing else we can do, is there?"

"Not for now, Captain. I expect I'll have to get in touch with your headquarters sooner or later for a full report. Thanks for your help."

Everybody turned their backs on the sad scene at the harbour side. All sorts of comments could be heard; some critical of the time it took the lifeboat to arrive; some in amazement at yet another apparent premature loss of a young life. However, most of them would be thinking why did Pete go out before the storm had blown itself out properly?

Most of them were so intent on discussing Pete Williams, they failed to see Bill Hawkin frantically pedaling his bike in the opposite direction towards the harbour. Breathing hard, Bill fairly leaped off his bicycle right in between PC Vanstock , Gerry Halford, who was patiently waiting for a statement, and the tarpaulin-covered body. Bill Hawkin surveyed this odd scene. When he had caught his breath, he looked at the tarpaulin on the ground. "What's in that then?"

Before Vanstock cold answer, Gerry Halford cut in, "It's Pete Williams. The lifeboat found him but he was already dead."

"I might have guessed that." Bill Hawkin was breathing normally now. "Where's the woman then?"

Vanstock looked up, he was startled. "What woman?"

"Well, Mr Vanstock, I saw somebody else on the boat with Pete before he fell over the side, and thought it was a female. I told them up at Penrian."

"The lifeboat crew never mentioned anything about any woman and they're on their way back to Penrian now."

Gerry Halford, now a cold-blooded news hound, scented another story. "That would be Madeleine Tremayne, she was Pete's girlfriend, you know."

Vanstock was astounded. "Do you know that for sure, young man?" He seemed always to address Gerry as 'young man' when he was under pressure. Vanstock wasn't all that dumb. He could almost read Gerry Halford's mind, and envisaged another headline, *'ANOTHER TREMAYNE DEAD, THE BODY MISSING.'* And that's exactly what Gerry was thinking.

Whereas the village PC looked upon it as yet another unbelievable coincidence and a huge catastrophe for Trehorra, the young reporter, in contrast, was thinking that this was yet another opportunity to further his career as a journalist. He couldn't believe that this was all happening in Trehorra. It was odds on now that he would never get a better opportunity for a story which might help him achieve his ambition to join a London national newspaper. It could definitely be a career boost. He must make the most of it, so out came his notebook. It must have been his adrenaline that wiped out any thought of how selfish and heartless his approaches had become.

Vanstock, ever suspicious of Gerry, couldn't help warning him, "Now you be careful, young man. Don't you be jumping to conclusions about this 'ere accident." Vanstock attempted to sound emphatic. "This is an accident," and looking at Bill Hawkin with a sidelong glance, "Now, Bill, how long had you been on watch before you saw Pete out in his boat?"

"My relief was late, so I was two hours or more over my regular shift," Bill Hawkin ventured.

"Ah, well then, Bill, you must have been exhausted. You could be seeing things. It happens, you know." Vanstock was not being as clever as he thought he was. If he thought he could dispense with the missing female whom Bill had seen, it wasn't going to be as easy as that. He was being exceedingly naive.

Gerry had met with Police Constable Vanstock so many times he knew when to cease his questioning. He put away his notebook and pen.

PART 2 of The Devil of Trehorra

FIVE YEARS LATER

Chapter 27

Mr and Mrs Gerry Halford stood on platform 1 at the almost deserted Drewstone Railway Station. Not many visitors came to this part of Cornwall, so early in the year.

Motor cars were far more in evidence than when Gerry Halford was last in his home county. This was to be his first visit since leaving Trehorra five years before to begin a journalistic career in London. Having impressed the London Express during the Trehorra murder mysteries, he had gone to London despite his mother's objections.

During those five years, he had covered a great variety of stories. After what was called the roaring twenties, the thirties had arrived with an alarming depression. But not for Gerry.

He had never been to the capital before in his life and it was certainly exciting. He was in the right place to experience so many wild, weird and wonderful stories.

He had always been a determined youngster and he had revelled in his new-found adventures. It wasn't like a job to him. Although there were millions of unemployed, Gerry didn't notice. He covered simple stories at first. The installation of pedestrian crossings or Belisha beacons, named after the Transport Minister at the time. He had ridden on the streamlined Coronation Scot on its test run. This train had been named to celebrate the coronation of George VI.

His experiences were numerous and varied. His best 'scoop' for the Express was when a George

Andrew McMahon had tried to shoot Edward VIII. Gerry was actually on the spot when McMahon was arrested. But, in his Cornish mind, nothing could block out the shocking Trehorra deaths of all five sons of a country farmer, which he had experienced during his teenage years.

It all came back to him as he saw John Taylor, the Trehorra taxi man, waiting, still in his Austin Seven. No need to bring his larger saloon car just for two people.

No one else had got off the branch line train of only two carriages from Exeter. His bride of only two months had never been to Cornwall before, so she was looking forward to this early holiday break, which was also serving as a honeymoon.

Gerry had become a workaholic. Although time had softened his mother's attitude towards her only son, Gerald, he was hoping that Momma Halford would give a warm welcome to her new daughter-in-law.

John Taylor was still as attentive as ever, insisted on carrying their cases to the car.

Gerry's inquiring mind and his natural curiosity to find out who was who in Trehorra and what was going on there now, did not draw much out of the Adonis-like Taylor.

After answering most of the reporter's questions with enthusiasm, he suddenly blurted out, "The locals say you have come back to sort out that Tremayne do?" And he added pointedly, "Never did find out who did it, did they, but I have a few ideas, if you're interested."

Before Gerry could answer, he had pulled up outside the Halfords' whitewashed cottage. "Here we are then." He was noticeably paying particular attention to Sarah. "I hope you enjoy your stay here, and if I can do anything for you, Gerry, you know where to find me."

Gerry need not have worried over the reception his mother would give to her daughter-in-law. "Come right in, my dear, make yourself at home, you call me Mum."

Sarah felt quite at home immediately.

"I expect you'd like a cup of tea, wouldn't you dear?"

"Thanks, Mum. What's there to eat then?" Gerry could already smell the Cornish pasty baking in the oven. It had been a long time since he'd eaten a real Cornish pasty, and Sarah had probably tasted only the Cornish pasties made in bulk in London.

The meal over, Gerry hardly stopped talking for over an hour. He had kept in touch with his mother over the years, and he was keen to know if any of his boyhood pals were still in the village.

"I hope you're not going to go rushing around seeing them all, Gerald." Mother Halford could almost read her son's mind. You're supposed to be here to take it easy. I'm sure Sarah won't want to meet 'em."

Sarah had definitely made a good impression on Mrs Halford. "Oh, I don't mind, Mrs Halford, I just want Gerry to have a restful holiday." She added light heartedly, "If there are any more good lookers, like John the taxi driver, it will be interesting."

Momma Halford was not without a sense of humour "You know, Sarah, how that man stays single is a mystery. He has nothing to do with local girls, but they tell me he's a 'bit of a one', when the visitors get here in the summer."

Mother Halford already knew that Sarah had her own business. "I'm hoping both of you will be able to relax." Sarah had inherited her father's horticultural business and it was practically a seven-day week operation.

This suited their London lifestyle. She was constantly kept busy travelling between the early morning markets and her shop in the city. Gerry, of course, had to go where there was a story. Never a dull moment for him. He often remembered the advice of Percy Hunt, the Cornish Echo editor, "You can knock on any door, my son, you'll find a story behind it for sure."

So far, however, Gerry had never had time to knock on any doors. Perhaps back in Trehorra he would find himself wishing he *could* knock on a few doors. He was positive that the answer to the Tremayne story was behind one of the villagers' doors. He had harboured some ideas and he secretly wanted to solve the Tremayne murders. Not only for the news value, but maybe a book. He had some plans, but not right now.

Chapter 28

The next day he was up early. After a lovely, leisurely breakfast – bacon, tomatoes, eggs, fried bread and fried potatoes, of course – Gerry took Sarah to see the harbour. He related all the old stories of smugglers and of the ship that sank whilst bringing a church bell to Trehorra.

"That's why they call the St Minerva Church the silent church," he explained to Sarah. She was enjoying the walk, the views and Gerry's stories; some true, some old fishermen's tales.

He had, many times, told Sarah of the Tremayne murders and the failure of Scotland Yard even to get a suspect. He pointed out the spot where Sam Tremayne had been found in the sea. His young wife shuddered as she looked down at the foaming sea as the waves dashed against the rocks. Gerry was holding her hand.

"My God it's quite easy to slip here, isn't it?"

Gerry was delighted that Sarah was taking such an interest. "Yes, but it would be a damn sight easier to fall down into the sea if he was pushed. Wouldn't take much of a push would it?"

Momma Halford had insisted the young couple be back for lunch. "Sharp at 1 o'clock I want you two here," she had warned them. And sharp at 1 o'clock they returned to the cottage.

Gerry was saying how much smaller everything seemed. He could now look over walls and hedges, which in his younger days he was unable to. The roads, the streets and even the country lanes all seemed narrow.

"Mr Vanstock has gone, you know, Gerry, he's retired now." Mrs Halford seemed to know what Gerry was thinking.

"Where's he gone?" Gerry was hoping he could have a chat with the old copper.

"Oh, I don't know – somewhere quiet, Mrs Vanstock told me. Not very far away."

Her son smiled. "He thought Trehorra was going to be quiet, remember, when he came here. That seems donkey's years ago now. But he did not find it quiet, did he? He certainly didn't expect to work with Scotland Yard I bet."

"Well, it was years ago. Must be at least five or six years now. His two boys will be grown up by this time," Momma Halford continued.

"Like most of the villagers he has put that sad era behind him and preferred to think it was way in the past."

People no longer talked about the Tremayne deaths. They were rarely mentioned. If they were, Trehorrans would mostly shake their heads, keep walking, and never speculate. This was strange because village gossip is almost a tradition, and Trehorra was no different from most villages.

Perhaps they were too embarrassed to be talking about murder, which had happened so close to them. It must be overwhelming to have even one murder in a village, and more devastating to think that the murderer must be one of their own. Some people were praying at the time that there was a slight chance that some of the deaths could have been accidents with the odd one being committed by an outsider, probably a transient.

The fact that Scotland Yard had failed to discover anyone, meant they were in doubt.

Mother Halford continued, "I shouldn't go digging all that up again, Gerald. You must have got enough to get on with up there in London."

She too didn't want to be reminded of what was called the 'Tremayne Trouble' time. But she couldn't resist telling Gerry, "Everybody said it was somebody local in Trehorra but I couldn't think of anybody who'd do such a thing. Terrible it was, Sarah. Terrible."

"It must have been awful." Sarah was quite matter of fact about it all. She knew most of the Tremayne story from beginning to end. Gerry had explained all the problems to her lots of times. Sarah commented, "It's quite possible the murderer still lives in the village then?"

****

Gerry was already thinking, "Wouldn't it be perfect if he could solve the Trehorra mystery of how the five sons of John Tremayne had met their deaths."

COULD BE THE HONEYMOON IS OVER?

Chapter 29

After one or two days Gerry had craftily led Sarah all over the Trehorra peninsula, the mysterious valleys, the grand old harbour. He had even managed to talk to many of the youths he used to know, had met several of them in the Pity Me, the pub nearest his cottage.

The tinker's son, Tom Ward, did not look a day older. Unfortunately for Tom, his intellect was not a day older either. He made a beeline for Gerry every time he saw *him*, whether in the pub or outside.

John Stephens, too, would never forget he had discovered Colin Tremayne in that horse trough and he hung around near Gerry and the Halford cottage as much as he could.

Like most villagers, when Tom would talk to Gerry, he would still talk about the Tremaynes. He still maintained that they were murdered and that he knew "who dun 'em". Tom moaned that his stories had been ignored by Vanstock and the Scotland Yard men.

Talking to Gerry, Tom was still convinced that the person he saw on his training run was responsible for Sam Tremayne's fall over Black Cliffs. Gerry had given much thought to Tom Ward's story. He couldn't forget the night that Tom had rescued him when he was lost going from a boy scout campfire meeting, but with only the vaguest of vague descriptions of the person he saw running away, there could be no progress on that one.

As for Sarah, she said of Tom Ward junior, "I'm sorry, Gerry, but that guy gives me the creeps. I can't believe he could contribute anything."

"Oh, Tom is quite harmless, but I think sometimes he just might be on to something." Gerry, showing some frustration, kicked a dead branch out of their way.

They were on their way to Minerva Church.

Gerry couldn't resist showing Sarah the horse trough where Colin Tremayne had been found.

It was still overflowing and the ice-cold, clear water still trailing all across the small country lane and disappearing under the hedge on the opposite side of the road.

While peering over the hedge to see what was happening to all that water, the two heard voices being raised and invading the somewhat eerie quietness of the place.

"Wonder who that is?" Gerry climbed on to the top of the hedge where he had a good view of the church and churchyard nestled down in the valley below them. "It's the new vicar and the village gravedigger. Looks interesting. Let's go down and have a look."

Gerry jumped down from the hedge, helped Sarah down, and hand in hand they took the steep, rocky path which led into the churchyard.

As Gerry approached, the old gravedigger, Sam Teath, standing with his foot on shovel, said, "Well, I'll be damned if it isn't Gerry Halford."

"Hi, Mr Teath, I see you're still at it then." Gerry and Sarah picked their way through the old graves.

"Nobody else wants it, my boy." Sam lifted the shovel and threw another spadeful of earth on the other side of the hole that he was digging. "Can't understand 'em, 'cos they'd never be out of work!" Who Sam was arguing with had disappeared and this was a rare bit of dark humour from the gravedigger.

"What was that all about then, Sam?" Gerry was more than interested. Harsh words with Sam Teath were very rare. No one liked to cross the gravedigger, but he continued to shovel the earth. "What was what all about?" Sam Teath was obviously stalling.

"Oh, it was nothing really."

"Well, it seemed to me as if someone wasn't too pleased about something." Gerry adopted a typical newspaper reporter's attitude, a statement with a hidden question which invited an answer. It was getting to be a habit of his.

Sam Teath pushed his cap to the back of his head, wiped some sweat off his weather-beaten wrinkled forehead. "Well, Gerry, my boy, I wouldn't be telling anybody else, mind you, but this new parson, he is so damned pernickety." Sam seemed to be relieved to be able to tell someone about the new young vicar. He carried on. "I mean to say, that mound over there behind poor old Bolitho's grave has been there for years. Well, ever since he was buried really." He pointed towards an untidy heap of earth on which there were huge clumps of long grass, weeds, dock leaves and other wild plants all growing profusely. "I think it don't look too bad, especially in early spring when there's a few daffodils and bluebells on it."

Gerry understood what the old gravedigger was talking about. The whole churchyard was transformed in the spring when it would be covered with bright yellow daffodils, quickly followed by a blue carpet of bluebells.

"Looks something like another grave to me," Gerry said. He took a few steps towards this untidy grass heap.

"Well, it isn't, I can tell ' e" Sam Teath seemed suddenly not to want to dwell on the subject. "The truth is, Gerry, the Bolithos wanted to have iron railings around the grave of Stanley Bolitho and to leave a space for his missus when she goes. So that mound will have to go then, but I don't see the need to do it now."

Hearing the sound of the church door behind him, he leaned closer to Gerry and in almost a whisper, he added, "So that mound stays if I have anything to do with it, and I'm not going to move it."

Approaching them now, and quite near, was the parson. Gerry and Sarah saw a pleasant-looking man in a light grey suit with the inevitable dog collar. He lifted his trilby hat, "I'm assuming you're the young Mrs Halford, I'm pleased to meet you. My name is Salmond with a silent L, you know. Douglas 'Sammon' that is." He turned to Gerry. "I feel I know you already, Gerald. Your mother has kept me informed of all your adventures and, of course, I do read the Express from time to time."

He turned to look at Sam Teath, now leaning on the shovel. "Oh, I must apologise if you heard our somewhat raised voices a few moments ago. Mr Teath and I were having a discussion." He offered his hand to both of them in turn and impressed Gerry with a very firm handshake. "You must have left for London just before I arrived in Trehorra. I inherited the first Trehorra scout troop and learned a lot about the boys, including yourself. I believe you were one of the founder members. What a troubled time that period was for Trehorra?"

"Yes, it was, sir." Now Gerry wasn't sure if he liked the sound or look of this new parson. "Seems a bit too sugary," he thought to himself, "a certain bit of falseness there."

"Well, if you'll excuse me, Reverend, I'll push on through the woods. We have to work up an appetite. You probably know my mother likes everyone to be on time for her meals."

Douglas Salmond shook hands with Gerry. "I would love to have a further chat with you. Do you think you could come to tea at the vicarage whilst you are here in Trehorra?" He turned to Sarah, touched the rim of his trilby hat. "And, of course, the invitation goes to you, too, Mrs Halford. I do hope you will give me the pleasure."

Sarah forced a smile. Afternoon tea with a country parson would be a first for her, so she spoke for both of them "We'd love to, thank you."

"Splendid, I'll look forward to seeing you both."

With that, Douglas Salmond looked at the gravedigger with a brief terse, "I'll see you later, Mr Teath." He turned away and strode back through the thick heavy oak door of the St Minerva Church.

The three of them waited for the clang as the heavy door was closed. Gerry turned to Sam, "Now, what's all the fuss about that mound? That shouldn't be a problem for you, Mr. Teath?" Gerry had always been a bit indecisive as how to address this old villager as Mister or Sam. "Who put the mound there anyway?"

"Well, I suppose I did." Gravedigger, Sam Teath stared at the mound of earth with the weeds on top. "You see, my boy, it was left over after I finished clearing up Bolitho's plot."

Gerry still couldn't really see what was the problem, and Sarah looked as if she wanted to move on from the subject of graves, funerals, mounds, murders and leftover Cornish earth.

"I expect I'll be seeing you again, Mr Teath," Gerry added, "I'll be home for a while yet."

"Have you come to clear up those Tremayne murders then? Them old Scotland Yard people couldn't find a thing, could they?" Sam Teath seemed delighted to get one in on the London detectives. He lifted his cap to Sarah, "Look after him, my dear, he's a good 'un you know."

Sarah gave him a smile, "Oh, yes, I think so, Mr Teath. It was nice meeting you." She grabbed Gerry's arm and they walked up the steep path which led out of the churchyard.

They closed the iron gate behind them and started their walk, though fallen branches and loose stones made walking a bit difficult.

Sarah was getting increasingly fascinated that the villagers wanted to talk to Gerry about the Tremaynes, and yet they did not discuss it among themselves apparently. "I bet you'd love to find out more about it?" she quizzed. In truth she knew she would be disappointed whatever his answer might be.

"I think you may be right there," answered Gerry, giving Sarah a loving peck on her cheek. Inwardly he was determined to follow up any leads he might find.

Chapter 30

VICAR'S TEA PARTY

The invitation to the vicar's was not long arriving. "I think we'll start early and walk over there," Gerry told his mother while Sarah was getting ready in her bedroom.

Momma Halford, not a regular churchgoer herself, still had a 'thing' about parsons and preachers. "I shouldn't put too much make-up on, dear," she shouted up the stairs. "In any case, you're far too pretty to have a lot on." Sarah turned up her nose, but looked very neat in a green two-piece costume with a white blouse. She wore no jewellery.

Mrs Halford found it difficult to believe her only son was married. "I don't suppose you'll need any supper though, will you?" she called after the couple as they walked from the front door.

Sarah turned to give a little wave. "No, we won't, Mrs Halford. From what Gerry tells me, he's expecting a long evening." She winked her eye at Gerry's mother, who didn't quite get that.

"The key will be in the usual place, you know, just in case you're very late."

"I've been thinking about that mound of earth those two were arguing about," Sarah surprisingly blurted out as they turned the corner into the vicarage lane.

"Oh, that," he lied, "to tell you the truth, Sarah, I'd almost forgotten about it. I think old Sam was making a mound out of a molehill, if you'll forgive the pun."

Sarah was now used to his quips. "Very droll, Gerry, but I've been thinking. Why on earth, excuse my pun, was there such a lot of surplus over from just one grave?"

"I hadn't thought about it, whatever made you think about that?" Gerry was pretending to be only slightly interested.

"I happen to know that when you dig a pit or a hole to plant something, there is always a certain amount of earth, or whatever, left over. So if the gravedigger chappie had this earth left over after the coffin was put in the pit, surely that would be quite normal." Sarah was now drawing on her experience of her business.

She had dug plenty of holes for replanting everything from potatoes to pine trees and knew there was always a surplus.

"Ah, yes." Gerry pretended he was getting more interested now, and particularly pleased that at last Sarah was thinking about the situation.

Apparently, this mound of earth looked a hell of a lot more than usually was the case. He thoughtfully added, "Perhaps Sam overdid the clearing up bit, as it was the lord of the manor's grave. Still, it might be worth asking him about it. After all, he did seem a bit touchy on the subject, didn't he?"

They were now approaching the big gate which led into the vicarage. "Don't think we'll bring the subject up, though. This new parson might be a bit touchy as well. I think he's a bit starchy myself, because I don't think he enjoyed us interrupting his heated conversation with Sam Teath."

The Vicar came down the drive to greet them, looking good in a bright blue-greyish sports jacket. The only thing that spoiled his appearance, thought Sarah, was that he still had his dog collar on.

"I'm so glad you could come," he said, "and I have a surprise for you." He led them into the conservatory where the table had already been laid. It all looked delicious, particularly for Gerry.

"Saffron cake, I see. I haven't had any of that for a long time."

The parson smiled, "Yes, Mrs Menhennick does me well. I inherited her, thank goodness, from the vicar and Mrs Bowering, you know. Ah, here they are. My surprise for you."

To Gerry, it was a surprise. He did not have to look twice, it was the previous vicar, Eric Bowering, and his wife. He had thought that the Bowerings had been retired to a quiet little church up in the Cotswolds, and they were the last persons he expected to meet.

With the handshakes and the introductions over, the host vicar recommended where each of them should sit. There was a sort of awkward silence while the young vicar went out to fetch the teapot. To break the silence, Gerry rubbed his hands together and repeated "Saffron cake, I see, I haven't had any of that for a long time."

Vicar Bowering looked at Gerry, "That's one of Mrs Menhennick's specialties."

With that, the host vicar returned with a huge teapot. Sarah recognised the pattern at once. "Oh, what a lovely teapot." She recognised the big flowery design matching all the crockery which was on display on the table. "It's Portmeirion isn't it, Vicar? I've always loved that design. Botanical Garden, isn't it?"

The young parson looked delighted. "You have a good eye Sarah. But do please call me Douglas." He added, "I've have to admit, I inherited this lovely set too, from the Vicar Bowering and his good lady."

Mrs Bowering had barely spoken at all. She tended to look down at the table, and she seemed to be avoiding any eye contact.

"Help yourselves, please." Douglas Salmond joined them at the round glass-topped table.

The conversation flowed from boy scouts to life in London, to life in Cornwall, to flowers, which was Sarah's speciality, and to newspapers. The Bowerings knew quite a lot about London. Apparently both of them had spent several years in the capital in their younger days but always seemed to divert the conversation away from London whenever Sarah broached the subject.

Inevitably, talk turned to Gerry's earlier years in Trehorra, and the story of the Tremaynes could hardly be avoided. The incumbent vicar finally looked across at Gerry, "Haven't you any idea, Gerry, who could have committed those dreadful crimes? You must have done an awful lot of research in your time."

"All I know, sir," Gerry started, but he was immediately interrupted by Bowering. "The Tremayne deaths did you no harm, did they, Gerry? In fact, they were to prove beneficial to you, I believe."

Gerry ignored those questions and carried on. "All I know, Douglas, is that it was certainly a local person. The problem which confronted Scotland Yard was finding a motive. And, of course, the disappearance of the second Tremayne's body complicated things during the early stages."

Mrs Bowering, who had been looking bored at times, suddenly looked up. "If I remember correctly, Gerry, you sorted that problem out, didn't you?" She added, "It was you who wrote that story on the Beast of Bawdry Moor, wasn't it?"

Gerry thought he noted a hint of sarcasm in her attitude. With a sort of tongue in cheek, he looked at Mrs Bowering. "Yes I suppose I was responsible for providing a possible explanation on how the missing body could have disappeared."

Vicar Bowering raised his eyebrows. "You mean you had no proof of that story? But a lot of people believed you. Even the police were willing to accept it, I even accepted it myself."

Gerry was a little surprised and not a little embarrassed with these questions and doubts being thrown at him. He was becoming a little hesitant. "Well, it was all so new to me and it was so mysterious. I was quite inexperienced then, and I was only a part-time reporter. It wasn't my job to solve the murder, that was the duty of the police."

Mrs Bowering now appeared to be paying attention to Gerry's every word. He continued, "Until Colin Tremayne was found, it was generally thought that the older brother's death had been an accident. And, of course, when the other Tremaynes were found dead, it opened up a whole new set of possibilities. And that got the nationals interested."

Vicar Salmond had been listening to every word. "Now, come on, Gerry, do admit it, you're here for more than a holiday? Have that last piece of saffron cake, won't you?" Gerry avoided answering the question.

"Oh, I don't mind. Thank you, Douglas."

The new vicar then surprised Gerry. A lot of my parishioners, too, think you've returned to Trehorra to get a story. Your paper has reopened it, haven't they?"

Sarah quickly cut in. She placed her cup into the saucer very firmly. "I think it was coincidental that the reward story broke just as we came down here.

"We're here on holiday, Douglas. Really. This is supposed to be our honeymoon, and I don't think Gerry is intending to work during our stay here, listen yes, but not work." Inwardly, Sarah knew differently, but thought that this would put a stop to the Tremayne murder conversations and the pressure the Bowerings seemed to be putting on her young husband.

The new vicar cleverly changed the subject to flowers, knowing that this would arouse Sarah's interest. Gradually, the Tremayne stories were not mentioned for a while. The Bowerings, however, seemingly couldn't forget them and only stopped when the meal came to an end.

Mrs Bowering and Sarah offered to clear away, Douglas Salmond put his hand up. "No, no. Mrs Menhennick will be in tomorrow morning and she will do it. It's not a problem. We can leave it for now." He added, "She would have been in this evening but she's a grandmother now and had to babysit this evening."

Gerry turned to the vicar. "A grandmother? I didn't know Evelyn was married. "Who's she married to?"

The Bowerings were with Vicar Salmond standing at the front door and Eric Bowering informed Gerry in a very firm voice, "She wasn't married. She was already pregnant when the father, her Tremayne boyfriend, was killed at that motor rally, don't you remember?"

Gerry was surprised "I didn't even know she was pregnant." Mrs Bowering cut in quickly "Why should you have known, Gerry. That subject is not exactly in your domain is it?" "I suppose not but it is the sort of gossip I expect to pick up." Sarah tugged at Gerry's arm to warn him not to proceed with this conversation. Although annoyed, he took the hint and an apparent feisty conversation was brought abruptly to a halt, and was followed by a series of "Good nights" and "Thank yous" with a smiling Douglas Salmond. "Do please come again, Mr Bowering and Fiona will be here for a week or two yet, and I'd love it if we could all meet again. Please don't return to London before I arrange another get-together."

Sarah shook his hand. "Thank you, Douglas. I'm sure we'd like that" and remembered to say "Please tell Mrs Menhennick how much I enjoyed her saffron cake, won't you?" Gerry managed to add "And please pass on my congratulations to grandma Menhennick."

Chapter 31

It was a cool evening and with the breeze coming in from the sea, the young couple walked together as close as possible, arms around each other's waist. Gerry had certainly been slightly stunned by the last part of their conversations with the Bowerings.

Only a few yards down the lane leading back to the village, he muttered to himself.

"I'll have to ask my mother a few things when I get home." And then aloud, "Funny my mother hasn't said anything about Evelyn Menhennick having a Tremayne child."

Sarah quickened her stride. "Why should she? You were never involved with her, were you?"

"Good God, no. I was far too young for Evelyn." Gerry laughed, and gave Sarah an extra squeeze.

"Well, there did seem to be a few teenage girls around at that time – at least by all accounts the Tremaynes could find them." She then added playfully, "Didn't you have time for any of the local girls then, Gerry? You must have been like John the taxi man, then."

"Not really."

"What does 'not really' mean? No or yes or sometimes?"

Gerry laughed her questions off. "I never had time, Sarah," but thought this mention of John Taylor strange.

"Oh, come on, Gerry, I'm sure there wasn't all that much to do half the time." Sarah was teasing him now and she was enjoying it.

They were nearing the Pity Me pub now and they could hear the tinkling piano. "Let's go in and have a goodnight drink. Perhaps you'll tell me of your Trehorra past then, darling." Sarah knew Gerry wanted to be serious, but she didn't want to hear any more about the Tremayne murders.

There were quite a few people inside the public bar, including a dozen or so regulars. Gerry and Sarah grabbed a couple of three-legged stools before he went up to the bar. As he was ordering the drinks, he came under quite a barrage of good-natured banter. "What's married life like then, Gerry?"

"Are you going to introduce us to the missus then?"

"Trehorra girls not good enough?"

"Better keep her away from Bawdry Moor."

"Solve any murders lately, Halford?"

Gerry laughed at most of them and took it all in good part, then joined Sarah by the window seat that she had moved to. "Cheers," they said together, and clinked their glasses.

"It would shock them if I did come out with a real story behind those Tremayne stories, wouldn't it?" He turned to Sarah, and in all earnestness he added, "I think I've got something to work on seriously. This holiday may turn out to be profitable after all.

"And if that big payday is still on, it'll be worth my while."

Drinking her Grand Marnier, Sarah was feeling very relaxed in this old 14th Century pub. It was very easy with the very low ceilings and oak beams. There was still a little bit of life left in the old cast iron fireplace still glowing red, and comforting for evenings when at this time of year it could be decidedly chilly.

Gerry continued to look thoughtful and serious. "That tea at the vicarage has given me a few ideas to think about. Bowering letting on that Evelyn Menhennick had been pregnant before her Tremayne had been killed. And I can't forget how interested Mrs Bowering was in that 'Beast of Bawdry Moor' story. It was just a throw-away, and was jazzed up by Boucher." Gerry was in full flow now. To him the Tremayne saga was as if it had happened only yesterday.

"Now, I remember old man Dixie Dixon thought that when his daughter was pregnant it was by another Tremayne. That was the one whose body was never found."

Sarah could hardly stifle a giggle. "I know it's not a laughing matter but I always wondered what you country boys got up to during the winter, now I know!"

Gerry grimaced "These Tremayne lads certainly found plenty to do, I must admit."

"How many were there then?" Sarah had gathered there were several boys in the family but had not discussed it in detail with Gerry.

"Well, there were five boys and one girl. Even she was supposedly accidentally drowned in the middle of it all while out with her boyfriend on his fishing boat. She was found three weeks later washed up on a deserted beach."

Sarah was beginning to realise that it was inevitable that the Tremaynes stories were going to intrude even more into their holiday.

"Were they all found in the sea then?"

"Not exactly. But they all had a watery end." He added, "That would be a good little title for a book, wouldn't it, Watery End or Watery Graves?"

Sarah finished her Grand Marnier, put her empty glass down in such a way Gerry realised she wanted another one. She shuddered "Gerry, you're not thinking of doing any more serious work on the Tremaynes, are you?"

"Not really," Gerry said, as he got up to fetch the drinks. He looked at Sarah, "But Mr Boucher did say if I could get another worthwhile story about the murders whilst I was here there'd be a big cheque in it for me, and of course that reward cheque would certainly be welcome."

There was a hand on his shoulder. "Sit yourself down, boy. I've been watching you two and I guessed you'd want more than one drink. I'll get 'em in," Sam Teath had kindly butted in.

Gerry was taken by surprise. "Well, thank you, Mr Teath."

Sam Teath, still dressed in his working garb, was not known to buy many rounds of drinks. When on the odd occasion he did venture into the pub for a drink, he usually drank on his own. Must have been the nature of his job.

The gravedigger arrived back to the couple, dragged another three-legged stool over to join them at their window seat. "I've been meaning to catch you, Gerry my boy, before you go back to London. You be going back, aren't you?"

Sarah said, "Of course we're going back, what could Gerry do down here?"

"Well, missus" – Sam was showing none of the shyness, or the reserved side of his nature, which he usually had amongst company. He was on his third pint of Guinness so that probably made a difference to his demeanour. "Oh, I think he could find plenty to do. He could finish off that Tremayne business for one thing. I've got a bit of summit which may be able to help him find somethin' out if he minds to stay a bit."

"Well, that's great, Mr Teath." He was all ears now. "Can't you tell me now?"

The wizened old bearded gravedigger looked over both his shoulders, took the clay pipe out of his mouth and leaned over the small round table between them. "Outside, my boy, in my saddle bag, I've got something to show you. Do you want to see it?"

Gerry looked at Sarah, and he thought by her look that it was OK for him to go see what the old man had got. "I'll be all right here," she said. "Go ahead"

Sam had propped his bicycle against a sturdy old oak tree. The lights from the pub enabled them both to see pretty clearly. "Mind you, Gerry, I'm relying on you keeping this to yourself for a bit."

Sam thrust his hand deep down into his saddle bag. He held it there for a couple of seconds, looked around furtively before pulling out what to Gerry looked like a little piece of cloth.

"What in the devil have you got there, Mr Teath?" Gerry peered closer to the old man's outstretched hand. "Oh, I see now – it's a rubber glove."

"Yes, it be a glove, all right." Sam could see he had Gerry's undivided attention. He dipped his hand into to the saddle bag once again, and again he looked over Gerry's shoulder before pulling out nothing more than an empty cigarette packet.

Gerry was amazed. "Well, Sam, you've got me now. A dirty old rubber glove and a crumpled empty cigarette packet. What's the game then?"

"Ah, there you be, young man." The old gravedigger seemed determined to enjoy his 'fifteen minutes of fame' with this local lad made good, a journalist from London now. "It be where I found them what'll interest you, I bet." Sam had lowered his voice to almost a whisper.

"I can't think where," said the mystified Gerry, "Nearby or in a rubbish bin, I suppose, or perhaps they fell off Bill Bonny's rubbish cart!"

"Ah, there you be again, young man." Sam made a near toothless grin. "I found them under where that mound is on Bolitho's plot."

"Well, there's no accounting for people these days, Mr Teath."

Gerry could not see where this was leading. "They throw stuff down anywhere it seems."

"Ah, yes, they do. But it's when I found them that's the thing, my boy. This glove and this old cigarette packet I found on the day of Bolitho's funeral beside his grave." He crossed himself. "May God rest his soul."

Gerry was all ears now. "Could you let me have a look at them sometime?"

"Course you can, my boy, I'll be glad to get rid of them."

Gerry handled them gently. "Looks like a small glove to me Mr Teath."

Sam was buckling up his saddlebag. "You guessed right there, young Halford. Now, let's go back in and have another drink and I'll tell you something else."

They walked quickly back into the bar. The piano had stopped. The barman had barked "Last orders, please!" Gerry was surprised to see a group of men around Sarah, but got a signal from her that she would have just one more. "A Guinness, half a mild and another Grand Marnier, please." Collecting the drinks he returned to their table, where now there was just three of them. Sarah, Gerry and Sam Teath made a strange threesome. In the window seat Sarah and Gerry, and on the other side of the small round table, Sam Teath perched on a three-legged stool.

"Now, what have you two been up to?" Sarah asked. "Up to no good, I bet." She seemed quite light-hearted now on her third Grand Marnier.

Gerry answered, "Nothing much. But Sam has got one more thing to tell me, haven't you, Sam?"

"Yes, I have, and you'll hardly believe it." Sam Teath took another sip of his precious Guinness. "The only one round 'ere who used to smoke them cigarettes was old Parson Bowering's missus." He pointed to the crumpled cigarette packet still in Gerry's hand. "I know 'cause she used to give me the special card from inside the packet for my grandson."

Their conversation was rudely interrupted by the part-time barman, Bill Gibson. "Haven't you got any homes to go to?" He was ready to close the bar. "You ain't in London now, Gerry Halford. We ain't open all night."

The bar had soon cleared and there was a flurry of "Good nights", especially to Sarah. They were the only ones left. "Okay, Bill." Gerry ignored the slight sarcasm, or maybe it was envy, from the local barman. "We'll be moving along now. Mr Teath has kept me up past my bedtime."

"I suppose he's been telling you he knows who did those ol' Tremaynes in." Bill was ushering the threesome out of the front door of the Pity Me. "Pity he didn't tell those old Scotland Yard blokes then innit?" Those remarks were ignored.

Outside, Gerry shook Sam Teath's work-worn hand. "Thanks very much for the drinks, Mr Teath, and for the other stuff. I'll keep in touch, they could be useful."

Sarah smiled sweetly at the old gravedigger. "Thanks, Mr Teath, I'm sure we'll meet up again."

"I hope so, missus." Sam remembered to touch the peak of his dirty old cap and, leaning towards Gerry, said in a low gruff voice, "Whatever you do with them bits and pieces, remember you didn't get 'em from me." He turned and pushed his bike up the lane towards his whitewashed cottage.

Gerry lifted up the old yellow-white spar stone which he could remember being perched on the step of the front door of his cottage ever since he was a small boy. Underneath it was the key, and the two of them let themselves in quietly into the cosy little cottage.

"You sit down." Gerry gave Sarah a peck on the cheek. "I'll make some coffee." He walked into the small spick and span kitchen. He was not long and soon joined Sarah on the cottage sofa. "Well, what a day! What a night!" he exclaimed.

Sarah inquired, "Could tell me, what was the gravedigger so secretive about when he took you outside? Is that glove and cigarette packet all he had to show you?"

Gerry took the old glove and the crumpled cigarette packet out of his pocket, laid them carefully on the table "Yes, that's all he gave me."

Sarah turned up her nose. "Oh, my God, Gerry you're certainly clutching at straws. What on earth has that to do with anything?"

"And don't tell me, it's got something to do with those Tremaynes,"

"People won't let me forget 'em," Gerry replied, obviously feeling quite pleased with himself.

"I don't think you want to." Sarah seemed reluctantly resigned to the fact that the Tremayne saga was going to continue to have most of Gerry's attention, for a while at least.

"Well, to be truthful, the clues I picked up today have made me think more and more about Mr Boucher's offer of that big cheque. If I could solve even one of those murders," he went on, "it would certainly be a godsend for us. It's worth thinking about, isn't it?"

Sarah thought for a moment about the possibility of a big cheque. "Would the cheque be big enough to get us out of our rented flat and enable us to buy a house, Gerry?"

"Could be. Could be," he mused. The conversation was serious now. Gerry turned to the glove and cigarette packet. "Now, if what Sam Teath told me is true, he found these things alongside the open grave of the lord of the manor on the Saturday before the funeral was to be held on Monday. And he infers that they belonged to the Reverend Bowering's wife."

Sarah asked, "Well, if that's true, what does it mean and why hasn't he told the police if it was that important?"

"I really don't know yet, but what it does mean is that Mrs. Bowering must have gone outside the church on that Saturday morning and she probably meant to have a cigarette and it was the morning that Colin Tremayne's body went missing. But what I'm wondering is why she went to that open grave, or even if she did.

"I'll have to look up my old notes if I can find them. If I can, I may be able to find out who was in the church and see if they can remember anything."

Sarah yawned. "I bet your mother will know who helps in the church on those occasions. In any case, I've had enough of the Tremaynes for today, I'm going to bed." She was obviously getting weary with the Tremayne stories" and was not afraid to let Gerry know it.

"Of course your mother will know." Gerry ignored her last remarks, but followed her up the stairs. "She probably will, and I'll have to ask her about those pregnant unmarried girls. I'm sure those sort of things were frowned upon and were a definite no-no in these parts in those days." Sarah sort of lightened up for a moment "I don't know about it being a no-no, Gerry, but there did seem to be plenty of them in Trehorra." Gerry thought she was getting over her impatience with the Tremayne saga "You just have to have a dig at your country cousins don't you?" He was so disappointed that, after a long lingering kiss, Sarah turned over and deliberately turned her back on him and within seconds was fast asleep.

On the other hand Gerry's mind was working overtime. He was visualising Colin Tremayne's body hanging over the horse trough, while, a mere hundred yards away, Mrs Bowering and her lady helpers were inside the church preparing it for the Bolitho funeral. Did she nip out to have a cigarette? Did she notice the body at the horse trough? Vanstock could have been on his way back to his house to use the phone, John Stephens had gone to his scouts' meeting. IF she did go outside the church, IF she did see the body in the horse trough, and perhaps knowing how her husband felt about meeting Colin Tremayne with regard to getting married urgently to the pregnant Peggy Dixon. Knowing her husband's 'darker' side and presuming something had gone drastically wrong with that early morning meeting, she could have dragged the body to the open grave, covered it over and during what must have been a struggle, left her rubber glove and dropped her empty cigarette packet, only for Sam Teath to find it later. These were his last thoughts before thinking there would be a few loose ends to tie up tomorrow.

Chapter 32

Following their busy day with Vicar Salmond's tea party and completing the evening with the goodnight drinks at the Pity Me, where Gerry had been surprised with the revelations of Sam Teath, Sarah was now resigned to the fact that Gerry was going to pursue the mystery of the Tremayne deaths.

The fact that a big cheque from his paper was the possible reward for Gerry no doubt helped Sarah not to object too much to this intrusion on their first holiday as a married couple.

Breakfast was all done and cleared away. Mother Halford thanked Sarah for helping with the washing-up. "And what's on the programme for today, you two?"

Gerry's head was stuck in his old notebooks. Mrs Halford had never thrown any of Gerry's 'things' away, and all his cuttings were methodically kept in a bureau in his old bedroom. It didn't take Gerry long to swat up the finer details of the Tremayne era.

"Oh, I was thinking of taking Sarah down to Pentoran Beach and showing her those huge caves where all that smuggling went on years ago."

Mrs Halford looked surprised. "And a lot of other things have gone on there in recent years, I'm told."

Gerry winked his eye at Sarah. "Oh, yes, Mother. I wasn't going to mention that to Sarah, yet."

"Well, you be careful, Sarah. I hear it's very difficult to get down there, if not impossible these days."

Sarah couldn't help smiling. "What's all this crosstalk about then? What's so mysterious about this Pentoran Beach?"

Mrs Halford leaned forward towards Sarah and, in almost a whisper, said, "Well, my dear, they do say there's a lot of nudists get down there."

Gerry laughed. "I don't think there'll be many down there today, Mother. It looks a bit too cool outside, even for nudists."

Mother Halford joined in the laughter. "Well, I was wondering if you could call in at Widow Billings for me and collect a dozen eggs. It'll be on your way."

"Will do, Mother." Gerry got hold of Sarah's arm and they were out of the door before any more 'orders' were forthcoming.

It was a fair walk to Widow Billings's and took them a good thirty minutes before they were at the St Stithian's Farm and the old lady's front step. "Well, if it isn't young Gerry Halford. And who be this with you then?" she squinted at Sarah.

"This is my wife," Gerry shouted. He knew of the widow's deafness.

"Well, well. Come in, my dears, do come in and join me for a cup of tea." She obviously didn't get many visitors.

Thank you, Mrs Billings, but I'm calling for a dozen eggs for my mother."

"That's all right, my boy, they be all ready. Now, who takes sugar?"

Sarah and Gerry could see there was no refusing now, so they both sat down at the kitchen table which was littered with all sorts of pots, pans and plates.

Mrs Billings, dressed all in black, eventually sat down at the table. "Now, what be you doing back there in Trehorra, young man? I thought you had gone up to London after all that Tremayne business."

"Yes, I'm living and working in London now, but I'm down here for a holiday." Gerry was keeping his voice raised which almost echoed in this old high-ceilinged farmhouse kitchen with just the table and wooden chairs on the old stone floor.

"You finished with all that bother, then? You're not going to dig it all up again," the old lady quizzed.

"We didn't come down to resurrect that awful business." Sarah couldn't understand why everybody seemed to think that Gerry was some sort of London 'whiz kid' whose main duty in life was to discover who murdered the Tremaynes. Gerry, too, was surprised that it appeared that now everyone, even Widow Billings, seemed willing to talk about the Tremaynes whereas when the Scotland Yard men were in Trehorra everybody seemed to clam up. It was as if they knew it was one of them but did not want to admit it.

Ignoring Sarah's response, Mrs Billings went on. "Well, my dears, you know, of course, that postman Mawgan called the police from here after he found one of the Tremaynes in the Goran river."

Gerry, of course, did remember that bit of the story. But Mrs Billings continued , "Well, of course, I was quite shocked when he came and asked to use my phone. All of a rush he was, too."

Gerry was keen to keep the old lady talking. "I expect he was. It's not every day you find a dead body on your post round, is it?"

"Well, I never seen him get on his bike so fast. He was all over the road. If it had been the day before he would have been run over."

"That was the day of the motor rally, wasn't it?" Gerry remembered. "Riding like that, I guess he would surely have caused some problems for some of those cars, wouldn't he, Mrs Billings?" "Not only them but the vicar came to give me holy communion and he went down the road well before that lot started.

"Ever since Percy died, I haven't been able get to St Minerva Church so he used to come every Monday morning. This new vicar hasn't been yet, though."

"So Parson Bowering was here early on that bank holiday morning then, Mrs Billings? You sure about that?" He shouted a bit louder.

"Course I'm sure," answered the old lady. She was very emphatic about it.

Gerry quietened down. "Well, I didn't know that. I guess we'll be off now. Thanks for the eggs, Mrs Billings."

"Your mam's welcome any time. Now, you two mind how you go. It be dangerous down at that Pentoran Beach."

The young couple continue up the lane towards the cliffs and Pentoran Beach. "My God. What do you think about that then?" he exclaimed to Sarah loudly.

"There's no need to shout now," Sarah answered. She couldn't really see why Gerry was so excited.

"Well, don't you see, Sarah, Parson Bowering gives Widow Billings her communion, takes off down the road in his car, and perhaps accidentally crashes into Duncan Tremayne on duty as a rally steward and then could have dumped him in the river. That's got to be somewhere near the point," Gerry enthused. "You see, if I remember correctly, none of the rally drivers could remember a steward at the Blue Mills Ford and that's where Duncan Tremayne was supposed to be."

Sarah looked serious now. "You mean that the Parson Bowering we met yesterday at the vicarage tea killed that Tremayne?" She shuddered at the thought.

"Well, whether he meant to or not, I don't know, but it's certainly a possibility. I'll look up some more stuff on that tonight. But for now, let's go and concentrate on Pentoran beach."

"You mean the nudists don't you?"

"Ah well, them too!"

Chapter 33

Mrs Halford had planned to have high tea at 4 o'clock so that she and Sarah would then have time to get ready for their visit to the village hall. The Trehorra Women's Institute was presenting a play, a very ambitious George Bernard Shaw production.

Gerry said he would look up his notes on the Tremaynes and meet them afterwards for a drink in the Pity Me.

Gerry thought he had absorbed all the details at the time of the baffling deaths of the Tremaynes, but now found he had quickly to assess theories of Vicar Bowering running over Duncan Tremayne on the day of the rally, once Widow Billings had revealed she had received holy communion with the vicar that morning. Could his theories possibly hold water?

The telephone rang. Gerry was half startled, he was so deep in thought. He jumped to the phone. Annie Hambly was on the other end. "Call from London for you."

"Thanks."

It was Mr Boucher. "How's the holiday going?"

"Oh, fine thanks, Mr B," and, as sarcastically as possible, he added, "enjoying the peace and quiet, you know, amongst other things."

"I hope the other things are connected to that big cheque on offer?"

Gerry wasn't at all surprised at this question from his boss. "Haven't been able to think of anything else, Mr B. Everywhere I go the villagers seem to want to talk about the Tremaynes. In fact, I've had one or two helpful stories. Wherever I seem to go, the village people want to ask if I'm still interested." And putting on his 'posh' London-acquired voice "To be honest the village seems to have shaken off its usual languid normality, and I do sense there's a lot more to be learned from some of the locals. You know, they preferred not to talk very much when the deaths actually occurred, but it's quite the opposite now."

"That sounds promising, son. Any names yet?"

"Well, yes. I hope you won't think this is ridiculous, but I'd like a rundown on the vicar and his wife who were here in Trehorra at the time. His name is Eric Bowering and his wife's name is Fiona."

"Will do, my boy. How's your wife liking it down there?" Boucher scribbled Eric and Fiona Bowering on his priority notepad.

"Oh, she's enjoying it, I think, Mr B, and I am keeping her interested by continually reminding her of that big cheque on offer. It's still on isn't it?"

Gerry wasn't sure if she would agree with his renewed interest in the Tremaynes and he was sure it was not what she expected when the visit had been arranged.

"I'll call you later with the info on the Bowerings. No, better not, I'll do it as soon as possible, Gerry. Keep your finger on the pulse and the cheque is definitely on the card." Boucher smiled as he put the phone down. "This lad might just do something," he thought.

     Gerry gathered his thoughts together again. Could Vicar Bowering have run into Duncan Tremayne by accident? Supposing he had actually killed him. Perhaps he wasn't dead after the car had hit him. And by placing the body out of sight along the Goran River, this would somehow or other relate it to the motor rally and could imply that he could have possibly been rescued. On the other hand, supposing killing the Tremayne boy was deliberate? Perhaps there was another car. But where?

     He looked up at the old grandfather clock in the corner of the room. "Oh, it's gone 9 o'clock," he muttered to himself, "And I've only studied one death." He quickly stacked his notebooks in a neat pile on the table and hurried down to the Pity Me.

     Mrs Halford and Sarah had not yet arrived, so he ordered his usual half of mild and sat down in the window seat. There was the usual group of regulars in the bar. Most of them greeted Gerry congenially and he was soon engaged in a conversation with Petherick Carnack, still in his working clothes, his face still as black as a coal miner's, after a hard day's work at his forge. "My first chance of speaking to you, Gerry. How's things with you?"

     "Fine, thank you, Mr.Carnack." Gerry was pleased to sit down with Petherick, mainly because of his involvement with everything that went on in the village.

     He soon discovered he had no need to remind the smith about the Tremaynes. Petherick himself couldn't wait, it seemed, to speak to Gerry. "So you've come back to sort out those bloody Tremaynes, have you?" Petherick was not one to beat about the bush.

"I really came back for a holiday. But I'll be honest, Mr Carnack, people here still seem interested to know why those deaths happened when they did, who did them and are puzzled that Scotland Yard seemed to give up on the case."

"I wasn't surprised those Londoners couldn't crack it. They knows nothing about village life, do they?" Carnack was all things Cornish and probably had never been out of Cornwall except perhaps to Plymouth. He found it not difficult at all to criticise anyone outside Cornwall.

"Took them a hell of a while before anyone up country took any notice at all."

Gerry could see the Trehorran's point of view, but was slightly surprised at the apparent aggressive attitude shown by the village blacksmith.

"I know they still have the files open on those deaths, Mr Carnack, and they'd be down here in a shot if they got so much as a small lead." Gerry thought he must put the record straight.

"You think so, do you, boy?" Carnack looked Gerry straight in the eye. "And who's going to give them a lead? You?"

Gerry thought that he would be as straight as Petherick Carnack, so he was just as blunt in his reply. "I hope so, Mr Carnack. They're certain it was a local affair and are hoping still that a local will come forward with some information. I would have thought you might have some ideas, Mr Carnack."

"Oh, I have ideas, all right. But then, who'd listen to me?"

"Well, I certainly would for one." Gerry was quick to confirm his interest to Petherick.

"You be born here, I know. And you may be a bit young, but you're old enough to understand what's what in the village."

"I guess you're right there, Mr Carnack, but I can't see what you're getting at." Gerry was genuinely puzzled.

"Well, who do you think – with all your schooling in London who– would want to get rid of those Tremaynes? Not that they were any bloody good anyway." Petherick got out a cigarette. "Have you got a light, boy?"

"No, I'm sorry. I don't smoke. But I'll get some matches for you." Gerry did not want the blacksmith to leave the window seat. And more important, he didn't want Petherick Carnack to drift away from the conversation.

Before Gerry could make a move, Petherick had borrowed a lighted cigarette from 'Dixie' Dixon, who had just entered the bar. Having had the cigarette returned to him, the white-bearded Dixon turned to Gerry. "Are you still on about Tremaynes? Reckon there's plenty folk could tell you 'bout 'em!"

"Well, I think I know enough about them already. What I want to know is who hated them so much that they wanted to do away with them?" Gerry replied with just a little bit of impatience. He decided he was going to be blunt.

Dixie Dixon laughed devilishly. "Old Petherick, for one, can tell you quite a bit about them."

Carnack puffed on his homemade cigarette and inhaled deeply. "That's right, Dixie, I can tell 'e a few things about them buggers, all right. And my Catherine, God bless her, would tell you a lot more if she were here to tell ye." The openness of the hatred towards the Tremaynes shown by these two villagers stumped young Halford, and he suddenly felt a bit awkward sitting with these two solid old Trehorrans, neither of them seeming to have any wish to disguise their dislike of those Tremaynes. He would have preferred to continue the conversation, but his mother and Sarah walked in the door at the very moment, accompanied by John Taylor. Gerry was a little taken aback and quickly nodded towards the threesome. "Thanks for talking to me," Gerry addressed the two Trehorrans.

"I must see you both again for another chat."

"What can I get you while I'm at the bar?"

"Mine's a pint of bitter," said Dixie.

"Thanks, son, I'll have a bitter too," said Petherick and, turning to Dixie, he lowered his voice.

"I was thinkin' I was over Catherine but seeing young Halford has brought it all back."

"I think I know how you feel," Dixie replied.

Dixie Dixon thought he knew how the other man felt and was glad that his daughter Peggy had settled down after having had one or two teenage flings following her first bitter experience with Colin Tremayne. She had finally settled down with Tom Queen, Petherick Carnack's assistant.

Mrs Halford always enjoyed her half-pint of cider. Sarah had her usual Grand Marnier. They both had enjoyed their evening out. Sarah couldn't believe what acting talent Trehorra possessed. "It was very, very good," she told Gerry, "but a bit ambitious I thought, but John here was excellent."

"Oh yes I have no doubt about that," Gerry remarked icily but thought he'd offer him a drink "What's yours, John?"

His mother did not lavish such praise however. Her reasoning being, "Perhaps it's because I know them all around the village."

Gerry listened to his mother explaining who was who in the play and then suddenly interrupted. "Mother, what happened to Catherine Carnack? Only Petherick Carnack mentioned her name as if she wasn't still here in the Pity Me I mean. He seemed more irritated than excited."

"Why ever didn't you tell me?"

Sarah was embarrassed for Mrs Halford. "Your mum can't be responsible for telling you every bit of tittle-tattle from the village, Gerry."

"I don't think a young girl committing suicide is just tittle-tattle, Sarah." Gerry, obviously annoyed, picked up his notebook that he had left on the window seat. "I suppose you're going to tell us it was something to do with those damn Tremaynes." Sarah did not realise how near she was the truth.

Mrs Halford lowered her voice to a whisper. "She had a miscarriage a few months after that one Tremayne lad got drowned at that funfair thing. Of course, there was no proof that the Tremayne had anything to do with it, but there was a lot of talk about it. They did say she hadn't been seen out with anybody else." Taxi man Taylor thanked Gerry for the drink, gave Sarah and Mrs Halford a hug and thanked them for seeing the play. Gerry turned to his mother. He was amazed at Catherine Carnack's story. "Do you think there's anything in it then, Mother? Do you believe it?"

"Oh, I don't know, Gerald. Some of these ol' village people were willing to blame those boys for anything and everything around that time," His mother had obviously forgotten or didn't know her only son had had a brief spell with Catherine Carnack. Perhaps that was why he was so sensitive?

The bar was steadily emptying and there were some goodnights and cheerios and one or two sneering, "Happy hunting, Halford." Some just nodded their heads and some touched their caps to Sarah and Mrs Halford. Petherick Carnack and Dixie Dixon left together. The blacksmith looked back "You know where to find me, Gerry. I'll be in the smithy most of the time."

"Okay, Mr Carnack. Thanks very much, I'll certainly call on you. Goodnight, Mr Dixon."

The three of them, Mrs Halford, Sarah and Gerry, were walking the short distance to their cottage along the street. The two men went in the opposite direction to play their nightly game of drafts.

Sarah was first to speak. "I hope, Gerry, you had a profitable time. Have you learned any more apart from poor Mr Carnack's daughter's sad story?"

Gerry suddenly thought he hadn't told them about Mr Boucher's telephone call. When Sarah heard that bit of news, she realised now for sure what she had suspected for quite a while; the honeymoon was forgotten. "I guess that's tomorrow all spoken for then."

Gerry hesitated, squeezed her hand. "I'm thinking every day we're getting nearer that big cheque"

At this stage, not wanting to dampen his enthusiasm, Sarah returned the squeeze.

"To be honest, Gerry, if it means we can get a nice house, it would be great but how big an IF is it?" He realised he wanted to pursue the Tremayne story. He'd got to get that cheque and in desperation he said "It won't be easy, but I'm going to try."

Chapter 34

The next day Gerry was up bright and early. He had people to see, people to talk to. He made do with just a boiled egg for his breakfast. He was just going out the door when Sarah came downstairs. "You're up early."

"I won't be long, Sarah. I'm calling on a couple of people. I guess you know why." With just a "Bye, mum," he was out the door.

Mrs Halford turned to Sarah, "Now what will you have for breakfast, my dear? We can take our time and linger over the toast and coffee after one of my special fry-ups. You're not on a diet, are you, Sarah?"

"Not yet," Sarah laughed, "but I'll have to think about it when I get back to London if I stay down here much longer."

"Won't be long now. I can't believe you've been down here over a week already." Mother Halford sighed "Time passes so quickly these days," as she started to prepare the breakfast. Sarah responded "Yes and all we've done, it seems, is to drag up all that Tremayne stuff."

Gerry, meanwhile, was hurrying to his first call. Dr Hillfield. He needed to see the doctor before he saw his surgery appointments.

The doctor had known the Halfords for years and greeted Gerry warmly. "Now, what can I do for you, Gerry? Doesn't look as if there's much wrong with you, my man. I hear you've brought your new wife to Trehorra. Nothing wrong, I hope, with her, or you mother."

"Oh, no, nothing like that, Doctor. This is a sort of a business call, although I'm officially on holiday."

"Business? But fire away, young man." The doctor was puzzled.

"Well, I'll get straight to the point. I don't know how far your records go back, Doctor, but could you tell me if Catherine Carnack who committed suicide, I believe, was ever pregnant?"

"Oh, yes, of course I remember it. She and young Gerald Tremayne had both been to ask me to confirm what they thought had happened."

"And she was definitely pregnant?" Gerry did not know whether to be pleased or not and did his best not to show his feelings either way. He thought he was getting near a motive for the murders but was finding it hard to believe that Catherine had associated with a second Tremayne after her father had stopped her liaison with her first Tremayne

"Oh, my, Gerry, didn't you know the poor girl committed suicide. It must have been two or three years ago now."

"I can't believe it." Gerry was astounded.

"Did she have a miscarriage then?" "I'm afraid she did, Gerry, It was all very, very sad. I did all I could but when her father came to see me, I should have realised then that the poor girl wasn't going to have a good pregnancy." The doctor was busily flipping through his files. (No such thing as a secretary for a village doctor in those days.)

Gerry was all ears now. "What happened with her father then?"

"You don't know?" The doctor was surprised. "Well, of course, I understand you would be in London by this time. The stories in the village got to her father so much, it was almost more than he could take. It was the second Tremayne boy she had been associated with. Of course, then Mr Carnack started drinking heavily and he never let her out of his sight. That was Gerald Tremayne who was found in that funfair pool."

"Yes, I was here then, but I hadn't heard of what had followed."

"Well, she eventually took an overdose, poor girl."

"Good God, Doctor, I never knew any of that." Gerry was genuinely shocked. These were people he knew and grew up with. "I am shocked, but can you be sure that that Tremayne boy was the one who got Catherine Carnack pregnant?"

"Oh, yes, I have a record of their appointment with me. They told me they would get married as quickly as possible. In fact, they had been to see the vicar to arrange for the banns to be called. But I understand her father soon put a stop to that. After she had admitted that Gerald Tremayne was the father. It was a very sad time in the village, and Mr Carnack could barely take all the stigma."

Gerry was shocked but acknowledged that the doctor's sympathy was genuine. His mind was now working overtime and it was time to get to the 'nitty-gritty'. "What about Ethel Weare was it true she was going to marry Samuel Tremayne for the same reason? And can I presume Evelyn Menhennick's child was also fathered – excuse my expression, Doctor – by Duncan Tremayne? That's if I can believe what my mother has told me."

"Yes, I have to agree, Gerry, all that is fact. I don't believe Ethel Weare has got married as she left the village soon after you left."

Gerry was beginning to see a vague vestige of a motive now. "Forgive me, Doctor, but have the police ever questioned you about these pregnancies?"

The doctor seemed surprised "No, I have no record of any interviews at all. You realise, Gerry, that what I'm saying to you now is strictly confidential."

"Of course, Doctor," Gerry confirmed. "I suppose if I still lived here though, I would have gathered all this."

"Well, yes, I suppose you could have. The village has always been full of rumours about the Tremaynes ever since those times but only rumours, I can assure you."

The doctor looked through his office window. It was a familiar sight – patients to see him were sitting in the waiting room. Gerry could see it was time to go. "I'm sorry to have imposed myself on you, Doctor, thank you for seeing me."

"I'm glad to see you again, Gerry. Good luck." The doctor ushered Gerry out of the side door. "Remember this interview must remain confidential."

When outside, he couldn't help thinking "I wonder if those pregnancies mean anything?

"There's the common activity between three Tremaynes at least. Whether or not that turns out to be the common thread to link all the deaths, I'll have to confirm with a few more people. I wonder if Vanstock knows anything. Wonder where he is living now."

On his way back to his home, he looked in at the village forge. Petherick was hard at work shoeing a horse. As the horse was not a particularly well-behaved one, the smith was hurling a few swear words about as well as his hammer. Tom Queen, his assistant, was holding the horse's bridle and trying to soothe the animal. There were, as always, two or three onlookers around so Gerry decided not to stop. There would be a more suitable time to speak to Petherick Carnack later, although the Catherine Carnack story, he wanted to forget.

He joined Sarah and his mother and helped them finish off the toast and coffee. After sketching over his visit with Doctor Hillfield, Gerry asked his mother about PC Vanstock.

"Oh, he's only a few miles up the coast. Tregwithian, I think. There's only a few houses there and one hotel-cum-boarding house."

"Oh, good." Gerry thanked his mother. He looked at Sarah. "Fancy a trip to Tregwithian, Sarah?"

"Looks as if I have to," Sarah replied. She knew now that Gerry really had got the Tremayne 'bit' between his teeth and in a resigned tone of voice, misquoting the line from Macbeth, she added, "Okay, lead on, Macduff. Tregwithian here we come."

As they were leaving, postman Mawgan was doing his post round, still on his red bicycle. He pulled up at the cottage door. "Telegram for you, Gerry." He handed over the little yellow envelope.

"Ah, I've been expecting this." Knowing the reputation of the postman when delivering local telegrams, Gerry quipped:

"What's in it, Mr. Mawgan?" The postman went on his way oblivious to Gerry's intended joke.

He ripped the flimsy envelope open and read the message aloud to Sarah as they waited at the bus stop. 'Bowering spent nine years in Africa, Stop. Married Fiona during five-year stay in Clapham, Stop. Left Trehorra after four years, Stop. Now acting as a locum tenens, stop. Phone me for further details, Stop.'

"Is that information of any use?" Sarah queried. "What is a locum tenens anyway? I've never heard of that."

"It means he's filling in for other clergy. I think that's why he's here." Gerry was a little bit subdued. He had been expecting a bit more detail really. Aloud he said, "I hope the further details are better than this, although this is pretty sensational stuff, don't you think?"

"I can't say that I do" was Sarah's caustic reply.

Chapter 35

They discovered the retired Vanstock easily enough. He was sitting on a chair at the top of his small garden. "Well, if it isn't young Gerry Halford." He got up, looking extremely relaxed in his rolled-up shirt sleeves. "And who have you got here then?" He held his hand out towards Sarah.

"This is my wife, Sarah," Gerry proudly answered.

Out came Mrs Vanstock with a very friendly welcome. She hugged Gerry and then Sarah. "Oh, my word, Gerry, you have got a pretty wife."

All the small talk over, Vanstock's intuition took over. "I guess you haven't come all this way to show off your new missus. What's up, young fella?"

"I'll make a cup of tea or coffee. What would you like, dears?"

"Cup of tea, please, Mrs Vanstock." They both spoke at once.

The retired policeman joined in, "I'll have one as well, missus, with a 'you know what' in just to taste."

Gerry could see that the old copper had not changed his habits that much. He sat down on the chair beside him and thought he'd better come out with the reason for his visit. He just managed to say, "The Tremaynes, Mr Vanstock."

Vanstock sat bolt upright. "Good God, Gerry, haven't you forgotten that lot? I thought you'd have more going on in London than to think about that old to-do."

"Well, I'm down here on holiday really, Mr Vanstock, but the people in the village haven't forgotten it. They've been coming up to me ever since I got here and asking me about it. And to tell you the truth, one or two of them have been telling me a few things I didn't know. So, to put it bluntly, I'm hoping you can fill in a few gaps for me."

"If I can, my boy. If I can," the retired policeman repeated. "I certainly didn't like retiring with all the business happening and realising people thought we did nothing about it."

"Can I ask you, Mr Vanstock, when you found Duncan Tremayne in the Goran River, did you think a rally car could have knocked him over?"

Sarah, meanwhile, was being shown around by Mrs Vanstock. She was showing her the country flower garden which she had always wanted and was now very proud of.

"I didn't find him, Fred Mawgan did that all right. But when I saw him, yes, my boy, his legs were broke all right, and he had scratches all over his arms and down the side of his face. Proper mess he was, but I don't think it was a rally car, though. I think that the report referred to multiple abrasions and bruising as well as both legs broken"

Getting his notebook out, Gerry started putting questions to the policeman, "Are you sure he was knocked out during the motor rally before or after?"

"Well, I did think at the time that the first driver, who was, if I remember rightly, a newcomer, had something to do with it, but he denied everything. His car was inspected and cleared, plus the driver was adamant that he saw no steward at the Blue Mills Ford, nor did any of the others."

Gerry nodded. "Say if I were to tell you that another car had passed that way in the opposite direction sometime before the first rally car reached the ford?"

This presented Vanstock with a scenario he wasn't expecting. "Well, Gerry, I'm still as keen as you seem to be to nail those deaths, which I think were all murders, no doubt 'bout that. But that's a new one to me – another car going the opposite way." He added, "Of course, it would have been impossible to tell because of all those rally cars going through the ford. But I've never heard of any other car going the opposite way."

"Supposing I told you I know for certain another car did go down that road?"

Vanstock seemed more than interested now. "As a guess, I'd say that would be worth pursuing."

Gerry was enjoying this. "Supposing I told you without pursuing it, I know whose car it was and who was driving it?"

"Well, I'll be damned." The ex-police constable of Trehorra exclaimed, "I can't believe what you've just said. There wasn't many people who had cars in Trehorra round about that time so I suppose you couldn't be far wrong, whoever you say."

"I'm not guessing, Mr Vanstock, and I'm hoping you can remember some incident or somebody which or who will confirm my discovery."

"There's not much I forget. Even now, I can recall most of what happened. So at a guess, I'd say that that car would be that old Vicar Bowering's or taxi man John Taylor. Only what the hell any of 'em would be doing around there that time of morning, before the rally I've no idea. Can't see anyone wanting a taxi or the parson and certainly not Colton-Taylor on a Bank Holiday"

"So it's Taylor or Bowering, if you ask me."

"Maybe you've hit the nail on the head there but why those two?"

"Well, to tell you the truth, I never did see eye to eye with Parson Bowering, but he did make a few visits to the old country folk. When I told Bugannon I was suspicious of the vicar for stopping me searching the church and the churchyard on that Sunday before Bolitho's funeral, the inspector disagreed. I didn't press Taylor but do you recall he was never far away when the dead bodies were found? Of course the Yard entered the fray, and along with all the other people we suspected, they never regarded the parson as a prime suspect. So in the end, we were only left with a lot of half-baked guesses, on a lot of 'half-baked characters."

"And who were they, Mr Vanstock?" Gerry probably knew what Vanstock was going to say, but he continued to write in his notebook.

"I hope you aren't going to print all this, Gerry." Vanstock frowned, and for a moment looked a bit worried. "But you knew as well as I did, that young Tom Ward was one they thought about. But he was another non-runner as was old Myrtle Smith. Both of 'em were ridiculous suspects, as far I was concerned."

Gerry stopped writing. "I'm inclined to agree with you, Mr V."

"Although I admit, I thought Tom could have tangled with Sam Tremayne or Colin Tremayne on some of his weird runs."

"If you think that, you're left to go to the other."

With that the ex-policeman got up from his chair. So the two of them walked down the path. Any onlooker looking would never guess that the subject of their conversation was multiple murders.

The sun was shining. The two ladies were picking some sweet peas, the men drinking their mugs of tea.

"Now look here, Gerry, the official verdict on Sam Tremayne was, and still is, as far as I understand, that it was an accident. And as he was the first Tremayne to go, there was nothing else to go on, so they had to say that. Of course, when the others were 'done in' there would have to be some pretty spectacular evidence to reach another verdict. Now don't tell me you found something different. Because if you have, it'll be a whole big can of worms you be opening. I should leave it, young man; if I were you."

"Don't think I can, Mr Vanstock" Gerry smiled as he thought of that big cheque.

The two men had now joined the ladies. Sarah was holding a huge bunch of the multi-coloured sweet peas. "Your mother will love these, Gerry. Mrs Vanstock has kindly let us have them all. They are the season's last." She held them for Gerry to smell the wonderful fragrance of these popular garden flowers.

"Yes, she certainly will." Gerry winked his eye to Sarah. "What a pity Mrs Vanstock doesn't live nearer to London. She could supply your shop."

"You must be joking, Gerry Halford," Mrs Vanstock laughed. "Now, what have you two been talking about? It looked pretty serious to me, with you getting out your notebook."

"Gerry's found out a thing or two more about the Tremaynes, missus, and some of those Trehorra people have decided to open their mouths at last."

Mrs Vanstock turned towards Gerry. "You don't mean somebody knows who caused all those boys to die. Who was it then?"

Gerry was slightly embarrassed. "Well, not exactly, Mrs Vanstock, but I was just telling your husband that I have found out one or two things which surprised me, and I just needed some confirmation, which, thank goodness, he has been able to give."

"Oh, my dear, what a pity if you have to dig up all those bizarre happenings again. I thought it was all buried in the past. What are you going to do now?"

Sarah and Gerry had just made it back to the cottage in time for Mother Halford's 1pm lunch. They were greeted at the door by an excited Mrs Halford. "Your Mr Boucher phoned this morning. You're to ring him back, as soon as you can."

Gerry leant toward the phone.

"Not now, Gerald, eat your lunch first."

Although now a grown man and married at that, Mrs Halfords's only son obliged and returned to the table.

Sarah looked up with an ironic smile, "That's a good boy." She was not surprised that he simply gobbled up his lunch.

Out came his notebook as the chief crime editor of the Express answered Gerry's call, "Boy, have I got news for you."

"I'm all ears, Mr Boucher."

Finally, more than thirty minutes later, Gerry put the phone down. Sarah, who had been sort of half listening was still intrigued by Gerry's exclamations such as, "Never." "No." "Not again." "I can't believe it."

"Oh, my God." "Not again." "You don't mean it." And so on.

Sarah started to clear away the empty plates, but could not subdue her curiosity. "That sounded sort of interesting. What now?"

"It's hardly believable, but Boucher's search on the Bowerings finds that their background has not been a bed of roses all the way."

"Oh, I guessed that, after we met them the other day at the vicarage. I thought she was very cagey. Did Boucher tell you anything you don't know already?" Sarah sat down, made herself comfortable, and resigned herself that she was going to have to listen to Boucher's phone conversation in full. She appeared to be taking more interest and perhaps was now as keen as Gerry to get to the bottom of this Tremayne affair, if only to get on with her and Gerry's life together. No doubt the thought of that big cheque could be a contributing factor too.

Mrs Halford got up from her afternoon nap. "Good gracious, you two still here? That Boucher must have kept you on a long time. I thought you'd be going out again." She filled the kettle. "You'd just as well have a cup of tea with me now."

Sarah got out the cups and saucers. Mrs Halford continued. "I suppose he's still got you on to those old Tremaynes, hasn't he? Beats me why somebody hasn't come up with the answers. After all, Trehorra isn't all that big. "If I be hearing right what you've been saying and from what I can remember, there can't be too many suspects."

"It's more difficult than you think, Mother. Whoever I said if it was a local you wouldn't believe it, would you?"

"It would take a bit of believing, you're right there. With all the rumours going around, I think somebody should have sorted someone out. I can't believe Scotland Yard went back to London without finding out anything. They did, didn't they?"

Gerry could see that his mother was now getting serious and impatient about the Tremaynes for about the first time he could remember. Perhaps she was reminded that but for those murders Gerald would not have left Trehorra.

She hadn't finished. "Somebody in Trehorra has got to know who murdered those poor boys."

"They weren't exactly angels, Mother. I've found out for a fact that some of the village girls were found pregnant after going out with the Tremayne boys."

Gerry doubted that he should tell his mother what he had discovered from Dr Hillfield, but Mrs Halford still hadn't finished. "Well, what's that got to do with it? Getting a girl pregnant is serious enough, but not a reason to murder?"

Sarah agreed with Gerry's mum. "I think you're right there, Mrs Halford, but could it be a reason in the absence of anything else? Perhaps that is the connection what Gerry keeps referring to." Sarah had one foot in each camp now between Gerry and his mother. She wanted Gerry's thinking to be correct but inwardly thought it was a bit off the mark.

She asked "If that turns out to be the motive who could be the murderer?"

Mrs Halford stopped what she was doing, put her two hands on the table, looked very serious and straight at Gerry. "There's another thing. Have you thought about the money these Tremaynes owed all over the place? Petherick Carnack told me himself, he won't do any more work for them. They owe him so much money."

"Well, Mother, a debt for shoeing horses is surely a long way off murdering three young men, that can't be enough to kill for."

"Mrs Halford was determined to say her piece. She never got out much and the art of conversation was not one of her usual activities. "I don't know about that, Gerald, but there's another thing Petherick said. He said those funny old Pascoe twins were in with the Tremaynes with those tractors. That would be doing Mr Carnack out of a living, which isn't all that good anyhow. He said that soon there'll be no horses left for him to shoe."

"Oh, Mother, come on now, tractors, horses, they are also a long way from a reason to murder and you are all but naming Petherick Carnack!"

Mother did not agree. "Tractors and horses, maybe not, but don't forget MONEY. There's been plenty murders over that my son."

Gerry didn't want a shouting match with his mother "Come on, Sarah, let's get a breath of fresh air before the whole village comes under suspicion." With that, Sarah and Gerry walked out the door.

Mrs Halford wasn't done yet. She called after them, "According to you they are, aren't they?"

As they walked along the street, Sarah quizzed Gerry. "Do you believe the pregnancies could have anything to do with those murders? If so who would want to murder those brothers?"

"Well, I guess there could be one or two possibilities if the pregnancies had anything to do with the murders. Mr Boucher told me to look for a common thread, and that just might be it."

Sarah nodded in agreement, but questioned, "So if you decide the pregnancies are relevant, who could be the murderer or murderers?" She continued and attempted to answer her own question. "Could be the girls' other lovers, I suppose, or perhaps the girls' fathers? I know my dad would have been wild if I'd have been pregnant before I got married. My mother too. And Sarah added a late stinging remark. I've just thought, Gerry Halford, couldn't you be in the other lovers' group? Gerry chose to ignore Sarah's 'dig' at his brief association with Catherine Carnack.

They had stopped at one of the wooden seats dotted around the village for people to take the weight off their feet, usually under a shady tree.

"Oh I sometimes think jealousy could be a motive, but I can't say I remember any of the girls going out with any other chaps, although there was a lot of chopping and changing that went on, but perhaps I can check that out." Sarah couldn't help it "One of them will be easy won't it?" Gerry ignored that remark and posed another possibility "What about their own father, John Tremayne? I don't think he could be all that pleased, when and IF he discovered that his sons were having to get married to these pregnant village girls." Sarah cut in on Gerry's ruminations "That could also apply to the girls' parents, too." Gerry had to agree that it had possibilities but he didn't want to go along the route. "We are theoretically widening the situation now, but I know them all, and don't think it is at all possible, but then you never know, perhaps the disappointed fathers got together and decided to act as a group."

Gerry was now reminded of a conversation he once had with Boucher. He had been told that the perpetrator doesn't always look the part. Very often murderers are unique individuals, in fact most murderers do not look the same. The next one is always different from the one before.

Sarah was beginning to understand how complicated these village murders were, and the more she got to know, the more confused and frustrated she became. "It seems to me, Gerry, that there could be more than one murderer. Seems as if there were several people who had reasons to extremely dislike the Tremaynes, but not really enough to murder. Perhaps it's proving too difficult, even for Scotland Yard, because there is more than one perpetrator?" Gerry was more than slightly surprised at Sarah's contribution.

"There is also another common link that all the bodies were found in water. So suppose that after the first death in the sea, the rest were deliberately placed in water to infer that there was just one crazy killer. In fact I'm beginning to think there has got to be more than one. If there was a particular one, perhaps he or she could have had an accomplice?"

"Mr Boucher always told me, the murderers very often are not crazy. They're smart.

"Mother's last remark about all the money the Tremaynes owed could also be a lead."

The sun was setting., sinking nearer and nearer towards the horizon in a bright deep orange glow.

"Your mother mentioned tractors, Gerry. What was that all about?"

Gerry looked surprised at the sudden question. "Oh, it's to do with a couple of Brummies who suddenly appeared in the village, rented what was no more than a shack. As I remember them, never had proper jobs, but collected unemployment allowances, just mucked about with mending and repairing the few cars that there were in the village at that time. They were also trying to introduce tractors to the local farmers and they somehow got the Tremaynes involved."

Sarah had not heard much about these characters so she presumed they did not figure in the Tremayne saga. "It's a wonder no one tried to involve them, isn't it? Being strangers to Trehorra and apparently not too popular."

Gerry looked thoughtful. "Do you know, Sarah, there was one terrifying incident I remember now. Grandad Tremayne was driving an old tractor, which the Pascoes had loaned to them.

"He was driving it through the village like a madman. Apart from nearly killing himself, he almost ran over a dozen other locals, me included."

"What happened to him?"

Sarah looked horrified.

"Oh, nothing that I recall. Of course, he should not really have been driving the thing at all. Apparently the brakes had been tampered with or something, and as one of the younger Tremaynes always drove the tractor, it was thought, it wasn't Grandad they wanted to kill."

Sarah was so surprised that Gerry or anyone had not followed that story up. "Good God, Gerry, didn't it occur to you that the old man Tremayne might have been seeking revenge? I did, before I heard the brakes had been tampered with." She then reminded Gerry of his last remark to his mother.

"Tractors and horses are a long, long way from murder."

Gerry seemed slightly embarrassed. "Sarah, you might have something there. I really meant to follow up the tractor story, from a different point of view, but I was only a part-time reporter then. It's not too late though. I'll ring Vanstock." He looked at his watch, "We'd better get going, remember I promised to present those boy scout awards tonight."

"Oh Gerry, have we really got to go?" Sarah moaned "I'm so tired."

"I promise you this will be my last appointment."

"Well it had better be. Why is it so damned important?"

"Don't you remember I promised Douglas Salmond I would present the scouts awards, as a sort of appreciation for his hospitality." Sarah interrupted "No I don't remember, and I don't suppose it's anything to do with this Tremayne saga then?"

"I suppose I'll have to change. Who'll be there anyway?"

"Oh I don't know, just the parents of the scouts and a few of the patrons, some of the parish council, you know those sort of people." He could sense a change in her attitude recently and repeated "This occasion is no 'big deal' and I can guarantee you the name Tremayne will not even be mentioned."

"That's a relief, because it has seemed as if you are only here to re-hash the stories that got you to London in the first place."

Gerry seized the opportunity to lighten this conversation. "That's one thing I'm thankful for, wouldn't have met you would I, if I hadn't got the job with the Express!"

Mrs Halford was waiting for them. "Will you have a cup of tea and a bite to eat before going to the vicarage, I don't suppose there will be a lot to eat there will there Gerry?"

Sarah was still disgruntled about going. "Thanks, that'll be nice, I still don't know why Gerry wants us to go." "Oh it will be a change, for you dear, and he'll forget all about that Tremayne stuff."

"Yes, I suppose that'll be something to be thankful for, I've just about had enough of that."

Chapter 36

Gerry could see a minor storm ahead if he was not careful. He had made two quick phone calls and was delighted to know the newspaper offer was still on. He got up, smiling, "We've got to get our skates on or we'll be late for the presentations. I'll just give Bugannon a quick call." He turned to Sarah, "while you get ready."

Sarah replied, "I really don't want to go," but with an air of resignation she slowly went up the stairs. Gerry was soon put though to the inspector. "Hello, Mr Bugannon." "Hello, young man, back on your old beat eh?" "Not by choice, sir." Bugannon was quickly to the point. "Vanstock has told me you questioned him about the Tremaynes' tractor."

"Yes, sir, I wondered if there had been a follow-up after that drive through the village." "Certainly we did. Our assessment of the brakes damage was the same as John Taylor's, and the Pascoes swore they were in perfect condition when they left the machine early the previous evening."

"I was thinking, if you didn't find anything wrong with the Pascoes' story, do you think that old man Tremayne was trying to have a bit of his own back on the village?"

"No, no, no," Bugannon was positive. "Don't be ridiculous, the brakes were dodgy all right and they had been tampered with, but not by the Pascoes. No-one was hurt in the incident so we moved on. There were more important matters to deal with at the time, but you're welcome to dig if you wish. In my opinion it would be a worthless exercise, you must know that the

Pascoes were using the Tremaynes to promote tractors in the area, so they would hardly be likely to damage the brakes would they?"

"I guess you're right, there, Mr Bugannon, but thanks for the information. "Any time, Halford, any time." Gerry hung up the phone. "That's another full stop," thought Gerry. They were at the vicarage entrance as Gerry broke the silence. "I promise this will be it, no more interviews or investigations." Sarah just nodded, but didn't believe him. Before she could say anything in reply, both Douglas Salmond and Eric Bowering were there ready to greet them.

"So glad you've agreed to do this Gerry," beamed Douglas while Eric Bowering gallantly took Sarah's coat. All the pleasantries over, they entered the lounge, to be quickly greeted by Fiona Bowering, offering them glasses of sherry. "I'll need a couple of these before the presentations, as I think Douglas is expecting me to say a few words." The parson's wife smiled somewhat sympathetically. "Being in your profession, Gerry, I suppose you'd rather write them, wouldn't you?" Gerry didn't reply to that remark, put his arm on Sarah's shoulder guided her farther into the room. "Think we'd better mix a bit, Mrs Bowering." Sarah took her glass of sherry, shrugged her shoulders. "OK, if you must, Gerry, but I'm sticking close to you, so don't wander about away from me." She didn't appreciate the fact that the villagers, men, women, and boy scouts alike all wanted to get close to Gerry. She was thinking one of them was a murderer, perhaps two or three! One asked him for his autograph, so Sarah held his glass of sherry, didn't attempt to return it to him. She just smiled, mouthed "Cheers" and emptied the glass in one gulp!

Surprisingly almost all the village VIPs were there and a lot of not so VIPs The bearded Petherick Carnack was all dressed up in his "Sunday best". Close to him was his draughts buddy Dixie Dixon. Even Serina Smith had managed to get a night off from looking after her mother. She was caressing a glass of sherry, and surprisingly talking to Serina was the ever pompous Carlton-Ward and Eric Bowering. Even the rascal Pascoe twins were there trying to avoid getting too close to ex-policeman Vanstock. Apparently, they had become patrons of the Trehorra scouts. The large lounge was no way suitable to hold all the guests as well as the scouts.

It was a considerable crush with some people spilling outside the room. They all turned, and shuffled to look at Douglas Salmond as he stood on a stool to make himself visible. He introduced the occasion. "Ladies and gentlemen, thank you for coming and I do apologise for the lack of space, but the church hall had been booked ages ago, so I thought rather than cancel the occasion and disappoint the boys it would be appropriate to have the presentation here, particularly as we have the founder of the 1st Trehorra scout group here, your previous vicar, Eric Bowering." There was generous applause. "So, with no more ado, to present the awards, here is Gerry Halford, who was a member of the 1st Trehorra scouts and now a well known crime reporter on the London Express." A small ripple of applause and shouts of "Hear, hear" greeted this announcement. Sarah seemed more relaxed as "Adonis" John Taylor joined them.

Gerry squeezed through to stand beside Douglas Salmond and proceeded to present the awards to the smiling youngsters. The boys responded with a smart click of the heels and a precise boy scout salute. Douglas

Salmond gave each boy a few words of praise and encouragement. Gerry kept his words to a minimum. He thanked everyone with a few patronising phrases, stepped down from the makeshift dais. He intended to make straight for Sarah, and sidle out quietly. His mother managed to squeeze through a group and whispered "That was very nice, Gerald."

Gerry was looking for Sarah "Where is she? I thought she'd be with you."

"The last time I saw her she was with John Taylor, I can't even see him now though."

Gerry scanned through the crowded room but couldn't see Sarah or John Taylor. "Perhaps she's gone to the ladies' room," Mrs Halford suggested. "Of course, Mother, why didn't I think of that, it's upstairs isn't it? I'll go and collect her, I've promised to take her home straight after the presentations. See you later Mum." He thought for a moment how strange Taylor nor Sarah could be seen and raced up the carpeted dimly lit staircase, towards the bathroom. He bumped with Annie Hambly half way up, thought of retreating back to the bottom of the stairs, but decided to squeeze past the middle-aged rather plump post mistress. "Don't you know it's unlucky to pass on the stairs young man?" Gerry was nearly at the top by this time" "I didn't think you'd believe that old rubbish, Miss Hambly, by the way did you see Sarah up there by any chance?" "No I didn't" She turned into the still crowded room where the conversations were getting louder and louder, as the sherry had given way stronger stuff.

Gerry hurried along the landing lightly tapped on the bathroom door, "Sarah are you in there,

Sarah?" There was no reply. "Are you all right?" He was cautiously opening the bathroom door, when BANG! He managed to blurt out "What the hell!" He suddenly saw stars, the bathroom door looked decidedly wobbly as the concerned reporter slumped to the floor.

Chapter 37

"Where in the hell am I?" He was in a sitting position on some bare boards. His lips were dry, he was scratching his head and raking his fingers through his hair as if to get some relief. He was gradually gaining consciousness He had no idea of how long he had been knocked out, but he was gradually getting used to the darkness when he heard a soft moan from nearby. He couldn't guess how near, but he thought he recognised the sound "Sarah! What the hell is going on?" His gaze swept towards what he thought was a fireplace "But in a bathroom? Cannot be," he thought. By squinting he thought he could see the outline of Sarah's figure, also in a sitting position. He tried to lift himself up, but it was too painful. Rain seemed to be hitting the glass roof of wherever they were. The drops were monotonous, the silence was frightening. Sarah had managed to shuffle over nearer to him. Gerry's head was still swimming. "I feel as if I've been hit by a brick wall, and I've no idea where we are. Are you OK, Sarah?" "No, I'm not OK, and all I want to do now is get out of here. No doubt this is linked to those damned Tremaynes. You'll have to forget it, cheque or no cheque."

Gerry could now distinguish a door. "I wonder if it will open, if it doesn't, perhaps if we bang on it hard enough, someone will hear us." They both managed to struggle to their feet. Still unsteady they put their shoulders to the door, "OK, Sarah, on a count of three. One, two, three. They tried as hard as they could. Sarah was out of breath. "It's no good, these doors are too solid." They both stood back, in need of a breather. Sarah put her ear to the door. "Listen, I'm sure there's someone out there." She was scared now. Gerry also felt none too brave. Their banging on the door had attracted someone, but who? Sarah looked through a small crack in the bottom of the door. She looked more closely. "I can see a pair of black boots. I can't believe this is happening in a vicarage. Who the hell can they belong to, that is if we are still in the bloody vicarage?"

There was a voice from outside the door. "Hold on a minute and I'll get you out," the voice said almost in a whisper. "Oh my God!" gasped Gerry, "It's Tom Ward!"

"I knew it," said Sarah, "I knew all along he was a weirdo."

"Never mind that now, Sarah." Gerry turned towards the crack in the door. "Hurry up, Tom, for God's sake."

It took only a couple of minutes but seemed like a lifetime to the frightened twosome. They were soon brushing dust and cobwebs from their clothes and looking around, still dazed and attempting to get their bearings. "Come on you two," Tom's face was as white as chalk, "let's get out of here." Gerry was quickly regaining some sort of normality.

Enough to put a protective arm around Sarah who had suddenly gone very quiet. They were being carefully guided over some sort of pastureland. Gerry still hadn't a clue as to where they were. Tom Ward was silent as he kept himself in front of them. He was half-walking half-jogging, until he came to a full stop at what was a cast-iron "kissing-gate", many of which are dotted around the Cornish cliffs. Tom decided to go through first, then turned to the surprised bedraggled pair and, surprisingly for him, with a sweep of his arm, exclaimed in a sort of triumphant voice "You know what you're supposed to do now!" Sarah looked vague. Gerry knew what the tinker's son meant, but was surprised as Tom was not known to have much of a sense of humour. He turned around to Sarah "This is supposed to be a kissing gate" but Sarah was definitely not in the mood for these silly Cornish "routines". Tom quickly opened the gate for them. "You knows where you be then now" and with that he disappeared into the darkness with his own particular style of jogging. Sarah was still shaking all over. "That's it, Gerry Halford, I'm certainly getting out of Trehorra now, and I won't be coming back in a hurry." As if to confirm her feelings, she added, "You can stay as long as you damned well like, a big cheque or no cheque at all."

Chapter 38

The next morning, Gerry was up long before his mother, partly because he had had a sleepless night, and his head was still aching. The phone rang and he literally dragged himself to it.

"Call for you, from London," the weary Anny Hambly mumbled. Gerry managed to get out "Thanks" and whilst being connected wondered who the hell this could be. Couldn't be Boucher. He wouldn't be in a office this early, so he did not know what or who to expect, but surprise, surprise, it was Boucher! Before Gerry could get one word in Boucher was quickly in with not even a "Good Morning". "Is that you Gerry?" and before he could answer Boucher was saying "Great stuff, Gerry, great stuff, got your latest copy through, very very interesting reading too, the editor wants us to move and move quickly." Gerry stuttered, "but, but Mr Boucher." His boss didn't seem to hear him. "Gerry we've got to get our finger out, the editor wants us to produce a dossier for Scotland Yard." Not stopping for a breath it seemed, Boucher continued "We've got to move fast, so how about breaking your honeymoon for a few hours, have a word with the old man Tremayne and the father of those boys." Gerry was flabbergasted, to say the least, and was finding it difficult to intervene ."But . . . but, Mr Bouch. . ." There was no stopping Boucher. "I know it may be difficult, son but according to my notes and yours, these two haven't spoken a "dicky-bird" to anyone at length have they?"

Gerry was still stunned by his previous night's experience, and was dying to let Boucher know about it and to let him know he wanted OUT of the Tremaynes, but the crime editor rattled on. "I've cleared the stuff you sent, Gerry. We can go positive on the first Tremayne boy and the one who was never seen at the rally point, but the one that was found by the local bobby in the horse-trough is another story."

"But, but Mr Boucher . . ." The Londoner, however, was still not listening to Gerry. "Your suspicion about the second chappie is OK. But they have to have more than a suspicion, before they can get permission to exhume a body. "That bit of evidence you got from the gravedigger may not be enough, so we'll keep that on file for now. If your thinking turns out to be wrong, Gerry, it would be serious and in addition we would be the laughing stock of the whole of Fleet Street. Facts are what we require, we have to have facts."

Gerry was getting "steamed up" himself by this time and was at last able to jump in. "If you want facts, Mr B, you can bloody well have some." He proceeded to relate to Boucher his and Sarah's previous night's experiences.

The crime editor wasn't listening, almost ignoring Gerry's story except to say it would make "damned good copy". He simply passed it off with "Well you're dealing with damned devious people down there, Gerry, what can you expect, after four or five unsolved murders?"

Gerry was dumbfounded, he knew he was losing it now. "Expect? I know what to expect all right. I'll expect a cheque and a bloody big one, that's if I am to carry on with this stinking business. Not only that, Sarah will want one as well, as now she is involved." Boucher WAS listening now. "Of course you'll get a big cheque, and compensation for Sarah too, but you must finish the job first. I'll guarantee it myself. Now take my advice, son, and get out to see the senior Tremaynes. I find it very odd that they haven't spoken publicly to anyone yet. I know you'll have to stay on longer. "My wife isn't going to like that, she's already completely fed up with those bloody Tremaynes and to tell you the truth, Mr B, so am I, and I never thought I'd ever say that." "Tell her it's all a part of the job and you'll be on expenses from now until the job is finished down there, now get cracking Gerry". With that the phone went dead.

Sarah had now arrived downstairs, looking very much the worse for her experience the night before. "From what I gathered, Gerry, I assume you've been persuaded to carry on this hopeless business. Personally I don't think you'll ever do it. Why don't you and that horrible Mr Boucher give up trying to do what Scotland Yard couldn't do? Pack it in, Gerry, it's history now."

It had been a quiet day and in the evening Sarah got her head stuck into a book. "Not long to go" she was thinking. Mrs Halford discreetly pretended to snooze. It looked like a perfect quiet evening in the snug little cottage. They had had a very tasty dinner, Gerry's favourite

– shepherd's pie, followed by some raspberry jelly, with an obligatory dollop of Cornish clotted cream.

Gerry as usual was scrutinising and scribbling away in his notebook, but there was an "atmosphere."

Chapter 39

It was getting on for 10pm. "Was that a knock at the door?" Sarah looked up from her book, a startled look on her face. Gerry put down his pencil and walked to the door. He opened it just a fraction. On recognising the caller, he opened the door "Why if it isn't John, John Stephens."

"Goodness me, John, this is a bit late for a visit isn't it? Come on in."

"I can't stay, Gerry." John was obviously nervous. "I wanted to tell you something before you – before you go back to London, you ARE going back aren't you?"

"Oh, I'm here for a while, yet," Gerry said softly stepping outside and closing the door behind him. "Yes I'll be going back all right but if it's important, John, you can tell me now." Gerry had certainly not forgotten that young John had discovered the body of Colin Tremayne in the horse trough, and he may have something to offer."

John's nerves were obviously on edge. "Well, I wanted to show you something as well." John looked over his shoulder and in almost a whisper, "It's about when I found Colin Tremayne."

"Are you sure you won't come in?"

"I can't. I've been to scouts and I'm late already."

To say that Gerry was just curious would be to tell a lie.

"I'd better get going now." John took a step backwards.

"I'll walk back with you, John. If it's about the Tremaynes, perhaps I can help you or perhaps you can help me."

"I've never told anybody about this, but I did see Mr Bowering in his car coming away from St Minerva that morning."

Gerry was surprised and yet wasn't surprised. He certainly didn't want to convey his inner excitement at this bit of news. "Well, that figures, John, he had probably taken Mrs Bowering to the church. She was getting it ready for that big funeral, remember?"

John kept walking nervously. "Yes, I remember all that, but the scout master told me I wasn't to tell anyone."

"When did he tell you that?"

"We were on a swimming test that day. I was a bit late. All the other scouts were already there and he wanted to know why I was so late. I told him about finding Colin Tremayne's body and taking the policeman there.

"The scout master took me on one side when we got to Penporth and asked me if I was sure it was a Tremayne boy."

Gerry, attentive now, continued to walk down the darkened street with John. "What did you say then, John?"

251

"Well, I thought the scout master could have seen him in the trough, and I said, 'Didn't you see him, sir?' He said, 'No, I didn't, and I didn't see you either.' Then he said, 'and you didn't see me.' I answered, 'But I did, sir'. Then he got a bit stroppy. 'You want that swimming badge, patrol leader Stephens?' Of course, I said, 'Yes, sir," He patted me on the back and then said again, 'You did not see me, understand, patrol leader Stephens, your scout's honour.' And he made me say, 'Yes, sir, scout's honour.'"

"So did you go through with your tests?"

"Yes, but I didn't do very well."

Gerry could see what was coming. "But you got your badge?"

"Yes, I did. And nobody knows except you now, Gerry. You won't tell anybody, will you?"

"Of course I won't if you say so, John." Gerry thought that he had to say that but didn't know whether he could or not. "But tell me, John, why have you kept it to yourself until now?"

They had now arrived at John's house and his mother, who suffered from arthritis, had already gone upstairs to bed.

John picked up his key from under an ornamental green frog, and put it quietly into the lock. He turned back to Gerry, "It's because I received a message this morning it was pushed under the door and my mother said I ought to show it to you."

"Who was it from then?"

"That's it, Gerry, it was unsigned. Mother wouldn't let me take it to school. I'll show it to you tomorrow. It is all about the Tremaynes."

"I'll call tomorrow then."

"I'll be at school all day and then I'm going out fishing but I could show you after."

"Yes, okay. That'll have to do then."

John looked very relieved. Gerry wasn't too pleased "You'll be sure to have the letter?"

"Yes I will. We'll be back about 6 o'clock at number two quay."

"Thanks, John. Good night. I'll see you tomorrow then."

"Thank you, Gerry." John stood at the open door, turned to Gerry, and in almost a whisper, "My mother said I might get that reward offered by the paper." If the letter was unsigned Gerry couldn't see its relevance but realised he had to encourage the boy. "Yes, you could, John, yes, you could. I'll see you tomorrow then." He walked back to his own cottage.

Sarah was waiting at the door and greeted Gerry with a stern look. "And what was that all about? Those Tremaynes, no doubt."

Mrs Halford had discreetly already retired to bed.

"I'll tell you later," Gerry promised. "But the boy has got something which is interesting."

"Maybe it is, but if you ask me you are in something too deep for your own good and mine for that matter. I would have thought you've had enough, because I certainly have."

Gerry didn't seem to be listening.

"Now look, Sarah, we have a nice day out planned for tomorrow, any mention of the Tremaynes will be banned." Gerry anticipated this would pacify Sarah. How wrong he was.

Chapter 40

This was the day out Gerry had promised Sarah and his mother. He planned to show them some of the ancient monuments and castles which Cornwall had in plenty. Although now he really couldn't spare the time he had pre-arranged the trip with John Taylor and despite the nice sunny day, Gerry was wary of what could be an "atmosphere", and was somewhat surprised at how bright Sarah was.

As always the taxi man was right on time, calling at the Halford cottage immediately after their breakfast. He was driving his big saloon this time. The trip took them first of all to King Arthur's 12th Century castle up on the North Cornish coast. Then it was over the barren Bawdry Moors. Jamaica Inn was another famous landmark, which had to be included. Down in the south-west of the county, they were taken over the splendid Pendennis Castle at the seaside town of Falmouth. Although Gerry noticed Sarah's smiling reaction to John Taylor's remarks, she and the strangely quiet Mrs Halford were not showing much response to his running commentary, such as "That castle was built in King Henry VIII's reign." Realising the ladies were not responding, John turned to Gerry and suggested they should go to a little known flower garden. "Do you know where I mean?"

"A good idea, John." The driver immediately swung the car sharply to the left. "There is a short cut up here." He knew the area like the back of his hand. "I suppose you mean Giverny, don't you?" He weaved his way around a few narrow country lanes and soon arrived at the Giverny. The Giverny Gardens were in the tiny village of Trelorne. Here, Gerry thought Sarah would snap out of her gloomy mood towards him.

The entrance to the gardens had a fantastic accumulation of everything from laurels, ferns, even some Bella Donna lilies with a beautiful big screen of fuchsias. Further on were plum trees, apple trees, exotic palm trees, cacti, and even a cacao tree. Sarah was in her element. There were plants and bushes, even grass, from all over the world, and she was deliberately walking alongside John who was leading the way.

During the walk-through, Gerry's mum also brightened up, and was enjoying the description of the bright-coloured flower gardens much more than Gerry's description of Cornish history. This highly enjoyable garden visit was over all too quickly for the ladies, especially as John Taylor expressed a quite surprising knowledge of the horticultural world. It was time to head back to Trehorra, all too soon for Sarah, which was all too obvious to Gerry.

John Taylor had been dying to get Gerry on his own and ask him about the Tremayne murder mysteries. Because, like the rest of the village, he too had heard that Gerry's appearance in Trehorra meant that the whole thing was being aired again, but he sensed all was not well with the young Halfords and wisely kept quiet.

They arrived back in the village as the evening was closing in. Gerry was anxious to keep his appointment with John Stephens. "I'll be back for dinner later," he called to his mother and Sarah as they got out of the car.

"Don't be late," shouted Mrs Halford. Sarah ignored him.

Gerry had arranged for John Taylor to drop him near the harbour. "Here you are then, will this do?" John Taylor spoke at last. "Hey, Gerry, I wanted a word with you."

Gerry jumped out of the car. "Thanks, but I can't stop now," he managed to say, and ran along the rocky path towards the quay where he had promised to meet John Stephens. He didn't hear Taylor shouting. "But it's important, Gerry."

It was getting darker by this time and Gerry knew that as soon as the sun disappeared behind the overhanging cliffs on the harbour, it would become even darker.

As he approached the quay side, he thought he saw two shadowy figures hurrying away on the cobbled path on the other side of the quay but paid no attention to it. There was always someone around. Breathless by now he was sure he had arrived at quay number two in time, but there was no John Stephens.

He peered through the now semi-darkness. He could see no one and suddenly thought he could hear a stifled, gurgly cry. Looking even more closely at where the sound was coming from, it was definitely a pleading cry. It was bit muffled but sounded like "Help! Help!"

Stepping right on the edge of the quay, Gerry could just make out what he thought was a white arm several yards away with its outstretched fingers coming out of the black seaweedy water. There was only one option for Gerry.

He threw off his jacket, took off his shoes, jumped into the uninviting harbour water, and swam towards the arm which was momentarily disappearing and surfacing alternately.

As he got near he could see it was John Stephens. The boy's arms were flailing wildly in desperation now. Gerry was scared. As soon as he got close to the boy, the youngster grabbed Gerry's arm in a vice-like grip, so tight that Gerry knew he wasn't going to let go. So he swam the breast stroke with one arm, the other towing the panic-stricken boy behind him.

John Stephens looked bizarre with his head covered in seaweed and some hanging over his face. He was clinging to Gerry for dear life.

As soon as he had pulled John Stephens on to the wet cobbled stones, he did what he could remember of his lifesaving lessons in the scouts. He turned him on to his stomach and attempted to pump out some of the seawater that the boy had swallowed. He seemed to be recovering, but very slowly.

After John had been violently sick, Gerry asked "How the hell did you get in there?"

Before John could answer, a booming voice yelled, "What the hell's up 'ere then?" It belonged to Jim Proctor, who had taken John out fishing. By a strange coincidence, Jim was the man who had discovered the body of the first Tremayne in the sea off Black Cliffs a few years previously. He had been making sure his boat was safely moored while John had been left to tidy up the boat. Jim held up an ancient fisherman's lantern to get a clearer look at the scene. Darkness was creeping in fast now. The evening was very cool and Gerry was shivering. "Don't know yet, Mr Proctor. I had promised to meet him here. Thought I saw two people running away, then I saw John in the water, He was struggling so I jumped towards him and sort of dragged him out."

Jim Proctor bent his long lean bony frame down close to John. "Are you all right, boy? 'Cause you don't look so good.". John was still lying down and shaking and shivering.

The old fisherman took off his outer jacket and wrapped it around the boy. He turned to Gerry "He's in a bad way Gerry and you don't look so good either. So you saw those two people was runnin' away?"

Gerry was supporting John in a sitting position, "Yes, I did, but didn't pay any attention to them." He was thinking that violence seemed to be the name of the game now and thinking of his vicarage experience, was doubting if a cheque, however big, was worth pursuing this Tremayne saga. Suddenly the youngster's head dropped and he fell backwards in a dead faint. "Think we'd better get him in the warm."

"We'll take him up to my house, just up the hill, my missus will be in."

An alarmed Mrs Proctor opened the door. "Whatever has happened?" she asked, as she saw her husband and Gerry carrying the boy inside. John was blue in the face and still shivering as they laid him gently on to the sofa. Meanwhile, Mrs Proctor had got a blanket which they wrapped around him. John was now sipping some warm tea and Jim Proctor suggested that they get him to the Cottage Hospital at nearby Poliggan. Gerry guessed that John Taylor would still be in his garage, so it wasn't long before the dependable taxi man arrived at the fisherman's cottage. Jim offered to go with them, but Gerry was almost back to normal.

"That's OK, Mr Proctor, I'll go with him. Will you phone my mother, tell her I'll' be a bit late and also Mrs Stephens. Tell her not to worry, we're only taking John as a precaution." The boy was changing colour now, he was losing the blueness, but was still deathly pale. A few minutes into journey he half opened his eyes. "Have you got my school bag Gerry?" John was forcing himself to speak. "Can't remember seeing it John, don't worry about it."

"That letter was in there, the one my mother wanted you to look at."

Gerry was still concerned, as John Stephens closed his eyes. "Mr Proctor was there, and he probably picked it up." John half opened his eyes again and whispered, "It's about the Tremaynes" he managed to get out before he closed his eyes "Yes I know, don't worry about it."

Upon arrival at the hospital, Taylor and Gerry got their patient inside and he was taken straight to a bed. Gerry, having given the receptionist all the details, was allowed to leave after a doctor had said the boy was not in any danger, but they would keep him in overnight. On the way back to Trehorra John Taylor became unusually talkative. He was asking Gerry a virtual barrage of questions, all about the Tremaynes. "Were Scotland Yard still interested?

He wanted to know how far Gerry had got towards solving anything? Was he just interested in all the rewards still on offer? He went on to ask some very personal questions regarding Sarah. For once Gerry was non-committal. He was beginning to think that Sarah was getting a little too friendly with John, whose reputation with young ladies visiting Trehorra Gerry was well aware of. Also crossing his mind was Sarah's suggestion that he was out of his depth with these murder investigations.

"I've changed my mind," he suddenly blurted out. "Take me straight home." There was no point in returning to the harbour for John Stephens's satchel. Maybe he would be inviting more trouble as he remembered those two shadowy figures he had seen prior to discovering John Stephens in the harbour sea.

Neither his mother nor Sarah had waited up for him, so he turned out the lamp which had been left on low for him, blew down the globe to make sure the wick wasn't still alight, and tip-toed quietly up the stairs to his bedroom. Sarah pretended to be asleep, and Gerry, now fatigued, simply sank into the soft cosy feather mattress. Strangely enough his last thoughts were not of John Stephens or the Tremaynes, but were about John Taylor's apparent interest in Sarah.

Chapter 41

The couple's journey to Drewstone Railway Station was taken in almost complete silence. Gerry's mind was torn. Should he stay and finally attempt to put the Tremayne saga to sleep, or should he return with his new wife Sarah on the long journey back to London.

There were only a few isolated groups of twos and threes on what was known as the 'up' platform when John Taylor dropped them off. The London train was right on time. John placed Sarah's luggage into an empty carriage and, with Gerry watching closely, he gave Sarah a far too friendly hug and said softly "Please come again."

For the want of something to say Gerry mumbled "What a pity you can't stay." He tried to hold her close and give a good-bye hug, but she resisted. "You must be joking, Gerry Halford, don't you think it's a pity YOU have GOT to stay. In any case I've got to get back now and I don't want to stay another minute in Trehorra, thank you." She tried to remain cool, but was lost for the right words. Deep down she could understand Gerry wanting to solve those awful murders, because of the huge monetary rewards he would get, but had come to the conclusion that it was not only going to be an awful waste of time, but far too dangerous now.

Gerry took a step back from the train, as it was about to move off. Sarah leaned out of the window. "You've made a choice, Gerry, and I hope it's the right one, but I can tell you now it . . ." The guard's whistle drowned the rest of her words, and Gerry had no idea what she had said. Sarah simply sank back into her seat and just stared into space. To say it was a disappointing end to what was supposed to be a holiday-cum-honeymoon, was as far away from the truth as it could be. It really had turned out to be a disastrous first visit to Cornwall for her. Her London friends were not going to believe what she had been through.

John Taylor had patiently waited for Gerry to return to the car. "Looks like you're staying on then," he commented. "Thought you would have called it a day on all that Tremayne stuff, and returned with your wife."

The young reporter did not feel like making conversation, so he just said, "Looks like I'll have to soon. I'll give it a couple of days or so and if I don't make any headway I'll have to get back to London." Taylor nodded his head and said surprisingly "Maybe I can give you a bit of help!"

Gerry had noticed a sort of brightness in Taylor's voice.

"If you can, John, I'm all ears. I don't know how much time I can spend on it though but if you can help, please do."

"Say if I told you I know who doctored the brakes of Tremayne's old tractor?"

"You mean you know who it was?" Gerry had momentarily forgotten Sarah was on the London train. He realised if he'd got to get to the bottom of these Tremayne murders, then listening to locals like Taylor was as good a way as any.

"Now, I don't want my name mentioned, if it turns out to be right – or wrong, for that matter." John

Taylor reminded Gerry, "I live here and I have a business to run, you know. Like most of the folk around here."

He was playing safe, Gerry thought, and that was natural, he supposed. "Of course it won't, but I have some ideas myself, John. So don't tell me you think it was the Pascoes, for I don't think they had anything to do with it."

"Well, they did cross my mind," taxi man Taylor was looking straight ahead, "but I think it was Petherick Carnack who did it, but I keep wondering why."

Gerry did not give away the fact that he thought Petherick Carnack had a motive, so he let John Taylor keep talking.

"I found a broken pipe in that ol' tractor engine." Gerry was disappointed with Taylor's suggestion. "I know that, John, it was a brake pipe, wasn't it?" "No, no, not that sort of pipe, it was a clay smoking pipe." "I never thought anything about it at the time, thinking it was old Grandad Tremayne's, it was only when Petherick Carnack, some time later came into my shop for some cigarettes, that made me think otherwise. I just mentioned to him had he given up smoking a pipe, and he laughed. 'Only for a while,' he said and he sort of searched his pockets, 'just till I find me pipe'". Gerry was getting interested now. "That's it," he thought. He knew Carnack had a motive, but what about opportunity?

Another question to be answered: The Police had ignored the tractor incident, because no-one was killed, no-one was even hurt, so if it was Petherick who meddled with the brakes, the plan did not work. "I'll have to think about that John. If there is anything else that crosses your mind, let me know." The taxi man looked relieved that he had got that off his chest. Gerry gave him a generous tip, not always expected but appreciated by the taxi man. Gerry winked his eye "If there's any more bits of info, you know where I am". "Thank you, Gerry, but keep my name out of it won't you, I've got a living to make here in Trehorra you know, and by the way I do hope your wife changes her mind and will return some time." Gerry appeared not to notice John's remark. He spent the rest of the day out at Trewarmett, questioning the Tremaynes, but it was like getting blood out of a stone. It was late that night before he was satisfied he could find no more to send to Boucher. No phone call from Sarah so he went to bed sad and disillusioned. And full of self doubt now, despite the glimmer of a clue from John Taylor regarding Petherick Carnack. However, at the back of his mind he couldn't help thinking of the number of times the taxi owner had mentioned Sarah. Surely there was no need to be jealous?

Chapter 42

Oblivious to the fact that their tiny village had been making national headlines, the Trehorra churchgoers turned up in more than usual numbers to the traditional final early morning service of the summer season which was always held at St Minerva Church.

The service was being conducted by past vicar, Eric Bowering, who was standing in for the Reverend Douglas Salmond. The temporary return of Parson Bowering to the parish church had helped to increase the congregation. There was a full choir and the church was practically full of men and women in almost equal numbers, plus a few children.

Although the end of his tenure had coincided with the now almost historic Tremayne murders, parishioners were looking forward to hearing their old vicar preach. His sermons were not only interesting, to say the least, but were always extremely straightforward and always to the point.

Vicar Bowering always called a spade a spade. He was never one to hold back. He would refer to names if he thought it necessary. Today was no different. His sermon included references to the past, to his occupancy when he had been happy to serve the people of Trehorra.

After his introductory welcome, he went on to say, "Despite the one tragic period during my years in Trehorra, I hope you think as I do, that when I left the village, it was a better, more God-fearing place than when I arrived. I am so grateful to your new reverend, Douglas Salmond, for allowing me to conduct today's service. I know that all your lives here have changed dramatically since the death of your lord of the manor, Stanley Bolitho, and a lot of you have had to endure great hardships since that sad day. We must not forget as well that there was the appalling loss of lives in a local farming family not far from this very church. I am sure you are all very unhappy that there has been no success in apprehending the perpetrators of those unlawful wicked and senseless murders."

At this sad reminder of the Tremayne murders, there was a murmuring, too muffled and indistinct to assess whether they were agreeing or not. People did look at each other with several eyebrows being raised, and there were several looks in Gerry's direction. Why an earth was Bowering bringing that sad period up? Surely this was a bit much for a church sermon, even for the outspoken Vicar Bowering.

He looked up from his notes, which were resting on the thick church Bible. He raised his hand to his forehead and simply stared over the heads of the congregation towards the ancient oak doors. The solid iron latch had clanged, as it fell back into the notch attached to the door post. Standing inside this door on a sort of granite dais, was none other than Police Constable Vanstock accompanied by men all around six foot tall, all dressed smartly in suits, with collars and black ties. Their leader gave a quick nod of his head and four of them moved swiftly down the three steps, following Vanstock who walked determinedly down the aisle.

They surrounded the pulpit. The leader, in an extremely low voice, spoke directly to the stunned preacher.

"Eric Bowering, I'm Chief Inspector Barnes of Scotland Yard, I have a warrant for your arrest and I arrest you Eric Balfour Bowering on suspicion of murder and must warn you that anything you say may be taken down and used in evidence against you. Please come with me."

For once in his lifetime, Eric Balfour Bowering was almost speechless. "Did I do something wrong?" he whispered, his head bowed, staring at the gold grey stone floor. He walked quietly out of the pulpit, his clerical robes flowing, surrounded on all sides by the men from London.

As they approached the church door, the tallest of those men hesitated on top of the three granite steps, turned around, and addressed the now bewildered, astounded congregation. "Please stay in your seats until we give you permission to leave. I would appreciate it if none of you attempts to obstruct my fellow officers, who will now need to speak to some of you." He nodded to the remaining men, and Vanstock.

There is no other silence as silent as a church silence. The congregation was over two hundred, and the stillness was more than the absence of any noise, it was an eerie silence. It was truly uncanny.

The history of St Minerva Church was full of strikingly odd happenings, unearthly stories, but it had seen nothing like this. The Scotland Yard men were following PC Vanstock, who was walking along the aisles scrutinising the astonished congregation, smiling at some, simply acknowledging others with a nod of his head. Most of the amazed villagers looked very nervous indeed. Some quiet whisperings were going on.

Vanstock, who was accompanied by the plain clothes detectives, stopped at the pew occupied by the Carnack family. He pointed out Petherick and the Yard men spoke quietly to him.

Petherick, who was on the outside of the pew, stepped obediently into the aisle. For practically the first time since his arrival in Trehorra, PC Vanstock was showing a lot of control. Next he directed the accompanying detectives to the Dixon pew. They nodded to Dixie to step into the aisle. Police Constable Vanstock wasn't finished yet, and he politely touched his helmet to none other than the vicar's wife, Mrs Fiona Bowering, and invited her to join them.

There were loud gasps of consternation as these three people, were escorted out of the church. Two of the most upstanding, popular Trehorrans and the wife of their most popular vicar walked with heads bowed slowly out through the old oak door of the church.

As soon as they had disappeared out into the still fresh morning air, a uniformed officer took his place at the top of the steps. "I am Inspector Bugannon. I am sorry that this traditional final service of the year at St Minerva church has been interrupted, but I can assure you that in time you will discover that it has been entirely necessary. We needed to speak to some of you.

"As soon as I say, I would like you to leave quietly. And I repeat we are very sorry that this final service of this year at St Minerva is now over. Thank you."

There were some uneasy mumbles and a buzz of mutterings by some of the remaining members of the congregation. They still could not grasp the situation. Some of them had a slight suspicion of what was happening, but others were simply bewildered. In an attempt to defuse the awkward silence, the church organist had the presence of mind to play softly.

Widow Halford and Gerald Halford felt that some of the congregation were staring at them. As for the mother and her son, they both stood transfixed. Gerry thought he knew what this invasion of police officers was in aid of, but it was the speed of the action, the timing of it too, that certainly had surprised him. Surely this could not be the result of the reports he had been sending to Boucher? It wasn't like Scotland Yard to act with such swiftness. At the back of his mind, was the word 'dossier', but he dismissed this as he had no idea that his final contributions could be so swiftly transferred into a dossier, which he knew Boucher intended passing on to Scotland Yard. He also had no idea it had been already published that very morning. "If it had, it must have been pretty convincing for them to act so quickly," he thought to himself, and he dared not think of the consequences, if he had not got the facts correct. His curiosity got the better of him and he stepped into the aisle to ask one of the suited men what this was all about, but he was quietly ushered back to his pew.

Gerry, like the rest of the congregation, was feeling uneasy, though for differenet reasons. Inspector Bugannon was now joined by Police Constable Vanstock and still stood on the dais at the top of three granite steps leading to the now open old oak door that led into the churchyard.

Meanwhile, the cars containing the apparently arrested men and the one woman were worming their way through the narrow lanes to the main road out of Trehorra.

These were the biggest saloon cars ever seen in the village. The car containing Inspector Barnes and two more officers turned off the main road and headed for the village.

Upon reaching a small, whitewashed cottage standing back in a cul-de-sac just off the main street, the car stopped. Inspector Barnes and the other two men got out quickly. They knocked on the door and bowing their heads to get under the small cottage doorway, did not wait but walked straight into the always darkened interior belonging to Tom Ward senior, the village tinker.

After a few minutes, they emerged with the protesting son of Thomas Ward junior. With some difficulty, the detectives had to manoeuvre him into the rear of their car. The door slammed to. Inspector Barnes congratulated his men. "Good work, chaps." He issued instructions to the driver, "Over the moors now, son, we're on our way to Bawdry."

"I wonder if we'll see the Beast of Bawdry Moor," laughed the driver.

Inspector Barnes joined in the laughter. "Don't tell me you believe what you read in the Express."

The driver, a sergeant detective, answered "Well, not all of it, sir."

Tom Ward junior did not even smile. He wasn't that simple. He realised he was in a serious situation.

At Bawdry a special magistrates court had been assembled. The people arrested in Trehorra, Vicar Bowering, his wife Fiona, Petherick Carnack, Albert 'Dixie' Dixon, and Tom Ward junior, were joined by another man who had been previously brought in by Detective Sergeant Tripp. He was Rolland Davies, a traveller with the Barney Bamford funfair.

"Everything okay, Sergeant?" Inspector Barnes greeted his assistant.

"No problem at all, sir, Bamford was very helpful."

The magistrate, not too pleased with having his Sunday disturbed, did not take long to agree with the Yard request to have all these arrested persons remanded in custody for 48 hours on suspicion of aiding or abetting murder or attempted murder. It lasted only a few minutes.

The group of Scotland Yard detectives looked very pleased and relieved with their morning's work. They had travelled down from London during the night. It was now midday. They were obliged to stay until the 48-hour deadline was reached. No doubt the arrested persons would have obtained lawyers by then. So for now, all the Scotland Yard men wanted to do was relax. So they went down to the local police headquarters where they knew they could spend a few hours in peace before the press corps would arrive.

As soon as Inspector Bugannon allowed the people in the church to exit, Gerry could not wait to get out. He hurried back to the house, leaving his mother to walk home by herself.

Although he knew it was a Sunday, he immediately got on the phone to Boucher's office. No reply. The skeleton staff at the office had not seen him and were not expecting him. From Boucher's home number there was no reply.

Annie Hambly, the postmistress, who on Sundays was always in charge of the telephone switchboard at the small village post office, told Gerry she would keep trying Boucher's number. "Oh, and Gerry, were you responsible for that Tremayne stuff in today's Express, I can't believe that it's all true."

"Thanks a lot." Gerry was nervous. Not for long, however. No sooner had his mother arrived back breathless, the telephone rang. Gerry grabbed the phone. "Yes, Mrs Hambly."

The male voice at the other end of the line, "I don't know who Mrs Hambly is, young man, but this is certainly not the lady you were expecting."

Gerry put the earpiece to his left ear as if he couldn't believe what he was hearing in his right ear. "Mr Boucher! I've been trying to reach you. Where are you?"

The voice at the other end, "I'm right here in your own stamping ground, Gerry. I'm in Bawdry and I want you to get here as quick as you can. Things have moved quicker than I thought, Gerry, meet me outside the police station."

As always, John Taylor, not a churchgoer, was willing and was ready to take Gerry to Bawdry. It was surprising that there was not much conversation between Gerry and the taxi driver. Gerry was a bit too uptight. Taylor must have been suffering from the shock of the stories he had read in the Sunday newspaper which he passed on to Gerry to read.

He wanted to say "If it's true, it's great stuff" but all he said was, "I'm glad you kept my name out of it, let's keep it that way."

Strange, thought Gerry, but quickly dismissed Taylor's request from his mind. Boucher rushed over excitedly to Gerry as soon as he arrived at the Bawdry police station. "What a scoop, my boy, what a scoop!"

"Do you mean all this happened because of my reports?" "A lot of it anyway, my boy, but I put two and two together and the Yard made it FOUR."

Boucher took Gerry away from a group of journalists who were already assembling outside the police station. "Inspector Barnes accepted our story about Sam Tremayne and the one who was found in the horse trough. He's also going to get that lord of the manor's grave opened up. He's completely bought your story about the boy's body being in the grave.

"The fact that Mrs Billings told you the vicar had been to her house the morning of the rally has also been confirmed by the discovery of the record of his visit in his own appointment book, which his successor, Douglas Salmond, provided."

Gerry gasped. "After so long I can hardly believe all this is actually happening or actually happened. It's unbelievable. It's as if it was all in my imagination that is until today, when the Yard men came bursting into the church!"

Boucher smiled. "Oh, it's happening all right, Gerry, and you were actually in the church?" Boucher couldn't believe his luck. "I'll want your church story when we're finished here today, that will be the icing on the cake."

"All right, I'll get cracking on that. Nothing more is going to happen here today is it?" Gerry didn't want to hang around with nothing to do, if the church story was needed.

Boucher stopped walking. "I guess you're right, son, nothing's going to happen much. Most of these fellas are photographers, who will be hoping to get a shot of those people who have been arrested."

Gerry suddenly thought of Tom Ward's arrest. "I thought I'd left out Tom Ward and I see he's one of the arrested people."

Boucher looked puzzled. "Oh, there must be a reason. I understand the arrests are only on suspicion. And this guy, Rolland Davies as well. We don't know much about him, do we?"

"Of course we do. Don't tell me you didn't get my one interview I managed with Gerald Tremayne's father. Apparently, the fairground chap abused Gerald the year before, and this year tried it again. The lad ran away, said he was going to tell the police. This Rolland Davies could have panicked, and when he saw Gerald among the part-timers hired to dismantle the diving apparatus, it could be assumed that he could have forced the boy up on to the edge of the diver's tank and during the struggle Gerald Tremayne fell or was pushed into the diving pool.

It would be just a matter of time before morning volunteers found the boy."

Boucher nodded his agreement, "Yes, and it was your idiot friend, Tom Ward, I believe who was the person who found him." He added, ironically "It's a pity these Tremaynes didn't belong to the scouts, they could have at least learned to swim." Boucher had no feelings. He had seen it all before and chuckled at his own sick joke. "I'm thirsty, Gerry, let's get a drink, shall we."

Gerry smiled. "It'll have to be tea then, Mr B. There's no pubs open this time on a Sunday in Bawdry. It's not London, you know."

"Don't I know it, my boy. I had a devil of a job getting a hotel room to stay in. We'll go along there."

Boucher and Gerry left the crowd of press men meandering around the police station and walked towards Boucher's small hotel.

Boucher glanced at the crowd, turned to Gerry, "They'll get nothing today other than perhaps a few shots as they take them from the court to the jail. They'll be back in court on Tuesday and they'll probably all get bail, so I'll wait until then. Send the church stuff to my office, Gerry, they will know how to deal with it. I'll see you here Tuesday."

Chapter 43

The Sunday papers were always later than the dailies, so the Trehorrans who attended St Minerva Church morning service had not read the exclusive story which the London Express published as a front page lead, for they had already left for that fateful service before the papers had been delivered. The locals had been much earlier than usual in the church, for not only was this the last morning service of the summer season, there was the attraction of their previous popular vicar and former scout master who was to take the service of the invitation of the newcomer Douglas Salmond.

Malcolm Boucher, the London paper's chief crime reporter, had certainly gone to town with Gerry's report.

Headline: TREHORRA MURDERS – WE HAVE THE NAMES.

'We can reveal what has baffled Scotland Yard for years. We know who is responsible for the killing of a poor Cornish farmer's family of five sons. The unfortunate death of the family's only daughter, Madeleine, we think was an accident, but the circumstances of her end have yet to be confirmed.

It all started with the discovery of Sam Tremayne's body floating in the Atlantic surf alongside Black Cliffs near Trehorra, this idyllic Cornish village. Did he fall whilst hunting for birds eggs? Did he lose his footing while looking for a secluded spot where he could romance the love of his life, young village maiden Ethel Weare?

The official report said briefly, 'Accidental death,' and the incident was forgotten: 'One of those things,' they said.

However, we can now reveal that this young man's fall over the cliffs was no accident: he was pushed over! Why? We will tell you as we have told Scotland Yard, in a special Express Dossier.

Within weeks, his younger brother, Colin, was discovered in a centuries-old granite horse drinking trough only a few yards from the church of St Minerva. His sad, limp young body was first discovered by a local boy scout, John Stephens. The police proceeded to lose the body which has never been discovered. We now know where to find the body. We know who murdered the second Tremayne and we know who hid the body and why. We will tell you.

The killer had not finished yet on his obvious mission to rid Trehorra of those ill-fated tragic Tremaynes. Yet another Tremayne body was discovered dead. Here the plot thickens. The unfortunate Duncan Tremayne was found submerged in the Goran River by local postman Fred Mawgan. The unlucky boy's legs were broken. His young body covered in cuts, bruises and abrasions. Dozens of cars had passed the place he was supposed to have acted as a motor rally steward. None of the rally drivers admitted to hitting him or seeing him.

Scotland Yard was reluctantly called in by the inadequate local police force. Time was wasted. Locals were interviewed: some, again and again. Search parties were formed, nothing discovered.

The detectives of Scotland Yard were stumped, they didn't have a clue. Even if they had a clue, they didn't recognise it. When questioned officially, the locals, they stayed tight-lipped. Officers would say, "If we let out any news, who are we to communicate with?" To be honest, they had no news.

The villagers remained ominously silent. They were reluctant to reveal any information. To them, the Tremaynes were 'outsiders'. If there were some clues offered to the investigators, they were ignored.

The slayings of this family were not over. There came a few weeks of tranquillity, Trehorrans got on with their lives. The circus comes to town. The tourists come in extra numbers as the news of these murders spread: some of them 'rubberneckers' no doubt.

When Barney Bamford's annual funfair came to the village, the fun was short lived. As the fair was being disassembled ready to proceed to the next village, unbelievably, another Tremayne. This time it was unlucky Gerald, one of twin brothers.

Locals were questioned again and again. Some individuals were questioned at least a dozen times. Scotland Yard eventually returned to London with the announcement, "The files will remain open. The search for the killer, or killers, will continue."

Locals were amazed. How could the search for these murders be conducted hundreds of miles away in London?

Again, tranquillity was resumed in Trehorra, but not for long. The final Trehorra occasion of the holiday season, the autumn carnival, was to reveal yet another death of the Tremayne siblings. This time it was Gerald Tremayne's twin brother Joseph. He was found drowned in the pond of a local tourist attraction, the Olde Lanier Millwheel.

This time, crowds of people who had watched a carnival parade and a fireworks display were still around the area. While, many others had gone to the carnival ball. Again, for the fifth time, no one saw what happened!

This calamitous death brought a brief renewal of interest from the police. Headed by Inspector Bugannon, their efforts to find their elusive quarry ended in failure once again.

Despite a reward of £1,000 offered by the Express, no one had come forward. Years since the world outside had forgotten the Tremayne tragedies this pretty little old world village almost returned to somewhat quiet normality. However, the majority of Trehorrans had not forgotten.

The Express has not forgotten either. We sent our man, Gerry Halford, who actually lived there through that dramatic era, back to Trehorra to pick up the story again. He has unlocked the mystery of the destruction of this indigent Cornish family.

We have passed a dossier on to Scotland Yard with all the details. Whether they act or not to our story, we will divulge our findings in full in a special edition next week.

Mr and Mrs Landon Perry were completely exhausted by 3pm on that Sunday. This DOSSIER storey printed by the London Express could have sold more than five times their normal supply. Never had the couple experienced such a busy Sunday.

Chapter 44

Malcolm Boucher, chief reporter of the London Express, welcomed to his Kensington luxury apartment, his protégé Gerry Halford, whom he considered he had plucked from the depths of the deprived county of Cornwall.

"It's great to have you here, Gerry, I want us to put the finishing touches to this Tremayne business, or else it's going to run and run. Perhaps in a couple of weeks we can put it to sleep forever, as far as we are concerned. Of course we may be subpoenaed to verify the points we've presented to the Yard, in that dossier, so we must be doubly sure of our story.

Gerry accepted the drink his boss had poured him and they sat down to compare notes after Boucher had lifted his glass. "Cheers, Gerry, what a lucky stroke that you were actually back on holiday in Trehorra, and a longer one than you envisaged eh?"

Gerry grimaced "Wasn't much of a holiday was it? Sarah went back to London alone and since I've been back, things haven't been good, in fact it's been bloody awful, and no mention of any rewards yet, which is one of the reasons I'm here tonight."

Boucher, a lifelong bachelor, had never considered that Gerry was still in the first few months of marriage. "It's only a temporary blip, old man. When you get that big pay-day cheque, plus the other rewards, she'll come around, and bloody fast too, you'll see. Now where will we start?" He answered his own question. "The BOWERINGS — now their lawyers will obviously want to clear their names, and if they can come up with some stories which will cause reasonable doubt, the prosecution will have problems. Personally I think Bowering will be accused of the murders of Tremaynes' One, Two and Three. His wife for aiding and abetting in the No 2 murder, concealing the body and obstructing justice, and I think they will try to involve others, and we have to admit there are several characters in "the frame". They've hired one of the best defence lawyers in England, a fella who got Fiona's father off lightly when, as a London gangster, he was in trouble with the law on several occasions, way back when she was a child. The prosecution will do well to get him for the other two as well. Gerry was now beginning to see that it was not all cut and dried.

"Do you think he will be charged with all the murders?"

"Oh yes, I do, my boy. The same motive is there for all the sons, Bowering made no secret of the fact that he simply hated the thought of at least three of the Tremayne lads fornicating with those naive village girls, getting them pregnant and then having the bloody cheek to demand a "shotgun" marriage in HIS church. That's his motive for sure"

"Well what about Mr Dixon and Petherick Carnack?" I thought that in my notes I inferred that they also had a motive and also the opportunity."

Petherick was already at the diving platform when Gerald Tremayne was the first helper to arrive and there was that business of him tampering with the tractor. Dixie Dixon and Petherick were also at the top of the mill wheel, dealing with the fireworks display when twin Joe was found in the mill wheel pool.

Gerry thought deeply. "And what about the others who had a motive? Colton-Taylor had let the Tremaynes put off paying rent for the farm for months, so when the details of that debt are discovered, this estate rent collector could be in a load of trouble."

Boucher hesitated slightly but soon answered Gerry. "Ah yes, my son, he may have had a motive, as did several other Tremaynes. They couldn't have been anywhere near some of them.

"And remember, both Carnack and Dixon had daughters who had got into trouble with the Tremaynes."

"All circumstantial, Gerry. In fact, didn't you tell me that you had a mild flirtation with Catherine Carnack?"

Gerry ignored what he hoped was a throw-away remark by Boucher, and insisted "Couldn't it be said it's ALL circumstantial, though?"

Boucher was surprised at Gerry's lack of confidence in what was virtually his own report. He carried on. "Not by any means. Fact one: Bowering told Ethel Weare she could go home as he needed to speak to Sam alone and show him St Winn, the church where they were to be married. As you know, the path to the church was along the very edge of the cliffs. So one slip or one unexpected nudge and "bingo", number one Tremayne is over Black Cliffs. And your simpleton, Tom, saw Bowering returning alone along the cliff. (Gerry did not interrupt, but thought, Tom had never told him whom he saw.) Boucher continued.

"Fact number two: Almost the same method except a different church. Either by design or by accident Bowering makes an appointment to meet Colin Tremayne at St Minerva. He drops his wife off early for her to prepare for that Bolitho's funeral. He meets the lad in the lane. Seeing the horse trough, he again, adopted the tactic of surprise and opportunity and dumped the poor sod where that boy scout found him later. I have no doubt, Bowering was a supreme opportunist."

The door bell rang. Boucher passed his journal to Gerry. "That'll be the dinner I promised you."

It was his neighbour returning with the "dinner" – fish, chips and mushy peas. Bachelor Boucher had already placed the plastic plates, knives and forks on the dining table covered with a plastic table cloth with side plates of bread and butter.

He placed a bottle of expensive red wine on the table with a certain aplomb. "Do you know, Gerry, it's said that a glass of wine turns a snack into a meal? So enjoy the meal my friend."

"I agree with you there, Mr B." They clinked the beautiful crystal wine glasses, Boucher delivering a toast "Salud, dinero, el tempo, de frutado."

"I've heard that toast before," Gerry remarked "You've missed something out, haven't you? I think the word you're looking for is amor" Boucher laughed "You noticed eh? Never mind you'll get plenty in time!"

"As far as I'm concerned, there's been no amor for me since you told me to stay in Trehorra to finish the Tremayne story."

Boucher continued unperturbed, raising his glass again "Enjoy, my son." He knew he had pressurized Gerry into completing the story of the Tremayne tragedies. His thinking had been that as a Trehorra native, Gerry would be the one to open up those canny, cautious Cornish people. HOW RIGHT HE HAD BEEN! As for Gerry he had cracked the story to Boucher's delight and apparent satisfaction, and now the Express crime chief was trying to convince the young reporter that this was surely going to enhance his career as a crime journalist. Boucher's own career was his Number One priority, which is probably why he had remained single. Being a lifelong bachelor, he had found it difficult to comprehend how lonely a country boy could be when suddenly thrust into a city the size of London, Gerry Halford had been fortunate in meeting Sarah, and getting married very soon after. Now he was apparently on his own again after only a few months of marriage. Boucher had no idea that there were already serious signs of the permanent parting of the ways for Gerry and Sarah.

"Not to worry, son. Now, where were we? Oh, yes, Tremayne number three, the one everybody thought had been run over by one of those rally cars."

Gerry sipped his wine and seemed a little bit more optimistic. "I guess I was lucky there. I often think if my mother had not asked me to call on Widow Billings for a dozen eggs, I'd never have thought that Duncan Tremayne could be killed by a car going in the opposite direction to the rally cars."

"Everybody needs a little bit of luck. Prior to you going back to Trehorra, the perpetrator had all the luck that was going. No one believing the village idiot, Tom Ward, the young boy scout, too scared to tell his story, your taxi driver chap keeping 'mum' about Carnack's pipe in the tractor; plus, you had that scary dumb gravedigger saving that old cigarette packet for nigh on five years.

"You see, Gerry, it was logical that most people thought it was a local, even the locals believed that themselves, so who better to find the perpetrators than another local."

Boucher poured more wine and they clinked the glasses again. "As someone once said, it takes one to find one, or something like that," The wine was getting to Gerry.

"You're right, Gerry, most people guessed it was a local, so who better than a Trehorran to discover the truth. The biggest mystery, my boy, was why the senior Tremaynes didn't have much to say to the police. Most people in that situation would be on the backs of the police all the time.

"Whatever made you think they'd got something to hide?"

Gerry was getting more pleased with the story now, or maybe the wine was having an effect?

"It was when I talked to the father, John Tremayne. I asked to speak to the Grandad, and I was told he was down the valley milking."

"Milking in the valley I thought, that's strange? Then he suddenly slipped out 'He's milking the goat.'

"I knew when I was a young boy there were wild goats out on the cliffs, and I thought they had all disappeared before I left school. I had a good guess that the Tremaynes must somehow have managed to get hold of these goats and perhaps bred some. There were always whispers of special customers whom they provided with goat's milk and cheese. A rare commodity down there, at the time.

"When I asked if I could speak to the grandad, I could see it was a no-no subject. Then I remembered their uneasiness when Myrtle Smith had one of her upsets and ended up in the Trewarmett Farm. John Tremayne didn't want us hanging around, seemed nervous and fidgety. I thought at the time it was because of Mrs Smith's upset, that was embarrassing to them."

Boucher was intrigued. "So that's what it was all about – goats? You were still uncertain though?"

Gerry was really warmed up now, "Oh, the goats were only part of the story. I found out that they were illegally slaughtering their own animals, heifers, by poleaxing them, and they were even killing their own sheep by slitting their throats. I was told by Mr Mawgan the postman that he often saw headless hens and chickens running around the farmyard when he delivered the post. To the Tremaynes it was obviously a way of life, they thought nothing of it. At the same time, I think they knew it was illegal, so they didn't want police hanging around."

"My God, Gerry, so much for the country life. I might even turn vegetarian after listening to all that!"

"Remember, Mr B, it was just good guessing for half of it, the rest fell into place somehow. I had always thought the family as a whole appeared offish and nervous whenever there were people around the farm.

"You surely cleaned that up, my son, all because of your schoolboy memories of the goats. I guess that's why the Yard buddies didn't get anywhere with it, and the local bobby hadn't a clue. Don't suppose he ever went anywhere near the Tremaynes until the boys were dead or perhaps he had roast chicken and goats' milk every week!"

Gerry half-smiled. He was still finding it difficult to believe how critical his superior was of the Trehorrans. To Gerry, these people were real.

He couldn't forget how Tom Ward had rescued him way back when he thought, according to Cornish folklore, he had been pixielated, and when he and Sarah had been locked in a shed at the vicarage. He had never thought of Tom as a village idiot, simple perhaps, but not an idiot.

He couldn't think of Sam Teath as dumb. Scary perhaps, but not dumb. Even Adonis John Taylor had always helped him without a procuring thought, although he didn't like Taylor's obvious advances towards Sarah.

He also thought how kind Petherick Carnack was to old Myrtle Smith and her daughter, but thought the red-bearded smith had been unnecessarily cruel to his own daughter. He had always respected Police Constable Eric Vanstock. He was a true rural village policeman, who discreetly turned a blind eye to some of the villagers' 'antics'.

In a peculiar way, Gerry was beginning to regret exposing the village where he was born to the sort of stories the 'gutter' press would no doubt dream up about Trehorra.

Boucher didn't leave him with his thoughts for long. He had disposed of all the plastic utensils.

He sat down again, poured out some more wine. "Now, we come to the twins, Gerald and Joe. Pretty difficult this pair were."

Gerry had to admit he had been surprised at the arrest of Rolland Davies. "I can't believe Inspector Bugannon dug him up from the Barney Bamford contingent, although when John Tremayne did tell me about it at first, I thought it was worth a stab at a story, but obviously you didn't. At the time Vicar Bowering, was not a suspect, but that fairground diving pool was only a few yards away from the vicarage, so as Gerald Tremayne was there before anyone else it would have been comparatively easy for employee Roland Davies or for Bowering to nip over there once the coast was clear. Opportunity, you see Mr B!"

"When Barney Bamford told me Mr. Carnack had done an emergency welding job on the diving fixture at the crack of dawn it only served to confuse the issue. I had to include him as a possibility. The opportunity was there."

Boucher intervened. "I think you reported that it was simpleton Tom who found the body, so he wasn't out of the running was he?"

Gerry was getting a little annoyed at Boucher's persistent mentioning of Tom Ward as a village idiot. He had been convinced all along that Tom was not party to any of the murders and could never understand Boucher insisting on putting Tom into the equation.

"Look at it this way, Gerry, the police will try to implicate him. He admits to seeing someone running away from the cliffs the night we supposed Tremayne number one went over into the sea. He could have been the one running away. There are stories of his training runs all over the place." He paused to sip his wine.

"You yourself had an experience with him when he turned up out of the mist to rescue you from your journey home from a scouts' camp, when you said you were pixielated. He turned up to rescue you and Sarah during that scout presentation. He's also the one who discovers the body in the funfair water tank. I'm afraid, Gerry, that if they ever get him in the dock as a witness or as a possible perpetrator, he may not be very convincing, and if the Bowerings' lawyer ever gets the opportunity to cross examine him he's in big trouble."

Gerry was astounded. He had not reckoned on how the facts could be distorted so much and he was thinking that perhaps those big pay-days were not as sure as he had thought. Boucher could see how disconcerted Gerry was getting. "Let's finish this wine off." He topped up their glasses once again. "I'm giving you the worst scenario Gerry, so don't get too concerned."

Boucher referred to his journal again. "Ah, yes, the mill wheel episode. As you did in the previous instance. Gerry, your fact finding was great, but your Tom Ward was there again. He told Vanstock he saw Dixie Dixon talking to Joe Tremayne around the top of the mill wheel.

There's also a possibility that some of those local youths kidded this Tremayne into a dunking game. Boucher had completely lost Gerry now "What the hell is that?" He was certain now that his boss had had too much wine. "I've never heard of such a thing." Boucher, however, could hold the wine better than Gerry imagined, and, with a perfectly straight face, said, "I'm surprised at you. Gerry, a born Cornishman, and you're not conversant with one of the most popular games involving a mill wheel!" It was Gerry who was affected more by the wine and could not see that Boucher still had a sense of humour, and he continued in a serious voice "It's a very old country game, where they tie some individual on to the mill wheel he goes round and round in and out of the pool, and the one who goes around the most times is the winner – simple!" Gerry had at last caught on. "But that's preposterous, with all those people around, you really can't be serious, and I suppose you'll tell me next that Tom Ward told you about it! I really must have another good look at that dossier you've done, especially if my name is to be connected with it." "Now, Gerry, we've got millions of readers to satisfy, I simply painted the pictures, YOU provided the colours." "I certainly didn't provide that colour, Mr B." Boucher was sure he could wind Gerry up still further. "Surely, Gerry you must have realised it was carnival time. People had momentarily put all that doom and gloom behind them." Boucher was now pacing around the room, and assuming the role of an actor, he waved his arms around "I can imagine people wandering around this area in the semi-darkness, attempting to take in and make the most of this rare happy event in their mostly sombre lives. The smoke from the fireworks display continues to hover around the old millhouse, the wheel is still relentlessly circling around and around, and there in the area at the top of the wheel right in front of the fireworks platform is . . . JOE TREMAYNE!!

Boucher now reverted to a serious attitude "Now what was Joe Tremayne doing up there? He as far as I remembered wasn't one to help any of the carnival committee, and wouldn't be asked either. Agreed, young man? But, for whatever reason, he was up there, and who knows what he was up to? Whatever it was, someone apparently didn't appreciate his presence, and I suppose it could be that if he refused to leave, this someone could have pushed him either deliberately or accidentally on to the mill wheel. The fireworks committee men, including Petherick Carnack and Dixie Dixon, were still there, and apparently Vicar Bowering who was making sure that all his scouts who had been in the carnival parade, were still not hanging around, so you can take your pick of that lot."

Gerry drained his remaining glass of wine. He couldn't remember how many he'd had, but knew it was too many. He got up groggily, managed to say "I'll have to go now, so I'll leave you to your 'painting', I'm sure you've got enough colours, and you didn't get 'em all from me." Boucher patted Gerry's shoulder "Thanks for coming Gerry, I'll get you a taxi and don't worry any more about that cheque, and it'll be a bloody big one I can assure you. I have no doubts that that will be followed by your missing "amore", and remember this, mark my words Gerry, it's not love that makes the world go around, it's money, my son." He rang for the taxi. Gerry was certainly appreciative of this kind gesture, but not for Boucher's next statement "Oh and by the way Gerry, don't forget you HAVE to go to Trehorra tomorrow and tie up those few loose ends we discussed in the office today before the trial begins. "I'd rather not go this time."

Gerry wanted to protest more vigorously. "I was hoping to smooth things over with Sarah." "Don't worry about that blip, Gerry, I've told you not to be concerned, she'll come running when you show her that cheque, you'll see." "You must be joking, Mr B."

Chapter 45

It was a fresh, chilly morning. The sea mists hung heavily over the Cornish coasts. Retired ex PC Vanstock remembered his usual Friday morning routine. This would take him along Main Street, around the duck pond, where he used to always have a separate look at those two almost likeable rogues, the Brummie Pascoe twins. Over the 15th Century bridge, and on to the quayside, where a few local fisherman would usually be unloading their early morning catch of lobsters which would be boxed and sent up to London.

"Don't think the St. Prynn golf course will be open today, missus. I think I'll go inland a bit and knock a few balls on the old golf links"

"Is that the one that was never finished?" Mrs Vanstock was glad that her retired hubby was going to get out from under her feet and get some much-needed exercise.

"I suppose it's good enough to practise on, yes Eric, you do that but don't forget your waterproofs. If that sea mist moves that way it's likely to get very damp up there."

It didn't take him long to get there in his little Ford 8. He only met one vehicle, Taylor's taxi. For a brief moment he wondered what the taxi was doing way out there, and was even more mystified when he noticed that the passenger was Gerry Halford, but completely dismissed it before driving through the two huge granite posts, which would make a very imposing entrance to the proposed golf course when completed. He parked the car, and when he got out, he could smell the fresh grass, where the sprinkles of morning dew had dropped off the trees. After a short walk, and what he presumed was a good loosen-up, he suddenly felt the urge to have a cigarette. He always smoked John Players and was just beginning to enjoy the sort of relaxation the nicotine had on smokers, though he did limit himself to five a day, when suddenly he thought he heard something. What was it? He threw his cigarette down, quickly putting his foot on it. Surely I can't be hearing things he thought, but he could swear it was the sound of a car engine. Surely nobody could be stealing his car? No – but the purring of a car engine it definitely was and much to his relief it was coming from way down to his left. He put his lightweight golf bag over his shoulder and walked slowly towards the sound of what he thought was a car engine. "God damn it!" he muttered to himself "this bloody mist is coming down pretty damn fast now." Visibility was down to a few yards. The nearer he walked to the sound of an engine, the thicker the mist. He could only see a few feet in front of him now. It was as well that he had a rough idea of the geography of the area. "This is a real 'pea-souper' he said to himself, "I won't be able to hit any golf balls today." He peered through the thickening mist and was sure he could see the outline of a car. It was certainly stationary, and he was extra careful because he realised that mists and fogs in this particular area could play tricks on people. The heavy mists were swirling around the vehicle as if it wanted to hide it. He stumbled through an intended bunker and stealthily approached the rear of the car. It was black and the windows were all fogged up. He was reminded of his days in the police force, when he would often come across a similar scene, but it would nearly always turn out to be a couple sneaking a clandestine evening of love. He would have had a brief, but crafty peep and then move discreetly on.

This was different. It was morning, the engine was purring away gently. He wiped one of the windows with his glove, and he could make out what appeared to be the figures of a man and a woman cuddled up close to each other. He could now see the tell-tale tube leading from the exhaust pipe, which told him what had happened. The car doors were locked, so he took out one of his irons and smashed the front passenger window.

"Oh my God," he exclaimed aloud and switched off the engine.

Chapter 46

The atmosphere in the Pity Me was unusually thick tonight with heavy smoke from the pipes and cigarettes of the two darts' teams and their supporters. For this was THE Darts Match of the Season! The Pity Me versus The Riverside Inn. It had been a pulsating local "derby" match. The public bar was full. Besides the teams and their supporters landlord Percy Neville had to contend with his "regulars" as well. Once the match was over, the conversation got louder and louder and the landlord and his assistant Bill Gibson were kept busy pulling the pints and keeping the till bell constantly ringing. Busy as they were, Percy somehow thought tonight was different and he could not think why. Perhaps it was because so many of his customers were out on bail! For years the shadow of the Tremayne murders had hung over the tiny village. The locals had talked about them, but only in whispers. Now it was at last over, or was it? Gerry Halford, the local boy made good, had brought everything into the open with his stunning reports and revelations of the perpetrators, with the now famous London Express Dossier apparently being accepted by Scotland Yard. This in turn had made headlines because of that "never heard of before" Sunday morning raid during a church service. The upshot was that a few local suspects found that they were to appear in a Cornish murder trial. Now it seems that everyone and his dog knew all about the murders all the time! Farmer Archie Jasper usually so quietly spoken, was in earnest conversation with Tom Ward Junior of all people. Tom was likely to be exonerated from any involvement in the Tremayne murders and some of his evidence would probably be accepted by the jury.

"In all seriousness," Archie snapped. "If you knew so much Tom, why in the hell didn't you tell Vanstock before?"

The "village idiot" as crime reporter Boucher always so unkindly referred to him protested "I did, I did, but he never took any blooming notice of me, nor did that inspector fella from Waterbridge." Dick Saunders, the local policeman's neighbour at the time, butted in on Tom's behalf. "Young Tom be right, Archie, I saw 'im several times go into the policeman's house," Archie retorted.

"He'll have no excuse when he appears in court, then they'll have to listen him won't they?"

Petherick Carnack was having words with Sam Teath. "If you hadn't hung on to that bloody cigarette packet for bloody years the other three Tremaynes may not have been killed. It could all have been nipped in the bud there and then, and we would have been saved all that bloody aggravation."

Sam Teath, the gravedigger, not used to all this noise, which was gradually amounting to something more than good-natured banter. Trying to get a word in, he just had to be serious. "No bugger ever asked me anything, till young Halford came back." He turned around and looking straight at Petherick, added, "Anyway Carnack, you were damned lucky to get off scot-free, after fiddlin' with those ol' tractor brakes!"

Not known for his humour, newsagent Landon Perry interceded "And you didn't know you'd buried two bodies in one grave did you Sam, is that the only time you've done it?" There was plenty of loud laughter as the gravedigger tried to get a word in, so he too raised his voice. "Well look who's talkin', you did all right out of it didn't you, Landon Perry? Bet you never sold so many bloody papers in your 'ole damned life." Taking another gulp of his pint, he looked at the group now facing him. He added, "In any case, I knew who 'twas from the bloody beginning." More derisive laughter followed this last remark, but the newsagent wasn't to be outdone.

"Oh you did, did you, Sam, why in the hell didn't you tell somebody about it? In any case I heard 'twas you who stopped the search of the churchyard."

"No bugger asked me, that was all down to Parson Bowering." Sam Teath was giving as good as he got. "Somebody should 'ave smelled a rat then".

Dixie Dixon was nodding his head in agreement, and, with his draughts mate Petherick, shouted, "Hear! Hear!" Backing up Sam, he turned on the rest of them now. "If Sam had been asked to see them folks from Scotland Yard, it might all have been different."

Carnack, the smith, was puffing vigorously on a new pipe and in a now hoarse voice, "Yes, he's right and if young John Stephens hadn't kept his mouth shut all this time "bout seein' Bowerin' drivin' away from the hoss trough, it could have been another tale altogether."

Part-time coastguard Bill Hawkin sarcastically butted in with his foghorn type of voice, "IF IF IF that's all you bloody lot are sayin', IF Sam had opened his mouth at the time, IF the kid Stephens hadn't been scared to death of Bowerin',, even IF ol' widow

Billins' had told 'em 'bout the vicar goin' to her on that car rally mornin', and drivin' back t'other way." Bill had now quietened the noisy crowd down, so he continued as if on a political soap box. "IF Ethel Weare in the very beginnin' had told 'em she'd left lover-boy Sam Tremayne with Bowerin' at 9 o'clock at night, it's all bloody IF with you lot, if a bloody elephant had wings, 'twould bloody well fly". Bill was on his fifth pint, and after all that shouted to Percy, "It's my turn, Percy, set 'em all up with whatever they want."

Sam Teath was well-away by this time. "Wondered when you was goin' to get in a round, Bill, but 'twas a good job that maid's body got washed up on Northwinds Beach, three weeks after you said she was on Pete Williams's boat or they'd be sayin' you'd bin drinkin' on duty, cos nobody else saw 'er 'cept you."

Bill had now started on his next pint. "You be 'sackly right Sam, me boy, and while I'm thinkin' 'bout it, I'll put a bloody IF in for meself . . . IF bloody Vanstock had put 'imself 'bout a bit more, none of this would 'ave bloody 'appened." No one chose to answer that. The noise stopped abruptly. Bill had lost the attention of his "audience"! Suddenly everyone was looking at the now open door. A waft of cold air cut through the smoky atmosphere like a knife. Landlord Percy Neville was the first to spot who was standing in the doorway, and broke the silence by shouting "Last orders please, gentlemen.".He had no idea why a retired copper should make what appeared to be such a dramatic entrance almost dead on closing time. "Well I'll be buggered if it isn't Vanstock," he said to Bill Gibbons. The quick thinking landlord thought – "once a policeman always a policeman" – and he didn't want to go past the time his special extended licence for the darts' match allowed him. Fisherman Jim Proctor broke the ensuing awkward silence. "Yes 'twas a damned shame 'bout Pete Williams, but really he shouldn't 'ave been out there, though I think he was dead unlucky, poor sod" There was some sheepish laughter. Jim hadn't realised the pun he had just made. Now there was a crush at the bar.

Several voices in unison were calling "What be 'avin' Mr Vanstock?" "Have one on me, Constable."

"Is he still a constable then?" Landon Perry was the nearest one to Percy Neville behind the bar who had craftily put the towel up to signify that the last orders were in effect. "Have one on me, Mr Vanstock, Sam Teath seems to think I'm a millionaire!" offered the newsagent.

Bill Hawkin, as caustic as ever, could not resist.

"He can afford it, he's never sold so many papers in his life." A sort of gangway had been made for the ex-village policeman walking towards the bar.

"Make mine a double scotch, Landon". It was quickly served and just as quickly consumed! "Ah, but that felt good, Landon". He turned around to face the now apparently sobered-up villagers. "Well I can tell 'e all, he'll be selling plenty more tomorrow." He downed another Scotch which was already lined up ready for him on the bar. "You may not believe this, gentlemen, but even now I'm retired, I've found another two bodies." Before he could continue Bill Hawkin boomed out "Well it can't be a Tremayne can it, there ain't none left be there?" Most of the men groaned at the sick effort by the coastguard. They turned to Vanstock, eagerly awaiting him to continue his announcement. "Well, me boys, I'm up at the old golf links today." He was getting very dramatic now.

"No, Bill, it wasn't a Tremayne, but there was two of 'em and both of 'em was a dead as dodos." The intended serious statement by the retired policeman was hanging on too long for his listeners. From the back of the room someone shouted "Tell us who it bleedin' was then." Another one shouted, "Who the hell be it?" More joined in as the ex-constable seemed to be not a bit concerned at their eagerness to know who it was. He smiled a big broad smile, put his glass to his lips. Whilst he hesitated Landon broke the silence "I bet it's somethin' to do with my missus." This took the wind out of Vanstock's sails. He had had another whisky thrust into his hand. "On the bloody wireless was it? That'll be that bloody Halford lad I bet – for some reason or other he was up at the old golf links this morning, 'cause he phoned my missus to say he had been up there, but he didn't tell her anything, said he could only speak to me, but if anybody was going to be there, it would bound to be bloody him wouldn't it?"

Archie Jasper had pushed his way almost next to Vanstock, "Well Mr Vanstock, it was a good job he came back and sorted it all out wasn't it?" No doubt Archie was thinking of his own disappointment with his unsuccessful bid for a romance with Evelyn Menhennick and for some reason he couldn't resist a dig at Gerry Halford and added "I hear his wife won't be comin' to Trehorra any more though," and added with a sneer "unless of course it's to see John Taylor."

Petherick Carnack, who had brazenly got over all the criticism aimed at him over those tractor brakes chipped in "There's no fear of that, Archie boy. She'll come 'round and get back to Gerry Halford no doubt when he gets those big pay cheques, due to 'im for doin' Scotland Yard's job for 'em"

"You're damned right there, Petherick." Percy Neville had had enough for one night. He turned to the now the subdued ex-policeman "I'll tell you this Mr Vanstock for nothin', if Scotland Yard had made the Pity Me their headquarters they would have solved it in no-time!"

Vanstock laughed away with them all. "Come on, Percy, take that bloody towel off, let's all have one for the road, eh?" Come on gents have one on me. By the way, I only called in to see the darts match, who won anyway?"

TREHORRA WAS GETTING BACK TO NORMALITY!

The Tremaynes' murder trial was sensationally adjourned when the accused central figures in the case, vicar Eric Balfour Bowering and his wife Fiona, were discovered dead in their car on a half-constructed golf course by Gerry Halford, a London Express crime reporter. The Bowerings' lawyer had told the court that the deaths had apparently been agreed suicide and he wished the trial to continue in order to clear his clients of the murders of the Tremayne brothers. He went on to implicate the rest of the accused, who had been arrested on suspicion of either committing aiding or abetting the Tremayne murders.

Malcolm Boucher had now taken over reporting the trial from Gerry Halford. One by one, the accused characters appeared in the dock, were cross-examined. It seemed to be just a matter of time before the final decision would be reached. The fact of the Bowerings' suicides seem to point only one way.

When the jury announced their decision, Boucher lost no time in reaching the nearest phone to ring his London office. Gerry answered the phone. "Gerry, my boy, are you sitting down?" Boucher shouted down the phone, "'cause I think you ought to be before I tell you the verdict."

"Don't tell me it's all over, Mr B."

"Certainly is, my son, and you're not going to believe the outcome."

"Thought it was obvious, Mr B, we've got the copy all written up."

"Well you'll have to scrub it." Malcolm Boucher was almost breathless. "They've pinned all of the murders on your mate Tom Ward!"

"This must be the biggest blunder ever, surely there'll be an appeal?" Gerry was thinking of the cheques he was about to receive from the paper. His editor must have been thinking along the same lines.

"No, Gerry, no appeal has been lodged. He did not admit to killing the one found after the motor rally, but did say he found the body and placed it by the river Goran. He was assumed to be of an unsound mind, just think my boy, how lucky you and Sarah have been, must have been pretty close on that night when he 'rescued' you both."

"My God, Mr B, you're right, we were lucky."

"You'll never know how lucky you were."

"I have to admit, Mr B you have been right all along. Tom really was the village idiot!"

"I was waiting for you to say that, Halford." He rang off.

THE END.

ACKNOWLEDGEMENTS

It takes more than one person to write a book, and I have had help from so many that I will probably miss some, and hope they will accept my apologies. In no particular order these are but a few who helped.

• Sue and Mike Nuttall. Sue's faith in the story line and both their help encouragement and support during several periods when I felt like giving the whole thing up.

• My son Max, his wife Marika for adding a touch of professionalism to my task

• Grandson Paul who spent a lot of his vacation from Finland typing a lot of copy.

• Neil Archer my son-in-law for keeping my Computer working!

• Ken Dove a very good friend for over 30 years,also a computer wizz-kid !

• To Valerie and Gordon Stephens

• Steve Gordos without whom the book would probably never have got to the print and to Rick Bachelor for his work on the book cover.

• Finally to daughter Vanessa who typed many chapters although all the time was sure The Devil of Trehorra would never see the light of day.

Thank you ALL.

Made in the USA
Charleston, SC
28 March 2013